HIS CURVY INFATUATION

A SMALL TOWN CURVY GIRL ROMANCE

BOOK BOYFRIENDS WANTED
BOOK 13

MARY E THOMPSON

His Curvy Infatuation

Book Boyfriends Wanted, book 13

Ebook ISBN: 978-1-953879-56-1

Print ISBN: 978-1-953879-57-8

Audiobook ISBN: 978-1-953879-58-5

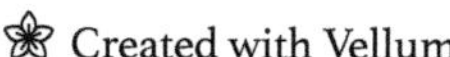 Created with Vellum

BOOK BOYFRIENDS WANTED

Fall is rolling in, and fun is on the horizon. Love is coming for the residents of MacKellar Cove, whether they're ready for it or not. Thanks for joining us for another Book Boyfriends Wanted story. Never miss a thing when you sign up for Mary's newsletter.

Romancing the Curves comes with subscriber exclusive freebies, sneak peeks, and a first look at everything Mary has to offer. Be the first to know about new releases and sales and all the curves ahead!

SUBSCRIBE NOW AT MARYETHOMPSON.COM

Happy reading!

1

BRANTLEY

My favorite day of the year was the first day of cross-country practice. I'd never admit that to the baseball team I coached, but I loved cross-country. Running long distances was exhilarating. And seeing new kids do it, watching them achieve something they thought they couldn't do, was the best thing ever.

I parked my SUV in the high school lot near the road so the parents and students would know where to meet. There was already a small gathering of seniors near a group of vehicles. I lifted my arm and waved, and they all waved back. They closed doors and grabbed bags, making their way toward me.

"Good morning," I said to them as they got closer.

"Hey, Coach P. Ready for this year?" Andrew was one of the top runners in the area. He consistently led the pack, most of the time running alone since no one else could come close to keeping up with him. Scholarship offers came in all summer from schools that had been watching him since he was a freshman.

"I'm ready. Are you? Have you been training?"

Andrew nodded. "Yeah. I need a scholarship." Andrew was the oldest of four boys. He always had good gear, but his brother, who was a sophomore, usually wore Andrew's hand-me-downs.

"It sounds like you've had a few offers. Anyone you're looking at seriously?"

Andrew shrugged. He was a quiet kid, one who didn't like being the center of attention, and realized the others were listening to our conversation. "Not sure yet."

I nodded, letting him off the hook. Choosing a college wasn't easy, and having more options didn't make it any easier. I'd pull him aside later and talk more about what he was thinking. When everyone else wasn't listening.

"How's everyone else doing?" I asked.

"Good, Coach P," they all said.

"How has summer been? Everyone keeping up with their training schedule?"

All of a sudden, there was a lot less chatter.

I chuckled. "It's going to be a rough few weeks getting into things. Seniors, make sure you're making the under-classmen feel welcome."

They mumbled their agreement as Jana McCloud, my co-coach, got out of her car.

"Hey, Coach M!"

Jana was new to coaching and to the district. She was in her mid-twenties and the young, fun coach the high school kids could relate to. She was also gorgeous and made all the teenage boys drool, but she was a professional and never out of line. She always ran with her shirt on, instead of stripping down to her sports bra like some of the girls did, and she never spent time one-on-one with any student. We spent so many hours with the kids that it could be tough to keep an emotional separation from them, but Jana was awesome.

"Hey, everyone. Are we ready to run?"

"Yes!" Their excited cheers for Jana made me smile. None of them admitted to her that they hadn't been training enough all summer.

More cars pulled in and more students were dropped off. I tried not to watch for Valentina Hayes's minivan but failed miserably. Valentina had been one of my closest friends since high school, and I'd been in love with her almost as long. She was also newly divorced and not ready for a relationship. She told me as much many times over the last few months. Work, kids, and friends were her focus now. Which meant I had to keep my interest in her to myself.

Story of my life. But it was for the best. Getting involved with her was not a good idea. I'd spent most of my life wanting her, and most of my life building up what it would be like to kiss her or touch her or tell her I loved her. It was past time to move on.

Or so I told myself when her daughters climbed out of another parent's vehicle.

Jana and I spoke briefly, confirming the plan we set for practice. We were fortunate that our elementary, middle, and high schools were all together, and the students could run a good lap around all of them and get in their distance without having to leave school property.

Once everyone was there, Jana and I called all the kids over. We took roll to make sure everyone had shown up and went over the rules for running. Even though school hadn't started yet, the kids needed to watch for traffic and run in pairs or groups.

"We're going to start you out with a time trial to get an idea of where you're starting from. You're only competing against yourself, so don't worry about your time. This will help us to pair you up going forward so you have someone to run with. For today only, your route is around the high school. We marked it out yesterday with flags, so it should be easy to follow. Coach M. and I will be on opposite sides of the school in case there's an emergency. Let's head over to the start line and do our warm-up before you run."

Jana led the kids in stretches and quick sprints to loosen their muscles, then told them to grab some water before they ran. It was a hot day to start the season.

The kids all lined up and got ready to run. Jana jogged around the corner to the other side of the school, leaving me to watch the start and finish line.

I counted them off and blew the whistle, setting the team off on their run. Day one. I loved it. Best day ever.

JANA and I smiled and waved to the last kids to get picked up. She turned to me and burst out laughing.

"I don't think any of them practiced this summer," she said. "Maybe Andrew."

I nodded. "He said he did, but the others? No. They definitely did not practice. It's going to be a rough few weeks getting them to where they can handle a three-mile run without wanting to die."

Jana chuckled. "Yeah. Lots of work to do. But we'll get them there. Great day, Coach. See you tomorrow."

"Yep. Get some rest, Jana. Lots of water."

"You, too."

Jana drove off in her car, zipping out of the parking lot and turning toward town. Since MacKellar Cove was like a rumor mill on steroids, I knew Jana lived in the condos by the water with her boyfriend, who, rumor had it, would be her fiancé soon. Nothing was secret in MacKellar Cove.

I let myself into my house and locked the door behind me. It still smelled like coffee since I forgot to dump the grounds before I left. I grabbed a bottle of water and chugged half of it before dealing with the coffee.

Before I lost track of everything on my mind, I grabbed my tablet and opened the document where I kept all my notes about the team. I added the times I'd recorded for each runner and sorted them based on their rate. As expected, Andrew finished the three-mile run a full two minutes before the next student. Paul Spear, Valentina's friend Goldie's son, was only a sophomore, but he was the second fastest on the team. Paul was going to dominate just like Andrew when he was a senior.

There were a few new students, including one would be in my physics class. I wasn't familiar with his name. He did well at practice, third place behind Andrew and Paul, but his transcript wasn't great. The only way for him to stay on the team would be to pass all of his classes, and that seemed to be a struggle for Kevin.

I finished my notes on all the students and started to make up groups that would be good to run together. When I finished the groups, I sent it over to Jana to review before practice the next morning.

With that done, I looked around my kitchen at the projects I had planned for the day. My house was the definition of fixer-upper when I bought it. I'd been there for almost a decade and had updated every space except the kitchen. It always felt like too big of a task, and I wasn't willing to tackle it, but I stupidly broke a cabinet door last week. My dishwasher died a year ago. And my fridge was feeling less cold than usual. The checkerboard backsplash, with chicken accent tiles, the previous owners installed had been chipping and falling off the wall almost since I bought the place. It was time. I knew it was time. But I didn't want it to be time.

Even as I stood there trying to decide if I was really going to do this, another tile fell off the backsplash. It clattered to the countertop without breaking and mocked me as it spun.

"Dammit."

I had a good idea of what I wanted the kitchen to look like. I'd been thinking about it for years. Of course, it was also Valentina's dream kitchen, but we didn't need to talk about that. It was just a kitchen. With a huge island where people could sit and eat, a six-burner stove, a new sliding door to the backyard that could be opened wide for parties that I never hosted, and a simple dining table for four.

Don't judge me.

Starting a project like that on the first day of cross-country, right before summer was ending and I was going to be back in the classroom every day, was almost as dumb as introducing my best friend to my roommate in college and sitting on the sidelines while they fell in love, got married, and built a life together. But clearly, I wasn't very good at making smart decisions.

I picked up the small sledgehammer and faced the backsplash. "Sorry, chickens, but it's time to say goodbye."

I barely had to hit the tiles for them to pop off the adhesive that was no longer doing its job. I collected all the pieces and dumped them into the trash bin in the garage. If I was going to do this, I needed a dumpster and a plan and some help.

Dammit.

Twenty minutes later, still sweaty from practice with the

added stink of renovation on me, I walked in to Al's Hardware. Knox Randall and I had become friends over the years. That happened when you spent half your paycheck at a man's store.

"My favorite reno expert is back," Knox said with a laugh in his voice. "What are we fixing up now?"

I glared at him, and he faltered.

"No. Are you kidding me? You're finally doing the kitchen?"

If a grown man could get excited about something like home renovation, it was Knox. I was fairly sure he had more ideas about my kitchen than I did.

I grunted in reply, a noise that made Knox's grin wider and sent him around the corner of the counter to lead the way to all the things I was going to blow my next few paychecks on.

"Demo is first. But if you want to live there while you work, you need to do this in phases. I think—"

"I need to live there. And I need to eat."

"Okay, understood," Knox said as he continued to walk away from me. "You're going to need a dumpster, or maybe one of those bags. Those are pretty easy. And if you're doing it in phases, that'll make more sense than keeping a big-ass dumpster in your driveway. We need to talk cabinets and countertops. Are you keeping your appliances?"

He turned to look back at me, then shook his head.

"No, of course not. Those are horrible. So, we need those, too. Backsplash?" He glanced back again, then kept going. "Yeah. Your flooring might be okay, but if you change the layout, you're going to need to patch stuff in which usually looks like shit, so I'd say flooring, too. There's this vinyl plank flooring that's really durable and great for areas like the kitchen. I think you'll like it. Especially if you ever get a dog like you've been saying forever. What about—"

"Dude! Take a breath," I barked.

Knox chuckled and shook his head. "Sorry. I just want to get you started before you change your mind again. You've been talking about your kitchen for years."

"Yeah, and you throwing all this at me isn't making me more excited to do it."

"It'll be fine." Knox walked back to me and clapped me on the back. He was a good four inches taller than me and wider, with about forty pounds of muscle on me. A slap on the back from Knox about knocked the wind out of me.

"Shit," I breathed.

"Sorry." His cheeks turned red, a trait accented by his light skin and dark blond hair. He hated it.

"All good. But let's slow down a bit. The backsplash is gone. I'm thinking the whole thing is going to be a gut job, but I can't just tear it all out and get it all back together in a day or two. I need to take it in steps. Maybe one section at a time."

Knox rubbed his beard and stared at a spot above my head. He wrinkled his nose. "I'm not sure how you can do that. I'd suggest running flooring under your cabinets so there's isn't a height difference with your appliances. That means you basically have to gut the entire space and start from scratch."

I sighed heavily. "I was afraid of that."

"It's all right. We'll figure it out. If we can gut everything and bring in new appliances, you can use them even as we do all the work. Or you can use what you have and replace them all at the end. Up to you."

I nodded slowly. It wasn't ideal, but it was going to have to work. I had some money saved up to make the budget possible, as long as Knox didn't go too crazy, but the time was a bigger struggle.

"Okay. It needs to be done, so let's figure it out. Think we can knock it out by the end of the year?"

Knox nodded. "Probably in half that if you want to, but three months? Definitely. Let's get to work."

I SHOULD HAVE KNOWN Knox was so methodical, but until he sat me down and walked through everything step-by-step, I didn't know that about him. I walked out of Al's Hardware an hour later with a dent in my credit card and a plan to remodel my kitchen.

Step one was tearing everything out. Which meant removing everything from the cabinets.

I got to work when I got home, loading everything from the cabinets into the closet in the spare room. My house had four bedrooms, which always felt excessive, but when I bought it, I told myself I was ready to settle down and have a family. I'd always wanted kids. Growing up with a mom who was a teacher and a dad who was a paster, family was important to us. My older sister was one of my closest friends when I was a kid, and still was, even though she lived in Maryland and we only saw each other a few times a year.

As I walked down the hall between the kitchen and the fourth bedroom, I felt the same pang I always got when I thought about having a family. At forty-five, I could still have kids, but knowing I'd be well into my sixties when they graduated high school meant that dream was less of an option. It stung. Especially since I'd always imagined a life with Valentina. She was my gold standard, and I was single because no one had ever come close.

I had no right to complain. I never told her how I felt, and I never gave any other woman a real chance. Besides, I had hundreds of kids. Watching my students and athletes year after year achieve great things was something I would always be proud of. I didn't raise them, but I had a hand in molding them. A small one, but still.

When I finally cleared out the last of the items from my cabinets, I let out a breath. It was really happening. I was really going to tackle the kitchen.

My phone dinged with an incoming text. I picked it up and breathed a laugh when I read what Valentina sent.

> First practice and you're going to remodel the kitchen? Busy day! Girls said it was a great practice, though. They're excited about the season. I'm excited about the kitchen. Need any help?

> Practice was good. It's going to be a fun season. And I'm always open to your help. Knox went a little crazy today.

> Crazy how? Did he talk you into something weird like neon cabinets? Please say yes. I'd die to see that!

I chuckled and settled onto the couch. I flipped on the TV and typed out a response.

2

VALENTINA

I watched the three bubbles and waited for Brantley to reply. I missed seeing him at practice today. Goldie dropped the girls off, and Xavier picked them up. Goldie's son, Paul, was dating my youngest, Samantha. Xavier's daughter, McJenna, was best friends with my oldest, Bianca. Between the three of us, we were working out a schedule to get the kids to and from practice so we could all also work.

> No neon. What are you thinking, woman?
> Have you met me? Plaid all the way.

I laughed out loud when I read his reply. Brantley Pierce was the only reason I was still sane, although some people would argue about that fact. He'd been my best friend for most of my life, but in the last few months, he'd been the only person I didn't feel like I had to pretend around.

My girlfriends were great, don't get me wrong, but Brantley was the one I'd call if I needed to hide a body.

And he was the one I called for everything else. He was always there for me, and I was beyond grateful for him.

Ah, I should have known. All those plaid
shirts you wear were a huge clue.

Exactly. If it wasn't for that pesky teaching
job, I'd be a lumberjack.

I giggled. Brantley certainly had the body for it. Not that I was checking him out. But I'd known him forever. He was a strong man.

Before I could reply, another text popped up.

I think Knox has been planning to remodel
my kitchen as long as I have. He had more
ideas about what to do than I ever
considered.

LOL. He is the expert.

Too bad he's not the bank, too. I might need
to take on a second job to pay for this. Glad
I have some money in savings.

Isn't coaching your second job?

A third job then.

That's not good. We'll miss you too much.

I'll be fine. I'm mostly kidding. We're going
to take it slow so I can make it all work. I'll
just be ordering lots of takeout and grilling.

Sounds like what you do, anyway.

Mean. Accurate, but mean.

Not intended to be mean. Maybe you
should come here for dinner. We always
have plenty.

> You just need me to fix something,
> don't you?

I breathed a laugh and shook my head. My ex-husband, Dawson, had never been very handy. Handsy? Yes. Far too handsy with women who weren't me, apparently. But handy? Nope. I would ask Dawson to fix things, and after weeks of nothing, I'd give up and ask Brantley, only to have Dawson mad at me when he saw whatever project was already done. Then he'd make me feel bad about it.

Gaslighting 101.

> I'm joking. I am always happy to help you
> with anything you need, Vee. Never doubt
> that. No payment necessary. Although I
> won't turn down dinner with my favorite
> people either.

I didn't know how he knew I was second guessing the idea, but he always seemed to know what I was thinking, usually before I did.

> Thanks. I don't know what I'd do without
> you.

> Sure you do. You'd figure it out like you
> always have. You're the strongest person I
> know. Don't doubt yourself.

> Thank you. Okay, enough about all that.
> What did you think about the first practice?

I waited for his reply, the bubbles dancing while I imagined Brantley leaning back on his couch and smiling. He loved coaching. When he talked about the kids, he always had a huge smile on his face. Him being the coach was why both my girls joined the team. Bianca encouraged McJenna to join, too, and this year, Sam decided to try it. If they hadn't known Brantley, and known how amazing he was, there was no way they would have tried cross-country.

Practice was good. Not many kids ran over the summer, but that's okay. Summer is supposed to be their time to relax and have fun. There are a few kids that are surprises and a few that are going to hate the season, but overall, it's a great group. Not surprising since MCHS is an amazing school with spectacular teachers.

Especially the physics teacher.

I hear he can be a real hard-ass.

I think he's a softie underneath. An amazing man who goes above and beyond for the people in his life.

Softie is not the term most men want a woman to use when describing them.

LOL! I can't believe you just said that.

You're the one who said it. I'm just making sure you understand most men would be offended by that.

Then I apologize. You're strong and virile and not soft at all.

Better.

Good. Anything to make it better.

That's a far too tempting offer. Anything?

My body heated with the unintended innuendo. I knew

Brantley wasn't suggesting anything like that, but my mind went there, anyway. I knew better. It was Brantley. He was my best friend in the world. I was not going to drag him into the middle of my disaster of a life. Even if I was ready to consider dating again, dating Brantley was a horrible idea.

I loved Brantley. I would do anything for him. And losing him as my best friend would be miserable. I wasn't sure if I was ready to date. I was beyond done with Dawson, that had nothing to do with it, but I was so damn tired. Tired of trying to be everything to everyone. I needed a break from it, which meant dating was a bad idea.

But I missed having a partner. Someone to come home to. Someone to talk to about my day and hold me at night. It had been a long time since Dawson was that person for me.

Are lemon tarts on the table?

I chuckled at his text and shook my head. He wasn't thinking about sex. He was thinking about food. That was why I didn't need to think about dating. I had my vibrators, including the new one I just got for the shower. That was all the romance I needed. Meaning none. I hadn't had any romance in my life in years, so why start now? Nope. I was going to forget about men and focus on my daughters.

Always. I'll make some tonight and send them with the girls to practice tomorrow.

No, you don't have to do that.

I know, but I want to. I owe you. So damn much. I wouldn't have gotten through the last few months without you. Thank you for that.

I'll always be here for you, Vee. Nothing will ever change that. Even if I don't get lemon tarts tomorrow.

You're such a charmer.

"Mom, is dinner almost ready? I'm starving," Bianca asked as she came down the hall to the kitchen.

"Yeah, almost," I told her. "Is your sister ready to eat?"

"I'll check." Bianca went back down the hall. A minute later, I heard a knock, then muffled voices as the girls talked.

My phone buzzed with another text from Brantley.

Just being honest. I love you, Vee. Anything you need, I'm here. I promise you.

Thanks. It means the world. And same. I hope you know that.

I do. My pizza just arrived, but I'll talk to you later. If the girls ever need a ride, let me know.

I will. So far Goldie, Xavier, and I are making it work. I think we have it covered for this week.

Good. Happy to help if you need it.

Thanks, Bee. Talk later.

Yep. Enjoy dinner. I'm sure it's amazing.

You too.

I tucked my phone into my pocket as the girls came down the hall. I pulled the sheet-pan pork chops out of the oven. It smelled good. It looked like everything was fully cooked. I'd never tried one of those recipes because Dawson refused, but I was no longer cooking for Dawson and decided to give it a shot.

"That smells good, Mom," Sam said.

"Yeah, it does. What is it?" Bianca asked.

"Pork chops with Brussel sprouts and squash."

The girls exchanged a glance and shrugged.

"If it tastes as good as it smells, you need to make this again," Bianca said.

"Let's try it." I handed them each a plate. Dawson hated dishing food at the counter and carrying plates to the table, but it never bothered me. The girls and I had gotten into the habit of doing it lately. A lot had changed since Dawson's girlfriend showed up at our house to surprise him, and I kicked him out.

We all got drinks and sat down to eat. We exchanged looks. Everyone speared something different and ate our bites together.

And groaned.

"Oh, wow," Sam moaned. "So good."

"Mm hmm," Bianca agreed.

I nodded along with them. The seasoning blended together perfectly. The vegetables had a softness to them once you got past the crispy exterior. The pork was juicy and tender and an amazing compliment to the veggies.

"This is a keeper," Bianca said.

I'd been experimenting with recipes for the last month. Only one a week, keeping our family favorites on regular rotation. So far, we'd had one success, one epic failure where we ordered pizza, and two that were okay but not great. This was a second success.

"I agree," Sam said. "Dad would have hated this." She wrinkled her nose in a sneer.

"Dad hated everything," Bianca spat.

"Girls." I worked hard not to bad-mouth their father in front of them. I never wanted them to think poorly of him. Of course, his girlfriend showing up during dinner hadn't helped. They knew exactly what happened between us, and they were definitely old enough to understand. And given that Dawson had barely been in touch with either of them since he moved out was not winning him any favors.

"You don't have to defend him, Mom," Bianca said. "He's an ass."

"Language."

"He's still our dad, Bianca, but I can't say I don't feel the same," Sam jumped in. She turned to me. "Dad cheated on you, more than once. How can you possibly be on his side?"

"I'm not on his side. Why would you think I'm on his side?"

"Because when we're honest about him, you get mad at us." Bianca met my gaze with her own. Looking at my sixteen-year-old was like looking in a mirror, but with shoulder-length curls instead of my pixie cut. I had so many hopes for my girls, but the anger they experienced because of their father clouded all of that.

"I'm not mad at you," I breathed. "I don't want you to hate your father. What he did had nothing to do with you two."

"Really? Because it doesn't feel that way. We barely talk to him. He left—"

"I told him to leave."

Bianca sighed and shook her head. "That's what I'm talking about. You're taking the blame for kicking him out. Where's his blame? He's the one who was with someone else. He's the one who made me say no to Andrew when he invited me to the prom last year. He's the one—"

"Wait, what?" I looked between my girls. Sam studied

her plate, and Bianca looked like she hadn't meant to admit what she said. "What are you talking about? Someone asked you to prom and your father told you not to go?"

Bianca looked at Sam, but Sam just shrugged. Bianca sighed. "Dad didn't tell me I couldn't go with Andrew, but he's the reason I said no. How am I supposed to date? How am I supposed to look at any guy and trust he's not going to cheat on me and break my heart? It's just not possible."

"Oh, Bianca, I am so sorry." I got up and hugged my oldest, feeling the anger and pain vibrating through her. "I didn't know you were having such a hard time. You know not all men are going to cheat, right? Not all men are like—"

"Like Dad," Samantha said. Leave it to the fifteen-year-old to be so succinct. "But some are. Paul said his dad was involved with someone else before he left his mom. And a girl in my math class said the same thing happened to her parents. I like Paul a lot, but when I see him talking to another girl... I'm with Bianca."

I sighed heavily and pulled both girls to the couch, one on each side of me. I wrapped an arm around each of them and kissed the tops of their heads. "Your dad wasn't happy. I can't explain why because I don't really know why. But your dad is not the model for all men. There are so many men who are good and faithful. Men who would never even think about cheating on a woman."

"Yeah, but how do you know which is which?" Sam asked.

I drew a breath and told them the truth. "Sometimes you don't. I loved your father. When we met, I thought he was funny, and he made me feel special. I wanted to be around him. He asked me on a date, and I liked the thought of a man who other girls thought was good-looking wanting me. Maybe that was shallow of me, but it's the truth. I never thought he'd end up cheating on me. Even when Haley showed up here, I was still in shock. But if I could go back and do it all over, I would. I'd still choose to marry your father because even though it ended badly, we had good times. Having both of you, moving into this house, seeing you two grow up. I loved your father."

"I don't think I'm as strong as you are, Mom," Bianca whispered. "I don't think I can do it."

"I'm not strong. I am just doing what I think is best right now."

"Are you going to start dating?" Sam asked.

That question. That one hurt. I could tell them anything about Dawson. How we met, how we fell in love, how we built a life together. But after twenty-two years with one man, a man who broke me and made me question everything, I was more on the side of my oldest. I wasn't sure I could trust another man. Or that I was willing to try.

"You're not. I can see it on your face," Bianca said. "You're scared, too. So why should we date?"

"I'm not saying you should." I brushed the hair back from Bianca's face and tried not to let the pain in her brown eyes break me. "You have to decide if you want to date someone. But I don't want you to stop living your life. I don't want you to refuse to go to the prom with someone you like because you're afraid one day he might not be faithful to you."

"Isn't that what you're doing?" Bianca asked.

I sucked in a breath and forced a smile. "I'm healing. I was married to your father for a long time, and we dated for years before then. I was with him for more than half of my life. It's not easy to turn around and let someone new in. To flip a switch and be okay with dating again."

"Do you think you will again one day?" Sam asked.

I shrugged. "I don't know. I have a job I love and I have the two of you. I don't feel like I'm missing anything in my life right now. I also don't know if I'm willing to make room in my life for someone else."

"Why isn't Uncle Brantley married?" Bianca asked.

"Brantley? Um, I... I don't know." The idea of Brantley getting married stung more than it should have. I had no claim over him. No right to wish he would stay single so I had a friend.

"I just wondered if he's like Dad. Or if he's a good guy," Bianca said.

"Uncle Brantley is an amazing man. He'd never cheat." The steel in my voice was something my girls didn't hear often, and they knew it meant I was serious.

"That's what I thought, too. But he's single. Why isn't he married or dating someone?" Sam asked.

"I don't know. You'd have to ask him." I stood, needing to end the conversation about Brantley. Talking about him dating shouldn't bother me, but it did.

"Is he coming over for dinner this week?" Bianca asked.

I picked up our plates from the table and shrugged. "Probably. He's remodeling his kitchen, so he's going to have trouble cooking. He might come over a few times. If you guys are okay with it."

They both nodded.

"Yeah, we love Uncle Brantley," Bianca said.

"Me, too."

The girls helped me clear the table and put away the leftovers. I asked if they wanted to help me bake lemon bars to take to Brantley at practice tomorrow, and they both agreed. While the lemon bars were in the oven, we piled onto the couch and started a movie. A romantic comedy where the hero definitely did not cheat.

The timer went off for the lemon bars, and I took them out of the oven. They looked perfect. And they smelled even better. I took a quick picture and sent it to Brantley. I got a reply almost immediately.

You're such a tease. I'm not sure if I can wait until tomorrow to try one.

They're fresh out of the oven.

I'm drooling.

You can come over. We're just watching a movie.

I don't want to interrupt your night.

No interruption. We were talking about you earlier. The girls won't mind.

Should I be worried? Why were you talking about me?

The girls were asking if all men cheat. We all agreed you're someone who'd never even think about it.

Agreed. Never in a million years. You all deserve better.

Thanks. They also asked why you aren't married or dating someone. I told them they have to ask you that question.

Throwing me under the bus. I see.

Not on purpose. I just don't know the answer.

Life's most difficult question.

I smiled. I wondered the same thing over the years, but

I'd never had the courage to ask him. Now that I had, I still didn't know.

I might never know why Brantley Pierce was still single. But I also wasn't sure it mattered.

> Are you serious about me coming over?
> Because I'm on my way if you are.

> You are always welcome here.

> See you soon.

I held my phone to my chest and tried not to be too excited. He was my friend. Just a friend. Him coming over had nothing to do with me and everything to do with the lemon bars.

But that's not at all why I made them. Not at all.

3

BRANTLEY

One week of practice was done, and so was one week of kitchen renovation. I wasn't sure which was harder. The huffing and puffing of the runners at the end of the week was enough to vote for practice, but my own huffing and puffing when I muscled the last of my kitchen cabinets to the trash said maybe the renovation took the top spot.

Either way, both sucked.

So did spending my Friday night, the last one of summer, alone in my empty kitchen. My life was not what I always hoped it would be. It was my own fault, but it was hard to know nothing had turned out like I'd hoped.

I pushed the melancholy thoughts aside and surveyed the empty space. It was huge without everything in it. Nice problem to have. And with the entire kitchen torn out, down to the studs, I was ready to start building everything back up.

It all came apart easier than I expected, which was why I pulled off the drywall, too. I'd done enough renovation to know there was always a reason when things were easy. My reason was an old water leak behind the fridge that went unnoticed for a long time. The rot was bad enough that it made sense to replace the insulation and to bulk up the framing in the walls. I needed to pull some of it out for the new sliders anyway, so it wasn't a huge hit to the budget, but it would change the timeline.

Knox still insisted I could finish by New Year's.

I was about to order dinner when a text came in from Valentina.

> Are you going to the movie tonight?

> What movie?

> The town is having a big weekend thing. All weekend there's something. Tonight is a movie in Catherine Park.

> I was just about to order dinner and jump in the shower. I look like I spent the day at the beach with all the dust on me.

> You should come with us tonight. I was going to pack a picnic dinner for the movie.

Valentina was inviting me to spend the evening with her. Why was I hesitating?

> Sounds fun. What time do I need to be ready?

> Movie starts in an hour. We were going to walk over soon.

> I can be to your house in twenty minutes if you can wait for me.

> That works. Are you sure?

> Always, Vee. I'll see you soon.

I undressed as I walked through my house, carrying my dirty, dusty clothes with me to the bathroom. I tossed my clothes into the hamper, then turned on the hot water. I set my phone on the counter, then stepped under the hot spray.

I hadn't run as much over the summer as I normally would, and my muscles were sore. Every other summer, I had nothing to do and no one to spend time with. I always saw Valentina and the rest of her family, but not as much as I did this summer. Without Dawson around, I spent more time with them than any other summer. I wasn't complaining, but between her sweet treats and my lack of exercise, I was hurting.

Not that I would tell my team that. Or Jana.

I took a fast shower, washing my hair twice to make sure all the dust was out, then turned off the water and snagged my towel. I dried off as I walked through my bedroom to the closet, choosing boxer briefs, shorts, and a tee for the night.

My shoulder-length hair was still wet when I finished getting dressed, so I tied it up in a knot and grabbed my keys, wanting to get to Valentina's as quickly as possible.

She opened the door a minute after I rang the bell and scowled at me. "I told you that you don't need to wait for me to let you in. You have a key for a reason."

"It's not my house, Vee. I don't want to catch you in a compromising position." I wiggled my brows to tease her as my dick hardened at the thought.

Valentina rolled her eyes and walked away. "Please. I'm not worried about that at all. Nothing to compromise around here."

"You might start dating one day."

She snorted. "Not anytime soon."

I followed her into the kitchen, letting the subject drop. I didn't want to think about her dating, anyway. Not Dawson, not anyone. It was painful enough to watch her fall for him. Watching her fall for another guy might kill me.

"The girls already started walking. They wanted to find their friends. Can you carry this for me?" She turned and handed me a small bag of water bottles and a bottle of wine.

"Got it. What else do you have?"

She grabbed the massive basket from the countertop and nodded. "All set."

"Let me carry that," I told her. She could barely hold the thing, let alone carry it.

"I got it."

"Vee, I'm right here. Let me help."

She hesitated, then handed over the basket. "Thanks."

Her soft voice was enough of a clue, but the way she avoided my gaze said I stepped in something. "Why are you upset about me carrying the basket?"

She shook her head and walked toward the door.

I followed her, basket and bag in hand. Whatever was going on felt important, and I wasn't going to let her get away with ignoring me. "Talk to me, Vee. What did I do? The last thing I intended to do was upset you."

She breathed a laugh and shook her head. "You didn't. It's just..." She looked up at me with watery eyes. "I was married for twenty-two years. Dawson and I dated for five years before that. I spent twenty-seven years of my life with him. Do you know how many times he offered to carry everything for me? How many times he tried to help when we would go to things like this? Hell, how many times he attended these events?"

I was pretty sure her questions didn't require an answer, so I just waited for her to finish her thoughts. Especially when I was also sure I could guess the answer.

"None. In twenty-seven years, Dawson helped me zero

fucking times. Nada. Twenty-seven years. Whenever there was an event, he said he was too tired from traveling. Of course, now I know he was too tired from fucking other women. He never did anything with me. Not the things I wanted to do. Why did I marry him?"

Again, I wasn't sure she wanted an answer, but then she looked up at me with those big brown eyes that made me feel simultaneously like the most important man in the world and the most insignificant. I mattered if she was looking at me, but this was Valentina Hayes. The woman who held my heart and made the world spin for me. People loved her. She was special and she was stunning and she was not mine. Which made me feel like I was nothing.

"When you introduced us, I had the biggest crush on you. I wanted to ask you out, but I was too afraid. I'm glad I never did because that would have just been a disaster. But then Dawson was there, and I sort of thought you were hoping I'd like him so I wouldn't be hanging all over you all the time. I was so shy, and I was so scared of college, and I know I was annoying. I always felt bad about the way I smothered you when we first went away. How I got in the way of you dating."

Everything she said jumbled in my mind like she spit it into a blender and turned it on high. I couldn't process any of it quickly enough. I knew I needed to respond, to tell her she misread everything, but there was so much in what she said that I couldn't figure out how to explain all that to her.

"Anyway, I just wanted to say I'm sorry for all of that years ago, and I wanted to make sure I'm not doing it again. When the girls asked the other day why you never got married, I realized I was doing the same thing I did back then. I've been monopolizing your time and cock-blocking you. I don't mean to."

"You are not cock-blocking me," I finally choked out.

She chuckled. "Well, lemon-bar-blocking you, or whatever. I don't want you to feel like you always have to drop everything for me. I know I'm the pathetic divorcée, but I promise you, I'll get my shit together soon."

"You are not pathetic. And you don't have to get your shit together at all. You're amazing. And I'm here because I want to be. I love you, Vee. You're the most important person in my world. I would do anything for you. Anytime."

She smiled up at me, her eyes shining with joy instead of the tears they held just minutes ago. "Thanks, Bee. I really don't know what I would do without you. But that doesn't mean I wouldn't figure it out. Sorry. I'm doing it again. Ugh."

"You're not doing anything. Now, tell me again how you had this huge crush on me when we went to college."

She laughed. "Oh, you so knew I did. I was so obvious." She ushered me out of the house and locked the door before turning toward town. She slung the bag of drinks over her shoulder and left me with the basket. She slid her hand onto my arm, walking close to me.

"I promise you, I did not know you liked me."

She shook her head. "I don't know how that's possible. I liked you almost all of high school, and when we both chose to the same college, I worried you were going to think I only went there because I knew you were."

"I knew you were going there before I chose it," I confessed.

"Oh, well, that's good. I didn't want you to think I was a stalker or something. But anyway, I just... I don't know. I always thought you were cute, and you were always nice to me. I guess I hoped when we were away from MacKellar Cove it would be different and I'd find a way to tell you I liked you. Then you introduced me to Dawson, and he swooped in and made me feel like I was bothering you if I asked what you were doing when we went out."

"He what?" My blood boiled at the thought.

"It was no big deal. He told me you were dating a lot and going to parties. I mean, that's what college was for, right? It all worked out. I guess. If you count both of us being single at forty-five. Shit, that's depressing."

I coughed a laugh.

"Not you. Dammit. I didn't mean you. I meant me. I'm depressing. You're amazing, and any woman would be lucky to have you."

"Even you?"

"Hell, yes, me. I am the luckiest of them all because I already have you in my life. You're my best friend, Bee."

"And you had a huge crush on me."

She groaned. "I never should have admitted that. Gah! But I know it's for the best that we never dated. I would have screwed it all up, and we wouldn't even be friends now."

"You don't know that."

She shrugged. "Maybe not. But I do know if I hadn't married Dawson, I wouldn't have my girls, and that's impossible to imagine."

"Yes, yes, it is," I admitted. As much as I wished I'd known about her crush decades ago, I'd never wish Bianca or Samantha didn't exist.

The noise of the crowd exploded as we turned the corner and saw the park. It was crowded. Not just busy, but overrun with people. Every square of grass was covered by a blanket or towel. The chairs were full. The sidewalks had people lined up on chairs. Even the streets around the park were wall-to-wall people.

"Damn. This is bigger than I thought. How are we going to find the girls?"

"We'll find them," I assured her.

Valentina's eyes grew wider as we walked closer to the crowd. She'd never been big on large groups of people, and this crowd was huge. Someone bumped into her, then apologized and said hello. Over and over again, we were jostled by others walking around, trying to find their spot and their people.

"Valentina!" someone shouted above the noise.

We both turned and saw Goldie waving to us from a large blanket. Karissa was next to Goldie on another blanket. We moved closer to them and found Bianca and Samantha.

"This is nuts," Valentina breathed as she hugged her friends.

"It is," Goldie agreed. "Patrick got here early and put our blankets down so we would have a spot. Xavier said this was the best place to sit for the movie."

Patrick was Goldie's assistant and her boyfriend. Xavier ran the MacKellar Cove Movie Theater and was married to Karissa. I didn't know either man well, but the few times I'd been to guy's night at O'Kelley's, they were friendly and kind. I appreciated that, especially from Xavier since I'd gone on a date with Karissa a while back.

"The kids wandered for a while, but it's almost hard to walk around here. This is so much bigger than I expected," Karissa said.

Karissa designed apps, including the top online dating app in the area. A ton of local couples got their start on Book Boyfriends Wanted. I had a few dates from there, including the one I went on with Karissa, but none stuck, just like everything else I'd tried.

"No one is ready to say goodbye to summer," Goldie said. As the Tourism Director for MacKellar Cove, she was in charge of making sure events like the one happening were a success.

"I'm not ready to go back to school," McJenna said. Xavier's daughter was sixteen, like Bianca, and on the cross-country team. She was smart, a good runner, and a nice kid.

The other kids nodded with McJenna before returning to their conversations.

Valentina lowered herself to a seat near Goldie, then patted the blanket next to her for me to sit. I set the basket down in front of her and sat facing her since the spot she tried to get me to squeeze into was too small.

Valentina smiled at me, a tinge of disappointment in her eyes. I wasn't sure what that was for, but I didn't have time to think about it before she was unloading the basket of food that would easily feed all of us and half the others in town.

We passed around cheese and crackers, sliced meats, nuts, and fresh fruits. Valentina had water bottles for everyone, but the others had their own drinks. They shared their food, and Valentina shared hers, and everyone talked about fall and school and getting back into routines.

I was the only one there who didn't live with a teenager, at least part-time. As they all talked, I just sat there and listened. I always saw the other side of things, the teacher side. I was the only one I had to worry about. I set my routines with no input or influence by anyone else.

All of a sudden, the loneliness of my life felt like it was too much. I excused myself and got up from the blanket. I wandered through the crowd, passing families and couples, and wondered what the hell I was doing there.

I laughed inside. I knew what I was doing there. I was playing house with my best friend. I was lying to myself and hoping she might notice me. I was wishing that the crush she admitted to having more than two decades ago was still simmering in the background.

I was a damn fool.

If she wanted me, she wouldn't have said us being together would have been a bad idea. If she wanted me, she would have told me. She didn't. She hadn't in a very long time.

"Are you okay?" she asked from right behind me, a second before her hand touched my shoulder.

I resisted the urge to shrug her off. I craved her touch, but not the touch of my best friend. I wanted the touch of the woman I loved. The woman I tried my damnedest not to love. The woman I was finally realizing I was never going to get over, no matter how many times I told myself it was dumb to love her.

"Yeah, all good," I forced myself to say as I turned to face her.

Her hand fell as I turned, but her gaze was spot-on. She narrowed her eyes and looked closely at me. "The parent talk getting to you?"

I shook my head. "Nah. I always wanted kids."

"You never told me that."

I shrugged. "There are a lot of things we never told each other, I guess. Like you having a crush on me."

She rolled her eyes and laughed, like I hoped she would. She leaned against my side and wrapped her arm around my waist. I draped mine over her shoulder and let her guide me back to the blanket where her friends and daughters waited for us.

She pointed to the spot she'd been in before and waited for me to sit, then sat a foot in front of me. My thighs cradled hers. It was intimate without being inappropriate.

She was my best friend. We'd sat like that before. But not in years.

And just that fast, I knew why I'd never get over Valentina. Because she was impossible not to love. And I had no hope of walking away from her.

4

VALENTINA

My body heated as I forced my focus to the movie that was starting on the screen. Why did I think it was a good idea to sit in front of Brantley?

I didn't think. That was why. Because Goldie and Patrick and Karissa and Xavier were sitting together, and I just slipped back into being one half of a couple. It didn't matter that we weren't actually together, we were there together.

I was so messed up.

I watched the movie without actually paying attention to it at all. Every time Brantley moved, I felt him. Every brush of his thigh against mine, every shift of his body, every long exhale, I felt. And all it did was warm my body even more.

As soon as the movie was over, I jumped up from my seat. Others around us were starting to move, so I didn't look too crazy. I glanced around for an excuse since our entire group was sitting.

"I need to run to the bathroom. I'll be right back."

"I'll go with you," Goldie said. "I drank way too much sitting here."

We turned toward the temporary toilets lined up on the

backside of the closest building. I hated using them, but with an audience, I couldn't just walk around for a minute and pretend.

"What is going on with you and Brantley?" Goldie hissed once we were a little away from the others.

"Nothing," I blurted. Too fast.

Goldie's brows went up, and her face pursed into one of those bullshit expressions. She knew me too well.

"He's my best friend." Wasn't that an explanation?

"And?"

I shook my head. "He's just there. He's been there for us. He was always there, but since Dawson left, he's been so much more than a friend."

Those brows shot sky-high again, and I realized what I said.

"Not like that. Nothing happened, and nothing is going to. Brantley is not interested in getting involved with a middle-aged divorced woman whose kids he coaches."

"Maybe not just any middle-aged divorced woman whose kids he coaches, but I think he might be interested in getting involved with you."

I scoffed and rolled my eyes. We stepped forward in line for the bathroom as more people crowded behind us. "He is not interested in me."

"Is that the only reason nothing happened?"

"No. I'm not looking to date. I'm not ready."

"Hun, I don't think you're ever ready. It's sort of like having kids. You just buckle up and pray you don't screw them up more than therapy can fix."

A laugh popped out of me. "That's the truth." I chewed on my lip. I had always had a thing for Brantley, but dating? I wasn't ready for it. Not when the only man I had any interest in considering was the one man I couldn't stand to lose from my life. What if it all went south, and I lost him for good? Not an option.

"I'm just saying you two looked pretty cozy tonight."

"We're just friends," I said.

Thankfully, the person in front of me stepped out of the bathroom line and I could escape the conversation. I held my breath and used the bathroom, thankful when the hand sanitizer was well-stocked inside and I could sort of clean my hands.

I waited to the side for Goldie, grateful when she didn't say anything else about Brantley on our walk back to the others. When we got there, the blankets and baskets were all packed up, and everyone was waiting for us.

"Ready to head back?" Brantley asked.

I nodded. We all said goodbye and headed out in different directions.

The girls walked a little ahead of Brantley and me, chatting about the movie and about practice. Their first meet was only two weeks away, and from the sound of it, they were excited.

"You're doing a great job with the team," I said quietly so the girls didn't hear me.

"Thanks. I love it. Running is what keeps me sane most of the time."

I laughed. "Having two teenagers, I can only imagine how taxing it is to have twenty or more of them at a time. Teachers are amazing."

"Yeah," he said in a way that made me think that wasn't the cause of his stress.

"You okay?"

He glanced my way and smiled, then slid his gaze to the ground. "All good."

"Hey." I put my hand on his arm to stop him and waited for the girls to walk a little farther ahead. "What's going on?"

He sucked in a full breath, his chest rising. He let it out slowly and met my gaze. His was heated, fiery, like he was holding back a desire I had never seen from him before.

I was drawn to it, like a moth to a flame. I'd never understood the expression before, but looking into Brantley's eyes and seeing that returned passion made me ache for him in a way I'd never known.

A giggle behind me snapped me out of the trance I was in. "Good to see you, coach. Ally said she's having a great time at practice. I can't wait to see you in action."

If someone had dumped a bucket of ice water over my head, I wouldn't have been more shocked. Brantley wasn't looking at me like that. He was looking at Ally's mom, Becky. Becky was young and pretty, with a tight, perky body that I was instantly jealous of. I'd never had a reason to be jealous of her, or any woman, before, but watching the smile curl Brantley's lips as he spoke to her made me want to claw the other woman's eyes out.

I was so foolish. There I was imagining Brantley wanting me, and all he was doing was checking out the hot mom behind me.

I forced a smile and turned to walk away. The girls were a full block ahead of us, and Brantley was talking to Becky, so I needed to go.

For the rest of my walk, I chastised myself for getting lost in a fantasy that Brantley might want me. I got my answer right there about why he wasn't married. Why would he settle down when he could sleep with any woman in town? Or every woman in town.

It didn't matter, though. I had no claim over him. I never had. I never would. Getting upset about it when I was the one who was married and unavailable for most of the time we'd known each other only made me a hypocrite.

Brantley caught up to me as I turned onto my street. He apologized for stopping to talk to Becky, but I waved him off.

"You don't have to explain anything to me. You're single and she's attractive."

He stopped me on the driveway as the girls walked into the house. "Do you seriously think I'm interested in Becky?"

I shrugged. "It's none of my business, Bee. I love you, and I want you to be happy. If she makes you happy, even if it's just for a night, then go for it. I'm not judging. I promise you."

He stared at me for a full minute without saying a word. When I squirmed, he finally spoke. "Sometimes I'm amazed by how little we know about each other."

"What do you mean?"

"I mean, you had a thing for me in high school, and you think I'm going to sleep with the parent of one of my students."

"I don't think that. I'm just saying I didn't want to be in your way."

"Trust me, Vee, you are never in my way. I will choose you over every other woman in town, every single time."

His words sent a spiral of heat deep into my belly. He didn't mean it the way I took it, but I wasn't going to push for him to clarify. Instead, I teased him and brought things back to how they always were for us. "That's just because I keep you in lemon bars."

He smiled, then breathed a laugh that felt forced. "That's nowhere near the only reason. I love you, Vee."

"I love you, too," I said, stepping into his open arms and letting him hold me close. The heat of his body warmed my skin in the slowly cooling night air. My heart pounded, the closeness of him relaxing me and exciting me at the same time.

It had been a long time since I'd been held. Sure, Brantley hugged me, but to be held like he was in that moment was different. So different that it brought tears to my eyes and made me wish things were different.

I sniffed, and he immediately pulled back. His far-too-observant gaze scanned my face before he wrapped me up again and kissed the top of my head. "I wish I could take all the pain away from you."

I didn't reply. I couldn't tell him about it. How would I? He already knew Dawson and I weren't sleeping together for a long time before we actually got divorced. Telling him not only did my husband stop wanting sex, but he stopped touching me altogether was a shame I wasn't sure I could voice. Talk about not feeling desirable.

And it wasn't just that, it was the fact that I stayed with him after that. I thought by fixing dinner and being a good wife, he would change. He would love me again. I believed it was possible.

I was a fool.

And that was why I wouldn't risk dating again. Not anytime soon. I couldn't put myself through that. I wouldn't.

"Let's get this inside, then I'll get out of your way," Brantley said, pulling back but keeping his arm around me.

"You're never in the way."

"Fine, then I won't get out of your way."

I laughed with him. He opened the front door and stepped back for me to walk in first. He went straight to the kitchen, unpacking the basket and putting things away. When he was done, he put the basket on the top of the pantry, where I kept it.

Dawson never would have known where everything

went. And he never would have helped put things away. He would have gone straight to the bedroom and taken a shower, leaving me to do everything.

"Want to watch a movie?" Brantley asked.

I smiled. "Sure." Normal. That's what things were like with Brantley. Perfectly normal.

I needed a little of that.

"GIRLS! The bus will be here any minute!"

It was the first day of school. None of us were ready. I told the girls to have their things packed the night before, and did they? Nope. Of course not.

So, we were rushing. I worked into the evening yesterday so there would be fresh treats for Cove Bakery to start the day. My boss, Harriett, always let me come in after the girls were in school. She managed the morning crowd on her own, knowing people were patient with her and no one in MacKellar Cove would be rude.

"Coming!" Bianca yelled. Footsteps raced toward me. At least one of them was moving.

"Me too!" Samantha shouted.

The bus was usually late on the first day of school, but I couldn't take any chances. I needed to get to work.

"Is the bus here?"

I shook my head. "Not yet. But we should get outside to wait. Do you guys want me to wait with you or pretend you don't have a mom?"

Bianca snorted and rolled her eyes. Samantha glanced at her sister.

"Mom, all our friends know you and love you," Bianca said.

"That doesn't mean you want me outside when you get on the bus."

"You're fine, Mom," Bianca said. Her phone dinged. "Ashley said the bus just picked her up."

"Let's go," I told them. Ashley lived around the corner, so the bus was almost to us.

We walked outside just as the bus made the turn onto our street. I wasn't sure if they had everything they needed for the first day, but I was hopeful.

Both girls hugged me. The three of us shared a laugh. "I love you, girls."

"Love you, Mom," they said together.

They let go and walked down the driveway to the sidewalk. The bus stopped, and I waved to the driver, then they got on and drove off.

I turned to my right and realized it was their first first day of school without Dawson. For all his faults, he was always there to see them get on the bus on the first day of school.

Until today.

I walked back into the house and sat on the couch. There were going to be a lot more firsts without him. I wasn't sad for myself, but my girls were going to miss their dad.

Unfortunately, I wasn't sure he was actually missing them.

And that broke my heart.

I couldn't go to work feeling so down, so I did what I always did on the first day of school and sent Brantley a text wishing him a good day.

Happy first day of high school! May your students be smart, your words be wise, and your colleagues be delightful.

LOL! Thanks. I don't know why, but I'm feeling a little off today.

Must be in the air. I'm right there with you. First time Dawson wasn't here for the first day of school.

Damn. I'm sorry. You should have told me. I could have come by.

It's okay. I can't have you playing dad to my girls all the time. It's bad enough you're the only positive male influence in their lives.

I'm happy to be there for all of you any time you need me. I love you guys.

We love you, too. Are you ready for today?

I think so. I realized it's my twentieth year of teaching. Crazy.

That makes me feel old!

Yep, me too. A lot of things I wanted in my life that I don't have yet. Lots of thoughts going on today.

You will get everything you want. You're too amazing of a man not to.

Hopefully one day.

Fingers crossed.

Are you working today?

Yep.

What are you guys doing for dinner?

Not sure. I was thinking I might do something special, like takeout. Want to join us?

I was hoping you'd offer. I'll pick something up after practice. Once I shower and change.

Sounds great. Thanks. I am so grateful for you.

Ditto. Gotta run. Kids are coming in. Have a good day.

You too!

I smiled at the phone. I was looking forward to dinner with Brantley. It would distract the girls from their father not calling this morning and not being home to send them off to school on their first day.

I was not going to think about the other reasons I was looking forward to a dinner with Brantley. He was my friend. That was it.

THE REST of the week went by much more smoothly. The girls were ready, no teachers assigned homework the first few days, and no one said anything about Dawson. It was all good.

Sunday night, I knocked on the door to Book Boyfriends Unlimited and waited. Goldie was next to me, reading an email on her phone.

Finley MacKellar, the owner and friend of ours, waved as she approached the door. Finley was married to Trent

MacKellar, the man whose family founded MacKellar Cove. They had an adorable fifteen-month-old son, George.

"Hi guys," Finley said. "How are you?" She hugged us both and led the way toward the back of the bookstore where a bunch of us gathered every Sunday night for book club.

Book club really being an excuse for us to talk about love, life, and relationships. A eat cake. That was why I came.

"Good," I said, knowing Finley wouldn't ask more from me. We didn't know each other well, and as the newly divorced one, no one dove too deep into my horror show of a marriage. They were all shiny and happy and loved. They didn't want to see their own relationship reflected in my disaster.

"I'm good, too. Just dealing with an issue Omar sent me," Goldie said, her focus still on her phone.

"Is he as good of a boss as you hoped he would be?" Finley asked.

Omar Knight was the new mayor of MacKellar Cove. He helped Goldie and Patrick get the previous mayor to resign. Long story, but it had a happy ending.

"He's great," Goldie said without hesitation. "The town is going to have an amazing summer next year with him in charge. He's creative and smart, but he's also open to ideas and is willing to spend money to make MacKellar Cove what I know it can be."

"That's exciting," Karissa said. The group of them had already started eating the cakes someone brought. Everyone took turns baking something for the week. Karissa shared when they first started meeting there were only a few of them and one cake was more than enough, but now there could be twenty women, so two people brought cake every week.

I didn't care how many cakes as long as I didn't have to bake them. When it was my turn, I bought one from work. I loved baking, but I hadn't been able to come up with many new recipes lately and buying something meant it didn't go to waste.

Goldie and I claimed seats and gratefully accepted slices of cake from Trinity and Elise. We all chatted about the start of school and the quieter feel to town now that tourist season was winding down. We were almost done with our cake when Finley said she didn't think anyone else was coming.

"Did anyone actually read this book?" Elise asked, holding up the paperback we'd all agreed we would read.

"I did," Finley said.

"Of course you did. You've read them all. Anyone else?" Elise asked.

"I did, too," Anna said. "It was amazing."

"Right?" Elise asked. "I couldn't put it down."

My cheeks warmed as I looked around the room. I hadn't had time to pick up the book, let alone read it.

"What's it about?" Karissa asked. "I didn't read it."

"It's about finding joy in the simple things. Knowing what makes you happy and living your life in that space," Elise said. "It really made me think about all the years I spent miserable after Andy and before Colin. I wasn't willing to dive deep enough to see what made me feel good."

"We all know what makes you feel good," Willow teased Elise.

Elise smirked. "Well, yes, but there's so much more than sex."

Willow gasped. "I never thought I'd hear you say such a thing."

Elise chuckled. The two of them were the ones who always turned every conversation to sex. Not that it took much encouraging in this group, but those two usually started it.

"Sex was the only thing that I allowed in my life at that time. I kept everything else at a distance," Elise explained.

"Like what?" Goldie asked.

I was grateful for her question because I was wondering, too.

"Everything," Elise said. "I didn't allow myself to find pleasure in anything. Fresh air, good food, time with friends, anything. I forgot what I enjoyed about life until I met Colin and he brought it out of me again."

"I went through the same thing after my divorce," Goldie said. "I found joy in some things, but pleasure was harder to reach for. I might have to read this book."

"You should," Anna said. "It felt like a guidebook for finding yourself. I wish I'd read it before I met Hudson. He's going to do a pleasure quest with me."

"A pleasure quest?" I blurted.

Anna nodded. "Yeah. We're really excited about it."

"I would be, too," Elise said with a saucy smirk.

Anna chuckled. "No sex."

"What?" Willow asked. "How in the hell do you experience pleasure without sex?"

I wanted to know the answer to that, too.

5

———

Anna chuckled. "Have you seriously never experienced pleasure that wasn't about sex?"

Willow raised one brow and looked at Anna like she had three heads. "Happiness? Sure. But pleasure? I think you're mixing up your words."

Anna shook her head. "Nope. Pleasure. It just means being pleased, finding enjoyment or satisfaction. It doesn't have to be about sex."

"And you're not having any sex?" Willow asked.

Anna laughed. "I didn't say that. I just meant we're not only seeking pleasure from sex. Come on. No one else has ever thought about what other things bring you pleasure?"

"Seeing George smile," Finley said.

"When Ian finishes a boat. The look on his face," Blake added.

"One of Valentina's desserts," Goldie said. "That brings me a lot of pleasure."

"A day on the water in the fresh air," Elise said.

"You're all insane," Willow insisted.

I thought they were brilliant. "I need to do this."

"You totally should," Anna said.

"You're joking," Willow said.

I shook my head. "I'm divorced. It's a barren wasteland in my pants right now. By my choice. I have no interest in sex."

"Not even alone?" Elise questioned.

"Sometimes, but I don't think I even know who I am right now. You're talking about this, and I'm like Elise before Colin. I can't think of one thing outside sex that would mean pleasure. Not one. After everything with Dawson, not to mention having two teenage daughters, I don't know what I like to do."

"You should do a pleasure quest," Anna said. "Hudson is having fun coming up with ideas. We can share some with you."

"Yeah, maybe," I said. The idea appealed to me, but I couldn't remember the last time I did something just for the joy of it. I wasn't even sure where to start.

"Well, I think you're all crazy. Just have more sex. That brings me pleasure all the time," Willow said with a saucy wink.

"One day you'll pull a muscle trying to get out of bed and you'll understand why I'm doing this," Anna told her.

"You pulled a muscle?" Willow asked.

"More times than you can imagine," Anna said with a groan.

Elise and Willow exchanged a glance. "We're not getting old," Elise said.

Anna, Goldie, and I snorted.

"You know the alternative is to die young, right?" Goldie said.

"Dammit," Willow hissed. "Well, then I guess I better enjoy being able to have sex for pleasure now. I can do a pleasure quest when I'm your age."

Those of us above forty snickered and shook our heads. To be young.

The conversation moved on around me as I thought about this pleasure quest. I took a bite of the cake I had and sat back, slowing myself down. It was good. Damn good. The way the flavors melted together and bounced around in my mouth made me want more. It also sparked a hint of creativity. Creativity I hadn't felt in a long time. Years.

I refused to blame everything that went wrong in my marriage on Dawson. He was the reason it finally ended, but over the years there were lots of things that happened. I stayed faithful to him and worked hard at making things right, and he didn't do either, but that didn't mean if he hadn't cheated our marriage would have lasted.

It took me a while to accept that. Not that an imperfect marriage was an excuse to cheat. There was no excuse. I would never forgive Dawson for that. But I knew we both held some of the blame for the beginning of the end of our marriage.

After so many years of being unhappy and doing everything possible to make the other three people in my family happy, I'd lost sight of the things I enjoyed. I used to come up with new items for the bakery all the time. I was still doing it, but mostly I was recycling ideas I'd had before. Or turning to the internet for inspiration.

My favorite flavor had always been chocolate, but I couldn't think of the last time I added something unexpected to it. Something new and different. Something—

"Earth to Valentina," Goldie said.

I looked up and found all of them watching me. "Hmm?"

"What were you thinking about?" Blake asked.

"Chocolate."

"Ooh, can I have some?" Finley asked.

I grinned. "Always. What did I miss?"

"Anna was trying to ask if you wanted to share ideas for the pleasure quest, but you were so lost in thought you didn't hear her," Goldie explained.

"Sorry." I flashed Anna a smile. "I'm trying to think up new recipes."

"I volunteer as a taste-tester," Elise declared, standing up and raising her hand.

I chuckled. "Sounds good. As soon as I have some good samples to try out, I'll let you know."

"You should bring something here next weekend," Finley suggested. "Then we can all try it."

Elise stuck her tongue out at Finley, who returned the gesture.

"I get first dibs," Elise said.

"Deal," Finley agreed.

I shook my head at them and chuckled. I liked the idea of trying out new recipes. But first I needed to come up with some. It couldn't be that hard. Right?

WHY IN THE world did I think it would be easy to create magic out of thin air? Crap. I was so stumped for ideas that I started scrolling social media. I followed a lot of bakers, and my mouth watered at the pictures they posted of their latest creations. Creations I should have been sharing.

Then I stopped. There was a picture of Dawson with another woman. Young, thin, and gorgeous. Dawson was always attractive, but it was hard to believe a woman as stunning as that one actually wanted Dawson.

It also hurt a little.

Okay, more than a little.

My brain knew we were divorced. Had been for months, and separated for months before that. Our marriage hadn't gone from amazing to disaster overnight. It took years of not communicating, not trying, and not working together to get to where we ended up.

But it still hurt to see him with someone else.

Yes, even though his girlfriend showed up at our house.

I couldn't explain it to my rational brain. It didn't make sense. It never would.

A text from Brantley popped up on top of my screen, distracting me from Dawson and his new woman.

> Any chance I can use your oven?

> Of course. You can also join us for dinner.

> I don't want to intrude.

> You are always welcome.

> What can I bring?

> Just your smile.

> I didn't ask what I should wear.

I choked on a laugh as the image of Brantley in swim trunks this past summer popped into my head. My entire body flushed. My breasts grew heavy at the thought of pulling those trunks off to see what pleasure lay beneath.

No! I could not think about him and pleasure. He was

my closest friend. We would not be exchanging pleasure. Not now. Not ever.

Just kidding. See you soon.

With clothes on?

Sorry to disappoint, but yes.

I wasn't sure how to respond, so I didn't. It was a disappointment, but I couldn't tell him that.

I closed the text app and lingered. I didn't really want to see Dawson and his new woman. I wanted to close that app and ignore him and his new life. He wasn't the man he once was. I wasn't the woman I once was, either, but I hadn't abandoned my family.

With a groan, I closed the app. Dawson was single. He could do whatever he wanted. Just like I could.

I pushed off the couch and went to the kitchen. If Brantley was coming over, I needed to cook. He could order a pizza himself or get takeout. He didn't come to our house for either of those options.

I scanned the fridge for something I could pull together quickly. My gaze landed on the hot dogs and sausages I bought on a whim. I hated using the grill, but I loved grilled foods. I told myself I needed to get over my fear and just do it.

I glared at the food for a minute, then slammed the fridge. It was something I enjoyed. But I was too chickenshit to make it happen. Was that how I was with everything in my life? Too scared to go after the things I wanted?

Before I could dig too deep into that, the doorbell rang. I knew it was Brantley and called out that the door was open.

A second later, he walked in. He whipped off his sunglasses and glared at me the moment he was inside.

His fury made me hot. I didn't know why he was mad, but I liked pissed off Brantley. His muscles corded in his arms and his neck. His wide set stance was one of protection and danger. And those eyes... His eyes did me in every time. The way they took in everything around us and then zeroed in on what mattered.

Me.

"Why do you have the door unlocked?" Brantley asked.

I tilted my head to the side. "What?"

"You are three beautiful women living alone. You shouldn't leave your door unlocked."

"It's MacKellar Cove. I'm not worried."

"I am. What if something happened to you? Or the girls? What if Dawson decided to show up and be an ass?"

At his threatening words, my body slowly chilled. Maybe I should have thought of all of that, but the truth was, I lived in MacKellar Cove because it was safe. There had never been a murder in town, or a home invasion. Major crimes didn't happen. But I didn't want to be the first victim of any such thing. Nor did I want my girls to be.

"Okay, you're right. I should keep the door locked. I will make an effort to do so."

"Thank you." Brantley exhaled loudly, all the fight going out of him.

I stuck my tongue out at him, and he chuckled. "I haven't started dinner yet. I'm still trying to figure out what to cook."

"You know you don't have to cook for me. It's late because of practice. We can just order in something."

I shook my head. "I'm not going to have you come over here and not cook. That's the whole reason you asked to use my stove."

"I should have brought something. I'll get groceries next week. Just get me a list of what you guys want to eat. I'll shop Sunday."

"You do not have to do that."

"And you do not have to feed me all the time. But you still do."

He grinned, and I couldn't help but return it. He walked over to me and wrapped his arms around me. I felt safe with him. Like no one and nothing could hurt me.

"Are you willing to show me how to grill?" I asked after a minute.

Brantley pulled back and cocked his head to the side. "Of course, but I'm surprised you don't know how."

"Dawson—"

"Ah, I didn't think of that. Okay, yeah. What do you have to grill? Want to start today?"

I chewed my lip and nodded. Did it count as part of my Quest for Pleasure if Brantley was helping? Did I care?

"I have hot dogs and sausages."

"Sounds good. Let's get started."

Brantley grabbed the meat from the fridge and led the way out to the patio. My backyard wasn't huge, but it was nice. It was fully fenced in with large trees in the back corners. A hammock sat in front of one tree, an old playground near another. We had a cornhole game in the center of the yard, and plenty of competitions all summer.

The patio had a basic grill and a large table that seated eight. We had a fire-pit at the edge of the patio with chairs surrounding it. My backyard was my happy place. Besides all the memories it held, good and bad.

"Do you know how to start the grill?" Brantley asked as he set the packages down on the nearby table.

I shook my head.

"Okay, come here. I'll show you. This one's easy. It's no different than turning on your stove. Each dial controls one part of the grill. I usually use all of them for mine so there aren't any cold spots. So, push in and turn."

The burner clicked, then ignited when he let go. It was just like the gas stove we had in the house. "Why was I so afraid of this?"

Brantley shrugged. "Because you haven't done it before. We're always afraid of things that are new."

I nodded, loving how he not only understood me, but didn't judge me. I turned on the other burners, and he adjusted all of them to make sure they would cook at the same temperature.

"Let's put the sausage on first since they're bigger. It'll take a little longer." He closed the grill. "We'll let that warm up for a few minutes while we get tools."

We both went back to the kitchen, and he explained why he used which tools and showed me the ones he'd use for other things. I smiled at his simple explanations that made something I was afraid of seem so easy.

I put the meat on the grill, under his supervision, and we chatted while we cooked. When everything was finished, he showed me how to turn the grill off, and we carried the food inside to eat.

The girls were on the couch and jumped up when they saw us come back inside. Both groaned at the scent.

"Thanks Uncle Brantley," Bianca said.

"Yeah, that looks good," Samantha agreed.

"Your mom cooked it all. I just supervised," Brantley told them.

Both girls swung their shocked gazes to me.

I grinned. "I figured it was time to learn how to use the grill."

"Can we have steaks next time?" Samantha asked.

I snorted a laugh. "We'll see."

The four of us worked together to create a quick green salad while the meat rested. When everything was ready, we fixed our plates and carried them to the table.

"How's practice going?" I asked the room.

They all exchanged looks, then nodded with their mouths full. They all grinned.

"Since you're all stuffing your faces and smiling, I'm guessing that's a good thing. The first meet is this weekend, right?"

Brantley finally swallowed his food and nodded. "Yep. Friday night. It should be a good one. Usually has about fifty schools, so it's not short, but it's a lot of fun. They have a huge bonfire and food and it turns into a party after the races."

"Dad said he's coming," Samantha whispered.

"What?" I blurted. "When did you talk to him?"

Samantha shrugged and stared at her plate. "I texted him. I wanted him to know I'm on the team."

"Why didn't you tell me?"

"I didn't want you to be mad at me."

Cue mom guilt. Damn. I made my kids afraid to tell me they were talking to their own father. That was not okay. "I want you to talk to him. He's your father. You should have a relationship with him. I'm happy to hear he's coming. It'll be good to see him."

Brantley's warm hand settled on my thigh under the table. I didn't know how he knew I was shaking, but his touch calmed me down right away.

I slid my hand into his and squeezed. He wrapped our fingers together and held on, eating with his left hand.

"I'm nervous about my first race."

"That's normal," Brantley said. "Everyone is. I'm always nervous at the start of the season. But once you get one race done, it'll get easier."

Samantha nodded. Bianca asked if she could sleepover with McJenna after the race, and we started talking about things other than Dawson.

But Brantley still held my hand.

When dinner was finished, the girls helped us clean up, then headed to their rooms to do their homework. Brantley leaned against the counter and crossed his arms over his chest.

"I'm sorry I got upset with you when I walked in tonight."

I shook my head. "You were right. I know it's safe here, but that doesn't mean I should take risks. When I get home, I just need to get into the habit of locking the door. No big deal."

"I couldn't handle it if something happened to you. To any of you."

I nodded. The look in his eyes made my breath catch in my throat.

"How was your first grilling experience?" he asked, changing the subject and shifting his gaze from mine.

"It was good. Easier than I expected. I've been fighting with myself for so long and now it just feels ridiculous to have sacrificed."

"What did you sacrifice?" His brows tugged together, and his eyes narrowed.

"Pleasure."

Brantley choked. Surprise registered on his face. "Did you say pleasure?"

"Yep. We were talking at book club the other day about finding pleasure in things that aren't sex. And since I'm having less than zero sex, I decided to try it. Do things that bring me pleasure."

"And hot dogs bring you pleasure?" he asked with a smirk.

"You have a dirty mind, but yes. I love hot dogs and sausage on the grill. I love a good steak on the grill. I love fresh chocolate and a rich, smooth ganache and cold ice cream on top of a brownie fresh out of the oven. But I haven't let myself have any of that. Dawson always made comments about how much weight I've gained since college. Especially after I had the girls."

Brantley growled. "Fucking asshole. You're just as beautiful as you've always been. More in my opinion. You have the body of a woman who's lived her life. Your curves would turn on any man with a brain in his head, although they'll also make him lose all the blood in his head. You're gorgeous, Vee. Don't ever let Dawson make you doubt that again."

My cheeks heated, and my body flushed. If any other man said those things to me, I would think he was saying he was attracted to me. But it was Brantley. My friend, my best friend. We loved each other, but it wasn't like that. Not on his side, at least.

"Thank you," I whispered, unsure how to reply.

He cupped my jaw and met my gaze. "I mean it. You're absolutely beautiful. Own it."

I smiled at him. He made me believe it. "Thank you."

"You're welcome. Okay, so you're trying to find pleasure in food?"

"Not just food. But in things that aren't sex."

"And you're starting with food. Understandable."

I shrugged. I didn't want to admit to him that very little

besides food had ever brought me pleasure. Including sex, although I wasn't looking to include that in my quest.

"Do you need any help with this pleasure quest? Because I'm more than willing to come over here and eat whatever you decide to cook up."

I laughed. "I just might take you up on that."

"I'll definitely look forward to it."

6

BRANTLEY

THE ENERGY ON THE BUS TO OUR FIRST MEET WAS ELECTRIC. The kids were ready, Jana and I were ready. It was going to be an amazing night. Absolutely kick ass.

The meet was at a school an hour north of us, so the bus ride was long, but the kids kept their moods high with music and talking. Once we arrived, they got serious.

Andrew was the last off the bus, as always. When he stepped off, like the others, he had his game face on. He was ready to smoke the competition.

Jana led the team to the wide open space where all the teams set up. We had a pop-up tent with our school name on it as a home base for the athletes. Jana and I worked with two of the taller kids to get the tent up so everyone could set their stuff down and start their warmup.

Jana led the team on a slow jog around the race path. It was good for the kids, especially the new kids, to see what it would look like. Flags marked the turns and white paint dotted out the running lane. Once darkness fell, the paint would be almost impossible to see, but the flags would keep the kids on the right path.

We checked in with race officials, and the kids got their numbers and their chips to record where they ran. Then we were ready.

The host school started their announcements ten minutes before the race was going to start. The runners were ready. Teams of four were running an extended relay, with each kid running one-point-nine miles. The first teams were called to the start line, and as soon as the announcements were done, they were off.

"They look ready," Jana said.

I nodded as our first group ran away from the start line. We encouraged them to pace themselves, and the first runners were right in the middle of the pack. Where I wanted them to be.

One lap came and went, then the second, and the second runner took off. Two laps and the third runner left. The last runners bounced around me, anxious to run and excited to start.

The first race finished and our kids did well. Our best team finished sixth overall, which was a huge success.

The second race started. Jana and I watched the kids go. I was so focused on them I didn't notice Samantha behind me until she tapped on my shoulder.

"Hey, Sam. What's up?" I asked.

Her face was tight, like she was trying not to be upset.

I looked around the track, wondering who said or did something that upset her. "What's wrong?"

"My dad didn't see me run."

Oh, shit. I'd forgotten Dawson was supposed to be at the race. That he promised her he would watch her run.

"Ah, man. That sucks. Maybe he can still hang around and get something to eat with you."

She shook her head, and the emotions started to spill over. "He's not coming at all."

"What?" That fucker. "Why not?"

Samantha shrugged, looking more vulnerable than I was used to seeing her. She was fifteen, but she looked much younger in that moment. A moment when the one man who should have always been there for her let her down. Again.

"He said something came up."

"What could possibly be more important than you?" I snapped.

"Coach," Jana hissed.

I looked around and realized we were drawing a bit of a crowd. The last thing I wanted was for Samantha to feel even worse about the situation.

"You got this?" I asked her.

Jana nodded.

I jerked my head to the side for Samantha to follow me. She kept up with my pace easily as I stalked to the other side of the football field, where few people lingered.

"I apologize for getting angry. I shouldn't have."

"I'm angry, too. Why did he do this? Why did he cheat on my mom? My mom is the most amazing woman in the world."

"Yes, she is. And I can't explain your dad's actions. I will never understand them myself. It makes no sense to me why anyone would ever throw away something great with a woman like your mom. She's perfect."

Samantha looked closely at me. "You think she's perfect?"

I cleared my throat and realized what I'd just admitted. "Of course. She's kind and smart, and she has two great kids.

Why would any man not want to be a part of your family? Plus, she's an amazing cook." I rubbed my belly and hoped my joking around with her hid the truth behind my words. That I'd give my left nut for the chance to call them my family.

"Why couldn't my dad see all that?" Samantha asked in a voice that held all the pain of a kid whose family was ripped apart by careless and selfish behavior.

"I don't know, Sam. I wish he could have."

She nodded and wrapped her arms around her middle. At practice, we kept things distant so it didn't appear as though I was choosing favorites, but at the moment, I didn't care about that. I couldn't.

I stepped forward and pulled her into my arms. I'd hugged Samantha and Bianca more times than I could count. I was the first person who wasn't family to hold each of them after they were born. I was their godfather and their adopted uncle and their friend. And I was not going to stand there and let her father being a class-one dick make her feel worse when I could do one little thing to make her feel slightly better.

She wrapped her arms around my waist and turned her face to the side, her head against my chest. She shook just enough to let me know she was crying. We were in the dark, away from the crowd, but she still didn't want anyone to know how upset she was.

I held her until I heard someone ask Jana if they'd seen her, then I pulled back and ducked down. "Someone's looking for you. Are you okay?"

She nodded and wiped her cheeks. If someone looked close enough, it would be obvious she'd been crying, but hopefully no one would.

I stepped to the side and looked back toward Jana. Paul

was with her, and they were both watching us. "Want me to wave him over?"

Samantha nodded. "Yeah. He knows everything."

I lifted my hand and saw Jana nod.

Paul sprinted the short distance toward us, reaching Sam's side in a few seconds. He looked from her to me, then back to Sam. "Are you okay?"

"My dad didn't come. He said something came up."

"What an asshole," Paul blurted.

Both kids looked up at me with wide eyes. I had a strict no swearing policy at practices and meets. The look in their eyes said they were waiting for the discipline I couldn't bear to dish out. "Agreed." Without another word, I walked away, leaving Sam and Paul to talk.

"Everything okay?" Jana asked.

I shook my head as I joined her. "Her dad was supposed to come today, but he bailed. She's just upset."

"Ouch. That sucks. You're close to the family, aren't you?"

I nodded. "Yeah. Valentina and I have known each other since high school. They call me Uncle Brantley when we're not at school."

"I'm glad you could be there for her. I wouldn't have known what to say."

"I didn't either, but it's not hard. They know how I feel about their father."

"He was a friend of yours, too, right?"

"He was, yeah. I haven't spoken to him."

She looked up at me and nodded. "I don't blame you. My mom cheated on my dad. I never really got over it. I will never understand why someone would promise to love another person and then take a dump on that promise and get involved with someone else, even just once."

"Yep. And sorry. That sucks. Maybe you would have known what to say to Sam. You've been there."

Jana shook her head. "Yeah, but I'm still that kid who wants to know what the hell happened. I wouldn't have known how to make it better."

"She just needed someone to listen." I glanced back and saw Sam and Paul still talking. He was holding her hand and looking at her like she was the only thing that mattered to him.

Good for her.

"Is he going to be able to run?" Jana jerked her head toward Paul.

I nodded. "He'll be fine. Sam might hang out here with us, though."

"No problem with me."

We watched the last of our racers come in for the current race, then Bianca and her team lined up with the other girls varsity teams. The smile on Bianca's face made me think she didn't know Dawson wasn't there and wasn't coming. I was not going to burst that bubble for her.

Their race started, and we cheered for our students running. When they finished, the varsity boys lined up, including Paul, Kevin, and Andrew.

Sam hung off to the side, watching Paul and glancing at Jana and me every so often. I caught her eye at one point and waved her closer.

"Want to watch with us?" I asked.

Sam nodded. "I wasn't sure if I was allowed to be here with you guys."

"Of course. As long as you don't interfere with the race, you're good," Jana said.

"I promise, I won't do that."

"We know," Jana told her.

The three of us stood there and watched as the runners made their laps. Paul and Andrew were on the same team. Paul was the third runner, and Andrew was fourth. As the two fastest on the team, they were poised to catch up to any team that was ahead of them at the start.

When it was Paul's turn, Sam cheered for him. He grinned as he took off, obviously hearing Sam's praise.

"Was that okay?"

"Absolutely," Jana told her.

Paul ran past us, his stride even and fast. He was close to the front of the pack already and would no doubt be able to catch up by the time he finished his second lap.

Paul finished, just a few seconds out of first place. Andrew took off at a sprint, like a rocket was on his back.

Jana and I exchanged a look and a smile. There was no way Andrew was not going to win. Especially with the ground Paul made up for them.

Paul jogged around the field behind us as Jana and I focused on the last lap of the race. Sam wandered over to Paul, walking near him as he jogged in circles around her.

"They're cute," Jana said.

"Yep. He's a good kid. He seems to be good for her."

She grinned at me. "You know you sound like a dad, right?"

"Not their dad."

"Sounds like their dad wasn't great at the job."

I grunted a reply. I couldn't disagree, but I also couldn't let myself imagine being a part of their family.

Andrew came around the first lap, fifteen seconds ahead of the second place student. Jana and I grinned and cheered him on. Andrew didn't break stride, picking up his pace a bit when he realized he was halfway through.

The kid could run. I'd never seen anyone with his skills.

Jana and I had trouble standing still. We knew he was going to be back around in about four minutes. We paced back and forth between the finish line and the start of the flags. As soon as we saw Andrew make the last turn, we looked at each other with matching grins.

"Go Andrew! Let's go! You got this!"

We cheered him on, yelling above the noise of the crowd. Paul and Sam and the other two kids on their relay team and half the MCHS team came over to cheer for Andrew.

He sprinted, separating himself from the student behind him even more. When he crossed the finish line, a full forty seconds ahead of second place, he threw his hands up in the air.

Paul and the other two boys on the team went over to Andrew and celebrated their team's victory. Sam hung around the edges with the other kids who were there to congratulate them.

Jana and I turned back to the rest of the race, exchanging a fist bump of celebration before we cheered our next team in, anchored by Kevin.

Once all the racers had finished, the bonfire started. The night air was getting cool, and the kids were all in their sweatshirts and huddled together with s'mores and water bottles.

I kept an eye on Samantha, making sure she was smiling and doing okay. I wasn't paying attention to anyone else until I felt a nudge against my shoulder.

"Hey," Valentina said.

"Hey." I grinned and put my arm around her shoulder. "I was wondering if you were here."

"Wouldn't miss it. They did well."

"They did. All of them. Have you spoken to the girls?"

"Yeah. Sam told me about Dawson. And about you saying any man would be lucky to call us family. Thanks for that. It made her feel a lot better."

"I couldn't exactly tell her he's a worthless piece of shit who doesn't deserve to lick the soles of her trainers."

Valentina snickered. "But you can tell me?"

"I can tell you almost anything."

"Almost?"

I nodded.

"Why almost? What are you hiding from me?"

I shook my head. "Nothing I'm going to reveal."

She stepped out from under my arm and faced me. She crossed her arms, her purple and white MCHS XC zip-up straining against her breasts. It flared wide on her hips and ended below the zipper on her jeans. "What are you hiding, Coach Pierce?"

"Wouldn't you like to know?" I mimicked her stance and smirked at her.

"Oh, so we're playing it like that. What if I guess? You have a secret family? No, I'd know about that. You hate coaching? No. Ha. Not a chance. You love this. You are in love with someone? No, I... Wait a minute. What was that look for?"

"What look?" Fuck.

"You're in love with someone. Seriously? Who is it? How do I not know this?"

"You're nuts."

"Tell me, tell me, tell me. I need to live vicariously. Are you going to ask her out?"

"No."

"Ha! I knew it. You do like someone. Wait, why don't I know this? Why didn't you want to tell me? Shit. It's because I just got divorced. Are you seeing someone? You can tell me about your happiness, you know. I'm not trying to make you miserable."

"Trust me, you don't."

"Then why haven't you told me about this woman?"

"There's nothing to tell."

"Then—"

"Drop it. Please, Vee."

She studied me for a long minute. Her smile slowly faded. She rolled her lips in and bit down on the bottom one. Then she nodded, just once. "Okay. Sorry. I didn't mean to cross a line."

Dammit. "You didn't cross a line. I just know it's not an option. She's not interested in me."

"That's not possible. You're a catch, Bee. You're everything a woman would want in a man. How can she not want you?"

"Vee, please." It was hard to stand there and listen to her. I knew she was trying to be a good friend, but it wasn't like it would change anything.

"Well then, fuck her. She's not good enough for you, anyway. If she can't see what a catch you are, she doesn't deserve you."

A laugh popped out of me. I nodded and decided a distraction was the only way to go. "Want to go closer to the bonfire? The kids are over there."

"Yeah, sure. Sounds good." She slid her arm through mine and pressed her body against my side. "Thanks again for being there for Sam. I have a feeling her need for his approval is never going to end."

"I think we're all that way. We want our parents to be proud of us. It just sucks when we don't get it."

Valentina nodded. "That's very true. God, why did I choose him to build a life with?"

"Nope. Don't do that. You can't change it, so don't regret it. Like you always tell me, you have two beautiful girls. You wouldn't have them if you hadn't married Dawson. I know you don't regret marrying him because of them."

She sucked in a breath and straightened her spine. My woman was back. "You're right. Thank you. He's an ass, but he gave me them. That's all I was meant to get from him. Not forever."

"Yep."

"I'm done. I'm done blaming myself for everything and trying to explain his behavior. There is no excuse for what he did. And I can't continue to be understanding. God, why did I try so hard for so long to make things right between us? Never again."

"Good. You deserve better, and now you can find better."

"Exactly."

"I'm going to grab us some s'mores. If you're up for it."

Valentina smiled. "Always. Thanks, Bee."

7

VALENTINA

I watched Brantley walk away, his shadow disappearing before too long as the darkness of night swallowed him up. I sucked in a breath and tried to calm the ache in my chest.

Brantley was interested in someone.

Dammit. I wasn't allowed to be upset by that. He could date. He should date. He was an amazing man with a lot to offer any woman lucky enough to catch his eye. Just because it had never been me didn't mean I was going to stand in his way.

I was a crappy friend. I was holding him back because I was the lonely, desperate divorcée who needed a man to be there for me. Shit. I hated being a cliché.

No more. I was done. Brantley deserved better than that. He deserved a real friend. Someone who would help him catch the eye of the woman who was foolish enough to not want him.

My mind whirred as I considered who it could be. I wandered a bit, trying to see if he was talking to someone. Maybe it would give me a clue.

"She's so desperate," I heard someone say. They weren't far behind me, but I didn't recognize the voices.

"I know. Have some self respect. Hitting on the coach when he's working. I mean, really?"

The first woman scoffed. "Exactly. I mean, he's gorgeous, so I get it, but at least wait a little while. Let him finish his job."

I wondered who they were talking about. I didn't want to be so obvious as to turn around, but it had been a while since I'd heard any gossip. Of course, with so many schools, it was unlikely I knew which coach they were talking about, anyway.

"He is gorgeous," the second one purred. "And rock solid. I picked Jenny up late one day, and he stuck around to wait. I made sure to give him a tight hug for that one. And slipped my number into his pocket."

"You did not! What is Henry going to say?"

Woman two snorted. "Oh, please. Henry is never going to find out. Mostly because Coach Pierce didn't do anything about it."

My ears burned. They were talking about Brantley. Oh, shit. One of the married moms gave him her number? And someone was looking desperate and hitting on him? I wondered if it was the woman he was interested in.

"He doesn't have time for you with Valentina chasing him around. First, she runs Dawson out of town, and now she's after Coach Pierce. She really needs to get over herself."

My heart pounded. My cheeks flamed. My entire body felt like my skin was too tight. They were talking about me?

Brantley had been my friend forever. I was allowed to talk to him. And I wasn't flirting with him. Was I?

Shit. I didn't want Brantley to feel awkward around me.

To worry I was clinging to him and making things weird. Dammit, that was why he wouldn't tell me who he liked. He thought I'd mess it up for him.

I couldn't stand there and wait for him to come back. I had to give him space. Let him live his life and not interfere. The bleachers weren't far away, so I turned toward them and made my way over. Most of the students were wandering around, and the parents were hanging around by the bonfire. The bleachers were quiet.

Thank God.

I drew a deep breath and let it out slowly. I was not going to cry. Sure, I was ruining my best friend's chance at happiness, but I knew better now. I was going to back off and give him space so he could find love. I wasn't going to be jealous or bitchy. I was going to be happy for him.

"What are you doing over here?" Brantley climbed the bleachers toward me, his hands full of s'mores supplies.

"I just wanted to sit down. Why don't you go back to the bonfire?"

"I need someone to help me eat these s'mores. I'll wait until you're ready."

"I'm good. You should just go."

"Why does it feel like you're trying to get rid of me?" Brantley's tone slid to a dangerous note that sent tingles up my spine.

"I'm not. I just thought there might be someone else you want to share s'mores with."

"Nope. Try again. What happened?"

"Nothing happened. I just want you to be happy. I don't want to get in the way of that."

"Who said you were?"

I sighed. "I heard two moms talking about you. They

were saying I was hanging all over you and looked desperate."

"Ah, so you think you need to back off?"

"Yes. Because I don't want the woman you like to think there's something going on between us. It's not fair of me to monopolize your time and cock-block every other woman."

Brantley snorted. "First, you're not now and never have done that. We already talked about that. I enjoy spending time with you. I want to spend time with you. I don't want you to ever doubt that."

"But—"

"And second, you are not desperate. You never have been desperate. We are friends. Great friends. And no one else gets a vote on who we are or what we do together."

"But—"

He put a finger over my lips and stared into my eyes.

I sucked in a breath, wanting to lick his finger. I wanted his hand to wrap around and cup my neck and pull me closer for a kiss.

I couldn't.

"Are you done arguing with me?" Brantley asked.

I nodded.

"Good. Don't doubt us, Vee. I would tell you if I needed space. Or if I didn't want to do something with you. I wouldn't agree to something just to spare your feelings or something. I thought we knew each other well enough by now to be able to be honest with each other."

"We do. I know. I just…"

"What?"

"You like someone. And not only do I not know who it is, I had no idea you even liked someone. What kind of friend am I that I don't know something like that?"

"You're my best friend."

"Then why don't you want me to know who it is?"

"Because it doesn't matter. She doesn't feel the same."

"How do you know?"

"Trust me, I know."

"But how? Maybe she doesn't know you're interested. Or maybe she hides it well."

"Let it go, Vee. I... it's never going to happen. I've accepted that."

I didn't want to let it go. I wanted him to be happy. He deserved it, more than anyone I knew. It sucked to hear him so defeated.

Maybe I could figure it out. Talk to her without him knowing. Talk him up and make her see what a great guy he was.

I just had to get more intel.

"Want to come over for dinner tomorrow?"

He looked at me sideways and raised a brow. "You're sure you're okay with being seen with me?"

"What do you mean?"

"You ran and hid. Just checking it's okay."

I bumped his shoulder with mine and shook my head. He wrapped his arm around me and kissed the top of my head.

"I love you, Vee. I don't want you to disappear on me. And I'd love to have dinner tomorrow night."

"Good," I said, my voice wispy and loaded with emotion. I wanted to lean into him and enjoy it, but I couldn't let those feelings control me. I had to make sure I was staying on my side of the line so when I figured out who he liked, she didn't think there was something going on with us.

"Since we have that settled... how about some s'mores tonight?" Brantley asked, holding up his supplies.

I chuckled and nodded. "Sounds perfect."

TEARS, anger, and stomping feet were the soundtrack for the next day. Samantha was still hurt that Dawson blew them off. Bianca was more flippant about the whole thing, but I knew it upset her, too. The two of them got into it a few times, with Bianca dismissing Dawson as a deadbeat dad who never actually cared about them.

"How many times did he show up for us when he lived here?" Bianca asked Samantha late in the afternoon during round three. Or maybe round four.

"I don't know," Sam murmured.

I wasn't getting involved, but we all knew the answer. Not many.

"He never acted like he wanted us. At least, I never felt it. And the way he treated Mom should have been a clue. I'm sure if we were boys it would have been different." Bianca crossed her arms, trying to look tough, but I knew the move was a defense for her. A protection when she felt like no one else was protecting her.

"That's not true," Sam countered.

"Okay, stop," I said, getting between them. "None of this is helping. Do either of you feel better?"

They both reluctantly shook their heads.

"Sam, I'm sorry your dad didn't show up when he promised he would. Unfortunately, this isn't likely to be the last time it happens. I hate it, but we all know it's true."

"Did he really not want us?" Sam whispered.

I shook my head and reached for my girls, pulling them both into my arms. "No, that's not true. He was so excited about both of you. When we found out you were girls, he never once said he wished for a boy. Your dad was a good man, he is a good man. When you were younger, things were better. But not all marriages are meant to last forever."

"Especially when he cheats," Bianca snarled.

"True, but your father and I weren't in a great place for long before that. We were drifting apart. I was trying to make it work, but it didn't."

"Why should it be on you?" Bianca pulled away to look at me. She stood a few inches shorter than me, but she held all the attitude I wanted to throw at Dawson. She was my protector, my fiercely loyal one who would stand up for anyone who needed it.

"It wasn't on me. It wasn't on him, either. It was on us that our marriage stopped working and neither of us tried to change that for a long time."

"But he's the one who cheated. You didn't cheat on him. Right?" Bianca's eyes widened as though she'd never considered the possibility Dawson was only reacting to my infidelity.

I shook my head. "I didn't cheat on your father. I never thought about it. I wasn't happy in our marriage, but I wasn't willing to throw it away either."

"Like he was," Bianca hissed.

I led the girls to the couch and sat with one of them on each side of me. I held their hands, letting them both know I was there for them. "Listen, girls, marriages are tough. All relationships are tough. And you will never know everything about another person. Even someone you share your life with. There are things about each other you don't know, even though you've lived your entire lives under the same roof. There are things about your father I never knew. Getting to know someone means trusting that the pieces they don't share are pieces you're willing to let them keep to themselves. Sometimes those pieces ruin the relationship, and sometimes they help it work."

"How could keeping something from someone make a relationship better?" Sam asked.

My mind immediately went to Brantley. If he knew I liked him back in high school, we wouldn't have stayed friends all these years. Same with now. I couldn't tell him. Especially now that I knew he was interested in someone else.

"Maybe you fail a test or get detention. Does telling someone about that make a difference in the relationship?"

The girls shook their heads.

"That's what I'm talking about. It's a piece of your life, but it's not a critical piece that defines you. Now, if you get detention every Tuesday because you're always late to school because you have to care for your younger sibling since your parent works nights, that's different. But if you get detention once, it's not likely something that will define you. Do you see the difference?"

They nodded.

"No one is perfect. The only thing you can do is find the person who's perfect for you. Someone who matches you and cares for you and gives as much as they take. Someone who wants to spend their time with you and supports you."

"Was Dad ever like that?" Sam asked.

I nodded. "When we were in college, I fell in love with him. He was funny and smart and kind. He made it impossible not to love him. Even after we graduated and moved here, things were good."

"But that changed," Bianca stated.

"Slowly. Over time. Small changes that went unnoticed until it was too late to dial things back. Him taking a job that required him to be gone all week. Me working at the bakery and not home a lot of weekends when he was here. We stopped prioritizing each other and lost touch. When we talked, it was about you two, not about us. And eventually, there was nothing to talk about. There was no us."

"That's really sad, Mom," Sam whispered.

I inhaled deep and let it out slowly. "It is sad. I'm sorry things didn't work out with your father and me. I wish we'd been able to find a way forward together. But once I met Haley, I couldn't accept that. I know some people can, and if that's right for their relationship, good for them, but it wasn't something I could handle. I am sorry all of that happened in front of you two, though."

Bianca leaned her head against my shoulder. Samantha followed suit a minute later.

"It sucked," Bianca finally said. "It was... It sucked."

"Yeah," Sam agreed.

"I know."

The three of us sat on the couch for a few minutes, all silent with our thoughts. I wanted to say something that would make it better for my girls, but there was no better. Their dad cheating sucked. Not just for me, but for them, too. Dawson was selfish and thoughtless. He never once asked me for a divorce or mentioned taking a break or anything. I knew things weren't good, but I didn't know they were that bad. If he'd talked to me, we could have tried to make things better, or we could have ended things amicably. As it was, we hadn't spoken since his girlfriend, Haley, showed up at our door.

"Is it okay if I hang out with McJenna tonight?" Bianca asked. "Mr. Xavier said we can go to the theater with him and watch movies."

"You were just with her last night."

"Yeah, but we crashed after the meet. We didn't really talk last night."

"Are you coming home after?"

"Yeah. I should be home around eleven."

"Okay. What about you, Sam? Are you having dinner with Uncle Brantley and me tonight?"

Sam shook her head. "I'm going out with Paul. If that's okay."

"Of course." My heart kicked. Dinner alone with Brantley. I shouldn't be excited about the option. But I was.

"I'm going to get ready," Bianca said, shifting forward on the couch. She stopped and looked back at me, then flung herself onto me in a hug that wrapped up Sam, too.

The three of us laughed. I held my girls close. It wouldn't be long before Bianca was going off to college, and Sam was right behind her. Our house was going to feel empty without my girls in it. The house Dawson and I always talked about growing old in. Seeing our grandkids play.

All those dreams were gone. Popped like a balloon with one ring of the doorbell. I didn't blame Haley, even though I struggled to like her. She was nice, and she wasn't the one who made promises to me, but it was hard to see her and know if she and Dawson never met our marriage might have survived.

Probably not, but I'd never know.

Bianca let go of Sam and I, then hurried to her room to get ready to go out. Sam hugged me once more, then followed her sister.

I sat on the couch for another long minute. It would take time for the girls to repair their relationship with their father. Bianca especially. But it would only happen if Dawson made an effort. If he tried harder with them than he did with me.

Was it my responsibility to tell him? I felt like he should know how to be a good father, but every time I thought that, he proved me wrong.

I pushed thoughts of Dawson away and went to my room to make myself a little more presentable. Not that Brantley would notice or care, but I didn't want to be in my pajamas when he showed up.

The girls left a few minutes apart, both hugging me tight before they ran out the door to be teenagers and enjoy their night.

I was more than a little envious until my doorbell rang, with Brantley on the other side of the door.

8

BRANTLEY

Jeans and a tee should not look so sexy. It almost wasn't fair. How was I supposed to resist her when she was my every fantasy come to life?

"Hey," Valentina said, tilting her head to the side and looking at me through narrowed eyes. "You okay?"

I nodded and stepped toward her. I must have been staring at her longer than I realized, fantasizing about stripping her out of those clothes and finally getting lucky enough to see what lay beneath her shields.

"All good," I said. I dropped a kiss on her cheek, just so I could linger for a long second and inhale the soft vanilla scent of her. "How are you?"

She shrugged and closed the door behind me. "Okay. The girls are still having trouble with Dawson not showing up yesterday."

Talk about a cold shower. Damn. Nothing like mentioning her ex-husband, and my ex-friend, to whither a growing erection. But it was necessary to remind myself, and my dick, that Valentina was not in a place where a new relationship was a good idea.

"Sorry, Vee. Want me to talk to them? Remind them that not all men are like him?" The offer popped out before I could think twice about it, but as soon as I said the words, I wanted to take it back. I wasn't their father, and even though she'd shared that they talked about me before, I didn't want to overstep.

She shook her head before I could retreat. "They're both out. But thank you. We talked a lot today, and they fought a lot."

"Why did they fight?"

She chuckled mirthlessly. "Sam is always going to be a daddy's girl and wants his approval. Bianca is much more cynical and less likely to give him extra chances, even though I know she wants his approval, too. It just made things tense today."

"Shit. I'm sorry. Are you okay?"

She looked up at me with a mixture of surprise and caution. "Me?"

I tugged on one of her short curls, then let it bounce back to shape. "Yeah, you, Vee. Defending him couldn't have been easy. And before you even say it, I know because you're a good person. You don't want them to hate him, even though they have every right to. You want them to still see their father as their hero. You want them to accept whatever love he's willing to give them."

"You make me sound like I can't see who he is."

"Not at all. You see him. You see him better than anyone else. But you see them, too. You know they need their father, even if he's not the best father in the world."

She sighed, the fight that rose up seconds ago sliding out of her. "I just hate that they're having to deal with this. Our marriage falling apart shouldn't have had such an impact on them. If they hadn't witnessed it—"

"They still would have known about it. There's no way it would have stayed a secret in MacKellar Cove."

"I know." She sighed again and went to the couch. She dropped her head into her hands and looked defeated. "It's just not fair to them."

"No, it isn't. But none of that is on you."

She sucked in a breath. Her back straightened. I sat next to her, and she looked over at me with a smile. "You're right. And I need to get over my pity party."

"That's not what I'm saying at all. You aren't throwing a pity party. You're being very honest about the shitstorm your life is right now. Dawson took a crap all over and walked away for you to clean it up."

She chuckled. "Yeah, he really did. And I'm kind of sick of it."

"Then stop making excuses for him."

She opened her mouth to argue, but I held up my hand.

"I know. You're not making excuses, you're trying to explain. Your marriage wasn't perfect before and it didn't fall apart because he cheated. I get it. But you're taking on a lot of the blame. Because you're the one who's here."

"Yeah," she breathed.

"So, instead of doing that, you need to remember that you did everything in your power to save your marriage. In the end, it was Dawson cheating that caused you to stop fighting for your marriage."

"You're right."

"I know I am."

She chuckled and shook her head. "You always make me laugh."

"Good. Then my work here is done."

"Does that mean you're going home?"

I snorted. "You invited me over for dinner, woman. You better get on that."

"Oh, shit," she said, jumping off the couch. "I never started anything."

I followed her into the kitchen and grabbed her arm, spinning her around and pulling her into my arms. I hummed a tune that didn't actually exist and swayed with her, dancing for a minute before she laughed.

"There's that smile I've been missing," I whispered. "Welcome back."

She exhaled, letting all the tension out. "I'm sorry I haven't fixed dinner yet. With the girls today, I just lost track of the day."

"You do not have to take care of me all the time. You're being far too generous cooking for me as much as you are. I owe you."

"But I should—"

"Fuck should. Don't even go there. I will never demand anything from you. Let's order a pizza. Relax. I feel like we haven't spent time together lately. Let's just chill. Like we used to."

"In high school?" she asked with a grin.

I nodded. "In high school."

We kept dancing around the kitchen, her hand in mine, my other hand low on her waist. The heat of her skin through the thin fabric of her tee called to me. I wanted to touch her bare skin, feel her body moving against mine. Kiss her and touch her and love her.

But she was my friend, not my lover, so I didn't have the right.

I spun her out, then pulled her back in, her back to my front. She laughed, and I gently eased her away before she felt the effect she had on me.

"What do you want on your pizza?" I asked.

"Same as always."

I nodded, smiling as I found the number on my phone and tapped to start the call. I ordered a large pizza with banana peppers, sausage, and extra cheese, our favorite pizza. I added garlic bread and a single order of teriyaki wings, and caved when they offered a small baked cookie pizza.

"Here in about an hour," I told her as I hung up.

"Thank you."

I looked closely at her and saw the exhaustion around her eyes. I knew better than to say something to her about it, but it killed me that she was so worn out. Being a single parent wasn't really new for her, but it had taken a toll in the last few months.

"Are you sure you're okay?" I asked.

She shrugged and looked up at me. "Dawson hasn't been here in months, and before that, he was barely around. I realized today the house is going to be really quiet a lot more."

"What do you mean?" I asked and took the seat next to her, close enough to feel her heat but far enough away that it wasn't awkward.

"Bianca is going to be gone in a few years, and Sam isn't far behind. Nights like tonight they're both out. I've just been realizing lately that I don't have anything in my life that's for me."

"You have your job. You love baking." I wasn't sure where she was going with this, but that was the wrong answer if the scrunch of her nose and the roll of her eyes were anything to go on.

"Yeah, but it's a job. I enjoy it, but I do it because it pays the bills."

"So, what do you want to do for yourself?"

"I don't know. That's the problem. If you weren't here tonight, I'd just be sitting here alone. I probably would have made popcorn and had that for dinner instead of pizza. I would have drank too much wine and regretted it. I just don't know what I like to do."

"Then figure it out."

A laugh hissed out of her. "You say that like it's easy. It's like the pleasure stuff we were talking about from the book at book club. I realized I have nothing in my life that I enjoy. Not outside of work and my kids. Nothing I do because I love it."

"Really? Nothing? What about book club? Or drinking wine? Spending time with me?"

She smiled at the last one. "I love all of those things. But I can't drink wine and monopolize you. It's not fair."

"Fair to whom?"

"To you. To the woman you're interested in. I can't drag you into my miserable life."

"I want to be in your miserable life," I said. "Wait, that came out wrong. I want to be in your life. More than you know, Vee. I love you. You're not getting rid of me."

"Good, but when this woman comes to her senses and realizes what a catch you are, she might not want me hanging around. I don't want to cause problems between you."

I grinned at her. If she only knew. But I couldn't tell her. Not when she was trying to figure out her life.

"If that happens, you'll be the first to know."

"Good."

"So, tell me about this book. I know you were talking about pleasure, but you didn't say it was from a book. I didn't know you guys read books like that."

She snorted. "Please. We meet at Finley's store. All she sells is romance novels, which are arguably all about pleasure. But this one was more about finding yourself. Pleasure that isn't just from sex."

"Ah, I see. That's where the conversation came from. Emotional and physical satisfaction."

"Yes. You get it. It really made me think, though. Since I'm clearly not having any sex, I've decided to go on a quest for pleasure."

My brain fed me images of Valentina feeling all sorts of pleasure. My tongue on her body, my cock inside her, my hands all over her. It didn't matter that she said she was thinking non-sex pleasure, that was all my mind heard when she said *quest for pleasure.*

"Is it dumb?" she asked, sounding far less sure of herself than she was a minute ago.

"To figure out what makes you feel good? Hell no. We should all know the answer to that."

She beamed at me, her brown skin glowing in a way that brought me right back to all the ways I would love to show her pleasure.

The doorbell interrupted any further conversation about pleasure. I wasn't sure if that was good or bad, but I was far too close to offering myself as her sexual pleasure quest partner, so it was probably a good thing.

We went to the door together to greet the delivery driver. I tried to wave off her offer to pay, but she shouldered me aside and handed the driver more than enough cash to cover our order and a good tip. I set the boxes on the coffee table and grabbed paper plates from the cabinet above the microwave so she wouldn't worry about doing any dishes.

An hour and a whole pizza later, I leaned back on the couch and groaned. "That was delicious."

Valentina chuckled and shook her head. "Best dinner I've made in a while."

I laughed with her. The pizza we ordered was good, but the company I got to share it with was even better. "How late are the girls out?"

"Bianca is supposed to be home around eleven. Xavier is going to drop her off after the last movie, but he has to close up. Goldie and Patrick said they'd bring Sam home around ten."

I stood and carried the pizza box to the kitchen. I felt her gaze on me as I moved. I knew where everything was in her house, so I helped myself to a bag to store the leftover pizza in and tossed it in the fridge before carrying the box to the trashcan in the garage.

"You don't have to clean up," she said when I came back inside.

"Least I can do since you bought dinner. Want to do something else, or are you ready to kick me out?"

"I'm never ready to kick you out," she said.

Her tone was light and teasing, but those words hit me deep. I knew she was still feeling the pain of her divorce, even though she claimed she was good. I carried the guilt of it with me. Dawson was my roommate, and I introduced them. I never expected him to be a first class asshole or to screw around on the most perfect woman.

If I was lucky enough to have Valentina, I'd worship the ground she walked on. Hell, I did anyway, but she didn't know it.

"Movie?" I suggested, to keep myself from asking if I could kiss her. It would be a mistake. She just got out of a marriage, and I was supposed to be her friend, not taking advantage of her.

"Yeah, sounds good. Nothing sappy and romantic, though."

"Wouldn't dream of it."

She handed me the remote, not flinching when our hands touched. It lit a spark inside me like I had sparklers in my pants. Nothing new.

I scrolled through the options and found an old favorite of ours.

"Ah, I haven't seen this in forever," she said as it started.

"Neither have I."

She tucked her feet under her and leaned toward me. Her head rested on my shoulder, her breasts against my arm and a smile on her face.

We'd watched movies like that more times than I could count, especially when we were in high school and unaware of our hormones. She never thought twice about me as anything more than a friend, but I always saw her as my future.

Too bad she built that future with someone else.

The movie played, and we watched, the past blending with the present and making me forget she was off-limits. My hand landed between us, right on top of hers, and all those neglected teenage hormones I didn't know what to do with leapt up and took notice.

She turned her hand under mine, wrapping our fingers together. My thumb brushed her wrist, stroking the rapid pulse that beat there.

"Brantley," she whispered.

"Yeah?"

"What are we doing?"

"Watching a movie." I was intentionally obtuse. I did not want to ruin anything. I couldn't. Telling her how I felt was a risk I wasn't sure I could take yet. Not when she was still hurting. Vulnerable. Not ready for what I wanted.

"Why do you come over so much?"

"Do you want me to go?"

"No," she blurted. "I just wondered why you aren't out on dates. Why you aren't married. You're an amazing man."

"I just haven't caught the eye of the right woman yet."

She shook her head. "She must be blind not to notice you."

I breathed a laugh. "Something like that."

She was silent for a few more minutes. The movie continued to play, but I barely noticed it.

"Thank you for being here, Bee. I don't think I could have gotten through the last few months without you."

"I'll always be here for you, Vee."

"I love you," she whispered.

"I love you, Vee. More than you know."

She smiled and nuzzled against me. I kissed the top of her head and inhaled her scent. I would miss it when I had to go home.

"I should have married you instead of Dawson," she said.

"What?"

She exhaled softly. "There was a part of me that hoped you'd stand up at my wedding and tell me not to marry him because you were in love with me. Obviously, it was dumb. But I was so crazy about you. Dawson was kind of my second choice since you didn't like me."

"No way," I blurted.

She nodded. "Yep. I loved him, but if I'd ever thought I had a chance with you, I never would have dated him."

I shifted so I could look at her and tucked my hair behind my ear so I didn't miss a bit of what she was admitting to me. "But you married him. You had kids with him. A whole life. Why would you do that if he wasn't your first choice?"

She sat up and shrugged. "I really thought you were trying to pass me off onto him. And I never met any other guys I liked as much as him. Except you, but that was never going to happen."

"I still don't know why you thought that."

She drew back and tilted her head, looking at me like I said chocolate was no good. "It was pretty obvious. You guys were talking about all the hot girls on campus, and Dawson was congratulating you about one who already asked you out. I figured you asked him to talk to me so I'd give you some space."

"That was the last thing I wanted back then. I've kicked myself for years for introducing you two. I had the biggest crush on you in high school."

She sucked in a breath, and her eyes widened.

"Dawson insisted on tagging along since he didn't know anyone else. When you started dating, I was so pissed at myself. I never had the guts to tell you how I felt."

She laughed, a timid sound like she was unsure. We'd known each other more than half of our lives. We'd talked about everything. But I'd never admitted liking her. "But you're telling me now?"

"You're the one who admitted it first. I just wish I'd known back then."

"My life would have been so different if I'd realized."

We stared at each other, the past and the present hovering in the space between us.

I glanced at her lips, and she licked them. Slick, wet, luscious lips that were begging for me to lean in.

I didn't know which one of us moved first, but we

collided in the middle. My hand went to her spiral curls, my fingers catching in them and tugging her head to my will.

She moaned softly, almost a sigh, like she'd been waiting half a lifetime for the feel of my lips against hers.

Same, Vee, same.

I licked along the seam of her lips, and she opened for me, groaning at the first taste. I sucked on her tongue, my hand landing on her hip and encouraging her closer.

She took the hint and straddled me on the couch. My erection pulsed at the feel of her heat right over the center of me.

"Fucking hell," I growled. The heat between us was supernova hot without even trying. All the time I told myself to forget her, to let her go, I was wrong. So fucking wrong.

A car door slammed outside. She pulled back, her eyes wild as she stared at the front door. Headlights shined through the windows.

"Sam's home," Valentina hissed. She scrambled off my lap, smoothing her finger-tousled hair away from her face and wiping her lips as though the motion could erase what had just happened.

She stood in front of the couch, watching the door, when Sam came in.

"I'm home," Samantha called. "Oh. You're right here. Hi, Uncle Brantley."

"Hey, hun," I said, turning to smile and wave at her. I couldn't stand. Not sure my bloodless legs could support me, but also not wanting to scandalize the teenager who'd no doubt notice the erection I was sporting, seeing as how it was trying to break through my zipper.

"How was dinner?" Valentina asked, her voice high and frantic.

"Good," Sam said. "Are you okay, Mom?"

"Yeah! Yep. Good. All good. We were just watching a movie."

Sam looked at the TV, frozen from when we paused it, and rolled her eyes. "Again? You love this movie."

"I do. So does Uncle Brantley."

Sam's phone dinged. "That's Paul. We're going to talk. Bye, Uncle Brantley."

"Bye, Sam."

Her footsteps hurried away, and Valentina sank to the couch next to me. "That was almost really bad."

Well, damn. That was not what I hoped she'd say.

9

VALENTINA

I DREW A DEEP BREATH AND LET IT OUT SLOWLY. I KISSED Brantley. Holy shit, I kissed Brantley. Or he kissed me. I didn't know, and I didn't care. We kissed.

And it was borderline orgasmic. A kiss shouldn't be that good. Was I just out of practice? It had been a long time since I'd kissed a man, and years of quick kisses from Dawson definitely left a lot to be desired, but I couldn't remember it ever being like that with him.

"I should go," Brantley said suddenly. He jumped up from the couch and paced toward the door.

"Oh, um, okay." I followed him, all the yummy feelings dancing around inside sinking like lead in my gut. He didn't feel the same things. I was trying to keep myself from smiling like an idiot and he was just ready to get the hell away from me.

God, I was such an idiot.

"Thanks for dinner. And the movie," he said.

Awkward. It was totally awkward. Things had never been awkward with Brantley before. I wanted to cry. Why did I tell him I wished I'd married him instead of Dawson? It was a lifetime ago. I never should have said anything.

"Brantley, wait."

He turned but didn't meet my gaze. The light scruff on his jaw made my fingers itch. His hair was tied back in a low knot. I wanted to smooth out the lines between his eyes and take us both back to where we were just a minute ago.

But the moment was gone.

"I don't want what happened to mess things up between us."

He smiled with his lips, a curl that would have fooled most people but didn't fool me. His smile didn't reach his eyes. Didn't light him up the way he usually did when he smiled at me. "We're good."

"Are you sure?"

He nodded. "Definitely. I'll see you soon."

"Okay. Good night."

"Night, Vee."

He kissed my cheek, lingering for just a second, then he was gone. Like it was any other night and nothing different had happened. Like he hadn't kissed me and made me wish I could go back in time and make one change. One change that would alter my life forever.

I stood in the living room, listening as he started his SUV and drove out of my driveway. I hated it. I hated knowing things had changed. Just that fast, things had changed. And I didn't know why or how to change them back.

I definitely should have kept my mouth shut.

I REFUSED to stress about Brantley. We would be fine. We always were. It had been us against the world forever. We survived my marriage, and my divorce, and we would get through my confession and stupid attack on him, too.

I just had to stop thinking about what could have happened if Sam hadn't come home when she did. Because that was definitely not doing me any good. Unless I counted the new toy I got and how damn good it was in the shower, especially when I closed my eyes and let myself imagine Brantley there with me.

No. I couldn't. It wasn't ever going to happen. So I had to stop.

Pleasure was supposed to be non-sexual. Dammit.

I shook my head and drizzled caramel sauce over the top of the brownies I just finished. Sea salt and caramel were always good together, but the chocolate I used was rich and decadent all on its own. I added a bit more salt to balance the richness and dusted the whole thing with powdered sugar for appearance.

It was good. Damn good. I could have eaten the entire pan, but I knew that would only make me sick.

Harriett was more than happy for me to try out some new things and was enjoying selling them up to the customers. A lot of people came in just to see what new items we had, and when I hadn't come up with something new, it was a disappointment for them.

New was good.

"Valentina, come here a minute," she whispered when I set the tray of brownies in the case.

There wasn't a line, but every table in the place was full. I smiled when I saw everyone had something different, chocolate to toffee to fudge to cupcakes.

"Look at the expressions on their faces," Harriett whispered. She knew I was trying out new things and searching for what made me happy. She had been trying to show me the way customers enjoyed their food for days.

I looked around and smiled. Eyes closed, lips curled up in hints of smiles. Groans and lips licked. Extending treats to family and friends to share, but quickly pulling it back for themself.

Bliss. That was the word that came to mind. They were enjoying my creations, my works of art.

My lips turned up in a smile for the first time in days. After Brantley walked out Saturday night, I struggled to see the joy in even the smallest things, but watching my friends and neighbors delighting in something I made allowed me to smile again.

"It's beautiful, isn't it?" Harriett asked.

I nodded. "It really is. Thank you for sharing this with me."

Harriett patted my hand. "You made it happen. This is my favorite part of the day. When everyone is enjoying their treats and can't stop long enough to have a conversation. When it's quiet in here because they're loving what you made. It's what keeps me coming in every day."

"This is pretty special. You've created an amazing place here."

She looked around and smiled. "I love it here. And I love having you here. You've made it more than I ever dreamed it could be."

"We both have."

The bell on the door chimed, and Harriett greeted the customers. I left her to charm them and retreated back to the kitchen.

Making others happy had been my passion for as long as I could remember. I wanted to see them smile, to see them enjoy things. But I wanted to enjoy things, too. I felt like a piece was missing. A piece that shouldn't have been so hard to find.

I spent the rest of the day working on new recipes for things I thought sounded amazing. By the time I left to pick up the kids from practice, I was exhausted but proud of the work I'd done. I wasn't sure I had the same blissful enjoyment as the customers, but I liked what I'd created. And I was happy to keep creating.

I parked in the lot, not far from Brantley's SUV, but not close either. I didn't want him to think I was trying to get him alone or something. We hadn't really spoken since he ran out of my house, and I wasn't sure what to say to him.

Practice was still going, so I dug out my phone and pulled up my email. Most of it was junk, but I hadn't checked it in a few days. I was reading about a new show created by someone I followed when there was a knock on my window.

I jumped, nearly dropped my phone, and screamed, all at once.

Then I looked up and saw Goldie laughing at me.

I put my phone in the cup holder and got out of the car. "What are you doing here?"

"I was going to ask you that. I thought I was getting the kids today."

"Really? Dammit. I'm so turned on. I mean, turned around. Ugh."

Goldie raised an eyebrow. "Um, are you okay?"

"No. Not even a little."

"What's going on?"

I realized what I was admitting and immediately backtracked. "Nothing. Sorry. It's just been a long few days. I'm good."

"You're full of shit. We haven't gotten together in a while. What are you doing tonight?"

"Um, I, uh…"

"So, nothing." Goldie was texting as she spoke. "We're going to O'Kelley's. Anna's going to meet us there. Dinner and drinks. Since I know you're not working tonight, you can't get out of it."

I scowled at her. I liked Goldie, a lot, but I wasn't sure I wanted to tell her what was going on. She'd already witnessed the absolute worst moment of my life. Did I really want to drag her into the second worst?

"Go home and get a few minutes to yourself. I'll bring the girls home. They can shower and change and Patrick can watch all of them tonight."

"I'm sure they'll love that."

Goldie chuckled. "They adore him. He's basically their age. But he has a credit card and can buy dinner. Anna's good. Said her boys are in."

"I can't—"

"No arguments. You have *I need help* written all over your beautiful face."

"Is it that obvious?"

Goldie nodded and squeezed my hand. "We'll get you all straightened out. Go home. I'll bring the girls soon."

"Thanks, Goldie."

She nodded and walked away, leaving me to do as she instructed.

I still wasn't used to relying on others, but Goldie was wearing me down. She had been there for me more than anyone besides Brantley in the last few months, and if I messed everything up with Brantley, then I was going to lean on Goldie even more. And Anna.

I changed out of my work clothes and debated on a

quick shower. I smelled like sugar and coffee, so I decided to just change my clothes and go with it.

Goldie dropped the girls off and told them they were all having dinner at her house. They took record showers and were ready to go almost before I was. When we got to Goldie's house, the others were already there and waiting for us.

Anna drove the three of us to O'Kelley's, chatting the entire way. We all hung out at O'Kelley's regularly. Anna's husband, Hudson, was the owner and a good man. They'd both been married before, but he was a widower, and she was divorced. They found each other and even though they did not get along, they fought until they liked each other.

Hudson already had a table for us with drinks and appetizers when we arrived. He gave Anna a kiss that made me blush, and made me wonder if pleasure could exist without sex because damn, did it make me hot.

"All right, what's wrong with you?" Goldie asked as soon as we were all seated and had our first sips.

"What?" I blurted.

"She asked what's wrong with you. She said you were a mess earlier. What's going on?"

I looked between them, casual as they could be, as they ate cheese curds and potato skins. I just wanted to break down. "Things got weird with Brantley and now I don't know what to do."

"What happened?" Goldie asked.

"I kissed him," I admitted. Ripping off the bandage.

"You what?" they gasped together.

"He came over for dinner last weekend, and we were talking, and I admitted I liked him in high school. He said he liked me, too, and then we were kissing."

"And then what?" Anna asked.

"And then Sam came home, and Brantley left."

"He left? Just like that?" Goldie asked.

I shrugged. "Yeah. We talked for a second, then he got up and left."

"What did you talk about?"

"Nothing really. I said it was almost really bad that Sam almost caught us, and I told him I didn't want us kissing to mess things up."

They exchanged a look that said loud and clear they thought I messed up, anyway.

"What?" I groaned.

"Telling a guy it was *really bad* after you kiss him is probably—"

"Really bad," Anna finished for Goldie.

"Yeah."

"But I didn't mean the kiss. The kiss was... It was just bad that Sam almost caught us."

"Did you explain that to Brantley?" Anna asked.

I thought back, then shook my head slowly.

"Do you want a relationship with Brantley?" Goldie asked.

"No. Yes? I don't know. I don't feel like I should get involved with anyone right now. I'm doing this Quest for Pleasure, and—"

"Whoa, what now?" Goldie asked.

"From the book a few weeks ago. Where they were talking about what brings us pleasure. Anna and Hudson are doing it, too. Aren't you?"

Anna nodded. "We are. Finding things we enjoy, things that bring us pleasure, that are outside sex."

"Okay, I remember now," Goldie said. "So, what does that have to do with Brantley and wanting or not wanting a relationship?"

I scowled and reached for a cheese curd. I definitely needed food to have this conversation.

Goldie and Anna kept eating, waiting patiently for me to explain myself.

I exhaled roughly. "I started dating Dawson when I was eighteen. For my entire adult life, I've been with him. Over time, I lost who I was, but there's a part of me that knows I never really took the time to discover who I was. I went from being a teenager living at home to a college kid in a dorm to a wife living with Dawson. There was no time to figure out who I was, who I am. And I feel like I need to figure that out."

"Without Brantley?" Anna asked.

I shrugged. "If I get involved with him, aren't I just opening myself up to letting him influence me? Aren't I just going from one man to another?"

Goldie leaned forward. "I think that's up to you. But if you're not ready or interested in a relationship with Brantley, that's okay."

"It doesn't really matter. He likes someone."

"Who?"

"I don't know. He didn't tell me. But I don't want to get in his way of having a life."

"Okay, so what are you looking for? What do you want?" Anna asked.

I thought about it for a long moment and looked at my two closest female friends. Both of them were divorced. They knew better than any of our other friends what I was going through. But I'd held back.

Time to stop doing that.

"I miss having a person. Having someone to come home to. Someone to talk to when I'm having a crappy day. Having a partner. Dawson wasn't that person for a long time, but he was my husband, so I told myself he would be there if I really needed him. I just never let myself need him. But when he moved out, it was hard. I hated him for cheating. I hated him for doing that to me. But I think the thing I hated the most was that he never fought for me. For us. I told him to go, and he did."

They each reached out and took one of my hands. I looked up into their eyes and saw the depth of understanding in their gazes. They really got it.

"When Charles told me he was leaving me, I begged him not to. I told him he could have his relationship but to stay. He knew I would hate him for it, and he was right, but in that first moment of weakness, when I saw my marriage disappearing, I was so scared that I wanted to hold on to whatever I could grasp," Goldie admitted.

Anna chuckled. "Nick came home so infrequently that I had many of those moments. When I found out I was pregnant with Matty, I didn't tell him because I knew he'd leave once he knew there was another kid on the way. I knew he was horrible for me, but I didn't want to be alone. I didn't want to admit that I'd failed at so many things."

"You didn't fail," I told Anna.

Anna smiled. "I did, but failures are part of success. If I hadn't married Nick and had Joey and Matty, my life wouldn't be the same. I wouldn't have realized what an amazing man Hudson was if I hadn't known how worthless Nick was. Well, maybe not, but you know what I'm saying. It makes me appreciate Hudson that much more."

"That's how I feel about Patrick. If I'd held on to my relationship with Charles, I never would have met Patrick or let him in. I never would have found this amazing new man who makes me feel like I'm the best thing that could ever happen to him."

"I'm just not sure I'm ready for that yet," I confessed.

"You never will be," Anna said. "I fought against falling for Hudson every second of every day. I despised him. But he was there for me. Over and over he was there."

"He wore you down?" I teased.

"No. He proved to me that all men aren't like Nick. Some stick around. Some don't cheat. Some are good and honorable and true to their word."

I sucked in a breath and fought back the tears prickling the corners of my eyes. That's what I thought about Brantley. But he wasn't mine, and he never would be.

"You should sign up for Book Boyfriends Wanted," Goldie said. "Karissa created it. It's a good app. You can just meet people."

"The dating app? Really?"

Goldie gave Anna a look I couldn't read, and Anna nodded. "You should. It's a good chance to expand your possibilities for the pleasure quest. Try new things. Meet new people. Expand your world."

"I'm not sure."

"Give me your phone," Goldie said.

I scowled at her, but she waved her hand at me to hand it over. "Fine."

Anna went to the counter to order more food and drinks, and to kiss Hudson a few times. Goldie peppered me with questions and created my profile. When she handed my phone back, Hudson delivered burgers and fries and more cheese curds and drinks.

"Do you ladies need anything else?" Hudson asked. He toyed with Anna's hair as he spoke.

"All good. Thanks, honey." Anna tilted her head back for a kiss, which Hudson delivered with a whispered word I couldn't hear.

I focused on my food. I didn't love the idea of online dating, but I wanted what they had. I wanted a partner again. A real one. Maybe not right now, but if I took the plunge and was open to dating, maybe someone would surprise me.

10

BRANTLEY

I NODDED TO HUDSON AS I TOOK WHAT HAD BECOME MY regular seat at O'Kelley's for the week. I was getting sick of eating bar food, but with my kitchen still a disaster and things with Valentina not great, I had no choice.

It didn't take long for Hudson to walk over with a glass of water for me. He'd gotten used to me being there and understood when I told him I didn't drink much during the season.

"Chicken sandwich?"

"Yeah. Thanks."

"Any sides tonight?"

"Got any salad stuff?"

Hudson chuckled. "Actually, Charlie said he could make you a salad. He doesn't have a lot of dressing options, but could do something if you're open to options."

"No shit."

Hudson nodded. "Trying to please our customers. We have lettuce, tomato, onion, stuff like that for burgers, so Charlie said he could chop it up and throw together a salad for you if you wanted."

"That's awesome. Thanks. Tell him thank you, too."

"You got it." Hudson started to walk away, then turned back to me. "Are you staying here or going to the table with the ladies?"

"What ladies?"

"Anna, Valentina, and Goldie are here. I assumed you knew."

I shook my head and sipped my water. My body flashed hot. I wanted to turn and get a look at her as much as I wanted to run out before she spotted me.

Hudson looked too closely at me. I avoided his gaze until he finally nodded and walked away.

I wasn't getting off that easily, though. He'd be back.

I drank my water and pulled out my phone, hoping I gave off a *leave me alone* vibe. Since summer was over, there weren't a lot of tourists hanging around, but I didn't want any parents coming up to me either. I just wanted to eat my dinner and go home.

Hudson came back with my food and a look in his eye that said he wanted answers.

Shit.

"So, what's going on with you and Valentina?"

"Nothing."

"You're a shit liar. What happened? Anna said you two were always close, but you've been here for dinner every night this week. What happened?"

"Nothing happened."

"Again, shit liar."

"Not looking to share my feelings," I countered.

"I didn't ask about your feelings. I asked what happened. I'm guessing you pissed her off if you're not willing to go say hi. What did you do?"

"I didn't do anything. She's the one who—" I cut myself off before I admitted anything. He was good.

Hudson looked closely at me and leaned on the edge of the bar. "She's single now."

"I'm aware. But she's not interested in dating. Especially not me."

"What makes you so sure about that?"

"She told me."

"She told you she doesn't want to date you?"

"After she kissed me, yeah. Her kid came home and Vee said us kissing was really bad."

Hudson's brows shot up, almost disappearing beneath the band of his baseball hat. He was one of the biggest donors to the MacKellar Cove Athletics Boosters, something I only knew from coaching. Hudson played for MCHS and was a star, but a knee injury ended his college career. He could have had my job as coach if he'd wanted it. He was twice the player I'd ever been.

"Damn, dude, that sucks. I assumed you had better moves than that."

I rolled my eyes at him as he chuckled. "Yeah, yeah."

"Well, you better pull your shit together, because she just spotted you."

"What?"

Hudson pressed his lips together and nodded, walking away to leave me alone with Valentina.

"Hey," she said, sliding onto the stool next to me.

I looked over and smiled. "Hey. I didn't know you were here."

"Same. Anna said Hudson mentioned you've been here all week. I wondered why I hadn't heard from you."

I shrugged. Our last dinner had gone so well, why would I try again?

"Is it because I kissed you? I'm sorry. I didn't mean to make things awkward between us."

"It's fine. That's not it."

"Then what is it?"

"I didn't want to be invading your space anymore. I have been taking advantage."

"Not even a little. You're my best friend, Bee. I always want you around."

I exhaled slowly, trying to let go of the hurt. She didn't really mean that, but I wasn't going to call her on it.

"Come over tomorrow night for dinner."

I hesitated. I was not interested in a repeat of the weekend before.

"The girls will be there. I promise. Nothing weird is going to happen. I will keep my hands to myself."

I forced a smile. That wasn't what I wanted from her, but it was for the best. We needed to be friends again. Nothing else. Just friends.

"Sounds good."

"Good." She looked at my plate. "Hey, how did you get a salad?"

"Charlie made one for me. I think he took pity on me since I've asked every night if they have salad."

"Nice. I'm going to have to work even harder to get you to come to my house for dinner if I'm going to compete with this."

I breathed a laugh and shook my head. "No competition at all where I'd rather be. Just don't tell Charlie."

She smiled and zipped her lips, locking them and tossing away the imaginary key.

"Thanks." I winked at her.

"I'm going to go back to Anna and Goldie, but are we good?"

I nodded. "Always, Vee. Have a good night."

"You, too."

She hesitated for a minute, then squeezed my arm and went back to her friends.

I refused to watch her walk away.

THE WORST DAY was always the day I handed back graded tests. Especially when there was one or two who completely tanked the test. Even worse was when the students who did were on my team.

Like Kevin.

I walked through the aisles of the classroom and handed out the tests. Many of the kids exhaled with relief when they saw their grade, but the tension ratcheted up as I moved through the room. When I got to Kevin's desk, I waited. Over his grade was a note asking him to stay after class so we could talk. He looked up at me and nodded, then I moved on.

I spent the class period going over the test so everyone knew what they did wrong. My expectation was for the students to follow along and do the corrections.

The bell rang, and everyone got up from their seats. I waited near the front of the room for the students to clear out, then I focused on Kevin.

He had his backpack slung over one shoulder, an annoyed look on his face, and pursed lips. His mind was made up. He was done.

"I know this is your first year here, so I'm unsure if you know the school athletics policy about grades."

"Yep."

"So you know this grade puts you below passing and

means you won't be able to compete in the next meet unless you bring your grade up."

"Whatever."

The urge to snap at him was strong, but I'd learned over the years that when kids behaved like Kevin was, the situation was more complicated.

"You're a gifted runner, Kevin. And you're a bright kid. I don't want you to give up."

"Why? Because I have such a promising future? You don't know anything about me."

"So tell me about you."

The bell rang for the next class, and a panicked look crossed his face. "I need to go."

"I will give you a pass. Talk to me. What's going on?"

Kevin eyed me like he didn't trust my questions. Like he didn't believe I wanted to help.

There was always a separation between students and teachers, but he was also on my team. That usually helped forge a better connection. One Kevin didn't seem to feel.

"I am available for tutoring after school. There's time before practice if you need help. The errors you made were all minor. Things that made it seem like you were rushing instead of that you didn't know what was going on."

"What difference does it make?"

"It makes a big difference. I want to help you."

"I don't believe that."

"I don't know how things worked at your old school, but here we help our students. I want to help you."

"I can't stay after school. I have to go to Spanish. I'm behind in that class, and she helps me."

"What about later? Or before school?"

"Don't worry about it. I can't do it. I need to go."

"Kevin—"

He walked out of the classroom without another word. Without a note. Without any explanation.

I wasn't okay with that. I understood him being frustrated, but why wasn't he willing to let me help him?

I WAS STILL TRYING to figure out the answer to that question when I got to practice. Kevin was warming up with his normal group, but he glared at me when I approached.

I raised a brow at him, trying to convey that I wasn't okay with the way he'd acted. Thankfully, he nodded. I took that as a good sign. Better than the attitude he'd given me earlier.

Practice was good. We had a meet the next day, so Jana and I scheduled a short practice to make sure the kids weren't worn out for the meet. When it was over, I approached Kevin.

"We still need to talk."

"Am I off the team?" he asked quietly.

"No. I don't want you off the team now, and I don't want you off the team in the future. I know how valuable it is to be a part of something bigger than you. Do you want to stay on the team?"

His head jerked up, surprise coloring his face. "Yes. If I can."

"Good. Then we need to figure out a way for you to bring your grade in my class up."

Kevin nodded. "Okay, but I don't know when."

"Do you have any study halls?"

Kevin nodded again.

"What period?"

"Seventh."

"Every day?"

He nodded once more.

"I have an open period then. I'll reach out to your study hall teacher and to your guidance counselor and get them to agree to let you come to my room. Are you okay with that?"

"Yeah. Um, thanks, Coach."

"You're welcome. I do want to help."

He nodded, then jogged away.

I watched until he got in a truck, and they drove out of the lot.

"Everything good?" Jana asked.

"It will be. He's failing my class, but I'm going to tutor him."

"Can he compete tomorrow?"

"Grades don't update until Sunday night."

Jana's brows went up. "You're holding off?"

"Yes, but not because of him. He'll be out next week."

"When we don't have a meet?"

I shrugged. "Just how the timing worked out."

She laughed. "Convenient."

"I'm not doing anything different than I ever do. I have years of history backing up my process. If I entered the grades now and updated them, that would be a variation, and that could be something that drew unwanted attention."

"You're right. It's okay. You'll get him back on track."

"I'm going to do my best."

She waved as the last student pulled out of the lot, then said good night and went to her vehicle.

I climbed into my SUV and remembered that I agreed to dinner with Valentina tonight. I should have been looking forward to it. I was. Sort of.

It would be fine.

I GROANED and rolled my eyes at myself. I was being dumb. Debating what to wear when it didn't matter. I could wear a three-piece suit, and she wouldn't care. Valentina didn't want me. Not really.

I grabbed a MCHS XC tee and a pair of shorts that were comfortable and casual. I was not dressing up for dinner with the Hayes's.

When I got to their house, I hesitated again. I'd never been nervous around her, but that changed now that I knew what it felt like to have her in my arms. To have my lips against hers. To taste her and touch her and relish her.

One and done. That was all I got. It sucked, especially because I was half-hard just thinking about it again, but I couldn't do anything about it. We were friends. Just friends.

I rang the bell and waited for her to open the door. When she did, I nearly lost my battle with the slippery fucker called willpower.

Valentina had her wild curls pulled back from her face with a stretchy headband that matched the purple tee she wore. Her cheeks were dusted with flour, and her shorts were barely long enough to be called shorts instead of panties. Her long, brown legs were thick and curvy and begged to be wrapped around my shoulders while I lost myself in her sweet center.

"Bee?"

"Yeah, what?"

"Why didn't you use your key? Or just let yourself in. I keep telling you that you don't have to ring the bell."

She chuckled as she walked away from the door, leaving me to follow her like one of Pavlov's dogs. Dammit, I would do anything to make her mine.

But she wasn't.

I followed her to the kitchen before I answered her question. "I don't want to walk in on something you don't want me to witness."

"Like what? If you dropped by and let yourself in, that might be weird, but if I know you're coming, what difference does it make?"

"We'll see."

She smirked at me, knowing that was the closest she'd get to me giving in.

"Bianca asked for ranch chicken tonight with potatoes and a green salad. Does that work for you?"

I nodded. "She's been listening at practice when I tell them about healthy eating."

"Yep. They both have been. They're enjoying trying new things. We had Brussels sprouts again this week."

"Seriously?"

Valentina nodded, her cheeks and eyes brightening when she glanced at me. "Yep. You're inspiring us to all eat healthier."

"Good."

"I'm chalking it up to part of my discovery. Seeing what I enjoy."

"How's the pleasure quest going?"

She wrinkled her nose and shook her head slightly. "Not great. For someone who always has a ton of ideas, I feel like I'm drawing a blank."

"How is that possible?"

She shrugged and avoided my gaze. "I don't know. I just feel like I've tried everything, you know?"

I coughed to hide my shocked gasp. "Like what?" I hated myself for asking the question. It was only going to torture me even more. But I agreed to help, and dammit, it was for research purposes. Yeah, research. Sure.

"Well, chocolate is obviously the easy choice. I've

blended it with salt and spices. I've done all kinds of things with it. Cheese is another one if you go savory. There's sweet and savory together. Rich, decadent, intoxicating flavors. I don't do as much with savory, but even that... I don't know. I just feel stuck."

I put the last plate on the table and looked closely at her. "You know pleasure can come from other things, right? Not just food?"

She rolled her eyes and turned away from me. "I know, but I just got divorced and I'm definitely not having sex right now so..." She trailed off with a shrug.

"Okay, first, your divorce was finalized months ago. Second, you said it was a year before then since you and Dawson... so you don't owe him any loyalty. And third, and most importantly, I wasn't necessarily talking about sex either."

She narrowed her eyes at me in question, like I was insane. "You're a hot, single man who every woman in town wants to sleep with. You can't possibly convince me you have any trouble with sex."

"Every woman?" I teased. I was fishing.

She rolled her eyes and swatted at me.

"I'm too old for casual, meaningless sex. It lost its appeal years ago. But I find pleasure in things every day. Things that have nothing to do with having an orgasm, although I do make it a point to have at least one of those every day, too."

She froze, something stalling her brain.

I waited, hoping I didn't push too far.

"You find pleasure in everyday things? Like what?"

Her tone suggested she didn't believe me. I guess I shouldn't have been surprised. Add it to the reasons I wanted to kick Dawson's ass if he ever showed his face in town again. No woman should go most of her life without a very clear understanding of what brings her pleasure. In bed? Absolutely. But in life? Yeah, that, too.

"I get pleasure from a sunrise run and watching the first light start to brighten the sky. I get pleasure from a long, hot shower. Clean sheets on my bed. The lightbulb going on for one of my students. Seeing a kid break their own personal record. Talking to my niece and nephews on the phone. Visiting my family. Having a drink with friends. Cooking dinner for people I love and seeing them enjoy it. Relaxing in the hot tub after a long day. Sunset and first kisses and massages, and well, yeah, orgasms that make my entire body tingle and my breath catch in my lungs and my chest ache for the chance to feel that good again."

Valentina sucked in a shaky breath. Her eyes were dilated, her nipples tight peaks under her thin top. She licked her lips and shook her head. "Yeah, I might need some more help. Because I don't feel any of that."

I smiled. "Then I guess we have work to do."

11

———

"We?" she squeaked. "You still want to help me?"

"Hell, yes. I said I would and I'm going to. Especially if you can't think of anything that brings you pleasure outside of food and sex."

"I just... I'm pathetic."

I shook my head and reached for her hand, grabbing it before I thought twice about the way touching her would zip up my arm and go straight to my dick. The demanding fucker perked up to get closer to her, and fuck if I didn't want to let him go all in. Literally.

"You're not pathetic," I whispered, struggling to keep my voice from betraying how desperate I was for her. "You haven't had to think about it. You haven't had time. I've been single forever. I've had to figure out ways to entertain myself."

"You dated that one woman a few years ago. Megan? Mandy?"

"Missy," I provided.

"Yes! That's it. I thought you two were good together."

We were good together, but Missy wanted me to move

when she got a new job in Pennsylvania, and I couldn't do it. I couldn't leave Valentina. Which made no sense, even then, but I couldn't.

"It just wasn't right. And regardless, we were talking about you. When's the last time you can remember not being able to stop smiling about something that wasn't food related?"

I watched her closely. She bit her lip. She pressed her hands to her cheeks. She avoided looking at me.

What the hell?

"Um, I don't know."

"You don't know? You look like you're thinking about something."

"Nope. Nothing. Nothing at all."

"What don't you want to tell me?"

"When we kissed, okay? When we kissed last weekend, I couldn't stop smiling, even though you ran out of here like your ass was on fire."

"Because you said it was really bad."

"No, I said that was *almost* really bad, and I was talking about Sam walking in on us. I was ready to... Never mind."

"Finish your sentence," I growled.

She looked up at me, her eyes wide and glazed over with lust.

I moved closer to her, needing to feel her heat. "Say it, Vee."

"I was ready to ride you," she whispered.

I didn't think, just reacted. I pulled her against me so fast she couldn't protest. My tongue plunged between her lips, taking the taste I'd been dying to get for a week. For a lifetime.

I tugged her hair to tilt her head, and she whimpered.

She did it again when I trailed my teeth down her jawline and sucked on the pulse racing at the base of her throat.

"This brings you pleasure, huh?" I whispered against her skin.

"Wh— what?"

"Me kissing you? This is what you were thinking about?"

"Yes."

"Good. I'm still going to help you."

"You are?"

I nipped at her jaw and squeezed her hip. "Yep. There are lots of things that can make you feel good. Maybe not this good, but good. And I'm going to help you find them."

"Not this?"

I chuckled and took a step back. The woman was potent enough to scramble my brain and make me forget she was my friend and not someone I would be buried in later tonight. "Not this. You aren't looking for this. You already said that."

"But—"

"Tomorrow morning. Sunrise run. Or walk, if you want. Are you up for it?"

She opened and closed her mouth a few times, blinking as she did. She was too damn cute, and too damn tempting. I needed a barrier. A separation. She was on the rebound, or something, and she wasn't looking for something serious. I was too far gone to resist her, even knowing it would destroy me when it ended.

But I could show her what pleasure felt like. Outside the bedroom.

"Walk," she finally said. "But sunrise?"

I nodded. "Best time of day. It'll be beautiful."

She grumbled. "It better be."

I laughed and kissed the side of her head as Bianca and

Samantha's voices reached us. Backup had arrived in the form of boner-killing teenagers.

Definitely something I never thought I'd be happy about.

I was back at Valentina's door just before six the next morning. I lifted my hand to knock, but I didn't want to risk waking Bianca and Samantha if they weren't up yet. If. Ha! I knew there was no way they were up.

I tried the knob, but it was locked. Thankfully. I dug out my keys and unlocked the door as quietly as I could.

There was a light on in the kitchen, and the scent of coffee filled the air. I'd brought water for us, but coffee was almost as good to wake up to as Valentina in the morning.

She walked out of the kitchen with a mug to her lips. She stopped when she saw me. She lowered the mug and smiled. "You finally listened."

"I didn't want to wake the girls," I said.

She nodded and went back to her coffee. "Do we really have to do this?"

I shook my head. "We don't have to do anything you don't want to do."

"But you want to do this." It wasn't a question. She was trying something because I wanted her to, not because she was interested in it.

"I'm not looking to change you. If you want to go back to sleep, I will go. No questions. I only wanted to offer some options you hadn't thought of yet."

She sighed and nodded. "You're right. I'm being a brat. Let me grab my sneakers, and we can go."

"You can bring your coffee."

She snorted. "Did you really think I was going to leave it behind?"

I laughed with her, smiling as she whispered to her coffee on the way to her bedroom.

It wasn't long before she was back, in blue sneakers that matched her black and blue leggings and blue zip-up top. She gave me a mock-glare and led the way outside.

I locked the door behind us as she finished her coffee and set it on the table on the front porch.

She turned to me, an eyebrow raised, and asked, "Where are we going?"

"High school, actually. There's a good spot to watch the sunrise."

She grumbled again. "Fine."

I smiled once she turned away. I did not expect her to be so frustrated to be up so early.

She climbed into my SUV and sulked while I drove. The sky was still that dark blue, murky color when we parked at the school. I wanted her to enjoy the sunrise like I did, even though she was clearly not a fan of mornings.

We made it to the baseball field before the midnight blue sky broke up. Wisps of light blue filtered across the darkness, with pinks and purples joining in. The clouds were stringy, stretched across the horizon like they rose up from it. Trees blocked some of the view, but the quiet of the morning always made me feel like I was the only person around. Like I had the world to myself.

"Okay, it's pretty," Valentina admitted.

I chuckled, shaking my head at her begrudging tone. "I'm so happy you could see the beauty of the world around us."

"I've never liked mornings. How do you not know this?"

I shrugged. "I guess because I've never spent the night with you."

I didn't mean for it to sound the way it did, but once the words were out, they hung between us. We teetered on the edge of something, something that could ruin our friendship or could make us more than either of us ever imagined. But I wasn't sure we had the courage to jump off that ledge and find out which one would happen.

"True," she said after a long minute.

"Let's walk. There's a lot of space here. Usually I run here from home, watch the sunrise, and then run back."

"Why didn't we do that?"

"You didn't want to run."

She shook her head. "We could have walked."

"That would have meant getting up earlier."

She scowled. "Good point. Let's walk."

I grinned at her stomping away and hurried to catch up to her. We walked side-by-side in silence for a few minutes. Every so often she'd look up at the brightening sky and smile. I didn't say anything, just let her take in the morning sun and the way it warmed us as we walked.

After a while, she unzipped her top and let it flap open. She wore a skintight baby pink tank beneath it, one that outlined her hardened nipples and accented her rounded belly.

"It's getting warm."

"Yep."

"Is that why you're in shorts?"

I laughed. "Yep. I'm used to this. I do it every Saturday before a meet."

"You're insane."

I didn't reply. I hadn't always loved mornings. When I was younger, it was painful to drag myself out of bed.

Teaching high school and being up and out the door just barely after the sun always felt like a rush. I started getting up earlier in the mornings, so I'd have time to relax and start my day the way I wanted to instead of hurrying.

"I do like the quiet, though."

"Me, too."

We walked a little farther, taking the route around the school and getting back to where I parked. If I were alone, I'd take another lap, but I didn't want to push it with her.

"Do you need to get home?" she asked.

I shook my head. "Not yet. What did you want to do?"

"Can we walk a little farther?"

"Of course."

We walked another lap around the school, enjoying the quiet instead of talking. She was the only person I'd ever been able to be quiet with. The only one I didn't feel the need to fill the silences with noise.

When we got back to the parking lot a second time, she drew a deep breath and let it out slowly. "Thank you for this. I'm not sure it'll become a routine for me, but I enjoyed it. Having the quiet to focus my thoughts is good."

"Good."

"Is this all you do? Every Saturday morning you run here, watch the sunrise, then go home?"

"Sometimes."

"What else do you do?"

"About once a month I book a massage."

"You do?"

I nodded. "There's a massage therapist at Dr. Monroe's office. They work together with some patients where he does chiropractic adjustments, and she does massage therapy. She focuses on my legs, sometimes my lower back."

"I can't even remember the last time I had a massage."

"We have an hour if you want me to give you one." The offer was out before I could think about it. Putting my hands all over her body? Yes, please. But keeping it non-sexual? What was I thinking?

"Well, if this is part of your recommendation for things I might get pleasure from, then I guess I can't say no."

I nodded, swallowing roughly. I was so fucked.

We went back to my house since the girls were still likely asleep. The bus for our meet wasn't leaving until nine, and Valentina said they'd be up closer to eight.

I let us in and debated where she could lie down. The bed was the obvious choice, but not a good idea. The couch?

"Can we go out onto the deck?" she asked.

"Good idea." I had lounge chairs around the hot tub and bench seating on one side of the deck. It was perfect.

Valentina chose a lounge chair and laid it flat. She stretched out on her stomach, pillowing her head on her hands. "Is this okay?"

I nodded. "Yeah. Perfect."

Her legs were completely covered in her pants, but she'd stripped off her zip-up, leaving her in the pink tank top. It rode up just enough to show off a sliver of skin between it and her pants, making me ache to trail my tongue across her back.

But I didn't. This was for her, not me. I picked up one of her legs, letting her knee bend. I sat down where her foot had been and propped her leg onto my lap. Using my thumbs, I pressed a line up her calf to the back of her knee.

She groaned.

And I nearly lost it.

One simple sound should not be so intoxicating, but it came out of Valentina, so it was.

I kept going, massaging her leg until all the tension left it.

I switched to the other one, repeating the process and leaving her boneless. I moved higher, working her hamstrings and glutes, then rubbing small circles on her lower back.

"We should have skipped the walk and just did this."

I couldn't have agreed more.

She flipped over, and I rubbed the front of her legs. Her shins were tight, and her thighs were warm. I used both hands to ease the tension in her thighs, being careful to avoid getting too close to her center.

"You feel amazing," she moaned.

I was barely holding back and needed to take my mind off of how good she would feel if I pulled her pants down and kept rubbing all of her.

"Did Dawson ever give you massages?"

She snorted. "Dawson didn't do anything. I don't think he ever gave me a massage in more than twenty years."

"That's crazy."

She shrugged. "He wasn't big into touch. Unless it was for sex." She cringed. "Sorry. You probably don't want to hear about this."

"You can tell me anything."

She sighed. "He's the only man I've ever had sex with. Do you know how crazy that feels?"

"I don't think that's crazy. He was your first love. And your husband."

"He wasn't my first love, but he was my first everything else."

I wanted to ask who her first love was, but I had a feeling I knew the answer. After her confession the weekend before, it sounded like we had that in common, but we were both too oblivious to have gotten it right back then.

I smiled to myself, feeling ridiculously happy with her

not-quite confession. "You thought you'd be with him forever. You'll find someone new when you're ready."

She propped herself up on her elbows and leveled me with a stare. "Can I ask you something?"

"Of course."

"How many women have you slept with?"

"What?"

"How many? What's your number?"

"Um, why do you want to know?" My heart raced at the thought of telling her the truth. I wasn't sure what she would think of me.

"I'm just curious. I mean, what's normal for someone our age?"

"Well, I'm probably not normal since I've never been married."

"So we average our numbers. Mine is one, and yours is..."

"Um... Twenty-three?"

"Twenty-three?" she screeched. "Twenty-three? You've slept with twenty-three women?"

"Tell all of my neighbors. Please." I got up and walked away from her. Back inside to my demolished kitchen. It looked how I felt.

I knew telling her the truth was a bad idea. I knew she wouldn't understand. She wouldn't get that I spent all of college trying to avoid seeing her and Dawson together, and then I spent the twenty-plus years since then trying to get over her. I did what everyone said and got under, or on top of, someone else.

And it never worked.

I heard her come into the kitchen, but I didn't turn around. I chugged the water I'd grabbed from the fridge and focused on that instead of on the shame rolling around inside of me.

"I'm sorry. I didn't mean to yell."

I jerked my head in a nod, but I didn't feel any better.

"And I didn't mean to sound like I was judging."

"Because you weren't," I said sarcastically.

"No. I mean, it sounded that way, but it's more that I'm..."

"You're what? Horrified? Ashamed? Because I fucked a lot of women."

"Jealous," she whispered.

"What?" I could not have heard her correctly.

"I'm jealous. I haven't had sex in over a year, and the only person I had sex with was Dawson. It was good, but it was never how some people talk about sex. It was sufficient. That sounds horrible, but it's true. I was barely interested in sex. That's why I didn't want this whole Quest for Pleasure to be about sex. Because I've never had rock your world, body tingling, chest-aching sex. I've never had sex that was nearly as good as kissing you was."

"Jesus," I breathed.

She took a step toward me, her dark gaze locking on mine and not letting go. "But you've had sex with twenty-three women. Twenty-three women who were lucky enough to be chosen by you, who got to experience the kind of sex you're talking about. I never cared much about sex because it's never been that good for me, but I'm jealous of those women, and of you. Because I was perfectly content to not bother with sex again until you kissed me. But now I want to know what else can possibly feel that good. What else can you do that has twenty-three women going home with you?"

"Vee..." I wanted to touch her, to reach out to her, but if I did, I wasn't sure I'd be able to let go.

"It's okay. I'm not asking you for anything. I don't want to ruin our friendship. Not because I'm curious how good an orgasm can be with another person."

"Fucking hell," I groaned. My cock jumped at her words. I wanted to see that. To watch her. To be there with her.

"What? Sorry, am I not allowed to tell my best friend that I enjoy solo sex?"

"Nope. You can tell me anything." I swallowed down that I was saving the rest of her confession for my own solo sex session.

"Thanks." She forced a smile that was as brittle as the distance growing between us. One tiny tug and it would snap.

I stared at her, my gaze drifting to her lips. I moved closer to her, unconsciously. I was almost close enough to touch her when an alarm went off from the living room, breaking the tentative connection between us.

Valentina looked away, disappointment and relief blending on her face before she hid both. "That's to get the girls up. I need to go."

"I'll take you home."

"Thanks."

"And, Vee?"

"Yeah?"

"I'm really enjoying your Quest for Pleasure."

She grinned. "Me, too."

12

VALENTINA

I was not nearly as tired as I expected by the time evening came. After being up before the sun, I figured I'd be dragging, but there was something about the sunrise that invigorated me.

Not that I planned to get up that early again, but it was a good experiment.

The girls ran well at the meet, and to celebrate, I told them we could go out to dinner. By some miracle, they agreed on where to go. Will Work For Burgers had always been a family favorite, but that didn't mean there weren't usually arguments about whose turn it was to pick dinner.

We all showered and changed after the meet, then went to the crowded restaurant. It took a while for it to be our turn, and while we were standing there, the girls saw half a dozen friends with their parents, too.

Finley, Trent, Xavier, and Karissa were just finishing dinner with their kids when we turned away from the counter. They waved us over and asked if we wanted their table.

"Thanks. And hi," I said, hugging all of them. "You guys

beat the rush."

"Barely," Finley said. "Thankfully, George also slept through dinner so we could enjoy it."

"He's so cute," Bianca said. She leaned over and cooed at the baby as he gurgled and laughed. He was quickly becoming more toddler than baby, but he still made me ache. A part of me always wanted more kids.

"Thanks," Finley said. "He's a good kid. Very happy."

"Yeah, we'll keep him," Trent teased.

Finley chuckled and shook her head at her husband. "He says that like he has a choice. He knows he'd go before the baby."

I laughed with Finley. I knew she was joking, but the remark hit home. I would have chosen my girls over Dawson any day, and in the end, I did.

"We've been talking about babies in health class," Bianca said. "I have to learn CPR. If you ever need a babysitter, I'd be happy to help."

Finley and Trent looked at each other and nodded. "Thank you," Finley said. "We will definitely let you know. I'll be honest and say we don't go out much, but it's always good to have babysitters."

Bianca nodded. Her gaze was glued to George. He had a hold of her finger and swung it around like he was conducting with her finger as his baton.

"He likes you a lot," Trent said, watching the two of them. "I've never seen him so drawn to someone before."

"Babies like me. I don't know why." Bianca shrugged.

"They always have. I think it's the older sister thing," I said. "Samantha was always interested in what Bianca was doing. Bianca would watch her sister and make sure she was watching everything. She's engaging."

"Mom," Bianca groaned.

"What? It's true. And you said babies like you."

Bianca rolled her eyes and dropped into a seat like I was the worst thing ever.

"Teenagers are great, aren't they?" Xavier whispered. McJenna sat next to Bianca, their heads together as they talked.

I shook my head. "I should have had a dozen more."

Xavier snorted a laugh. "Right? I keep telling J she'll understand when she has kids."

"I bet she loves that," I said with a laugh.

Karissa nodded next to him, rolling her eyes with humor and understanding.

"Oh, yeah. When she doesn't think it's gross I would even talk about it. I'm no fool, though. She's old enough for me to worry whenever she's not in my sight."

"All the time." It was good to have other parents who understood.

"Number three-four-nine!" the man at the counter yelled.

"Is that us?" Samantha asked.

I nodded. "Do you want to grab the food?"

"Yep." Sam jumped up and wove through the crowd to the counter.

"We should go. Let you guys eat. Good to see you," Finley said.

"You, too. See you tomorrow." I'd become a regular at book club and finally felt like I not only belonged but I enjoyed it.

One more thing for my pleasure quest that had nothing to do with food or sex.

"See you then," Finley said, as George started to fuss.

Sam came back with our food, and the three of us sat at one end of the large table to let another party take the other seats. We were halfway through our burgers when Bianca set hers down and looked around.

"What's up?" I asked. I saw the wheels turning and knew something was brewing.

"Finley and Trent got married after they had George, right?"

I nodded. "Yes. Why?" I knew the story, but I wasn't sure I wanted to tell my teenage daughters about friends who had a one-night stand and ended up pregnant and married later. It was a good story, but not what I hoped my kids would model their lives after.

"It just makes me feel better that things worked out for them. McJenna told me her dad and Karissa were college sweethearts, but he didn't want to move here. Sort of like Dad."

I set my burger in the basket and tried to formulate my response. Then I stopped myself. I owed my girls the truth, not some manipulated version designed to make their father look better.

"That's true. He complained a lot about moving here."

"Even after you guys moved?" Samantha asked.

I nodded. "All the time. I found a job here, and he didn't have one, so he moved with me. He was never happy about it, though. I don't think he was happy until he found a job outside the area and traveled for work."

"And met other women," Bianca grumbled.

"Unfortunately, yes."

"Why did he do that?" Samantha asked.

"I will never understand. But I don't have to. Like we talked about before, there are people who would never do something like that. Those are the people I want in my life."

"Like Uncle Brantley."

I nodded. "Like Uncle Brantley."

"I hope I find someone like Uncle Brantley or Trent or Xavier instead of someone like Dad," Bianca said.

I grabbed her hand and squeezed it. "Me, too, sweetheart. Me, too."

I WAS elbow deep in flour when my phone dinged with a text Tuesday afternoon. It wasn't the sound I'd set up for the girls, but that didn't mean it wasn't important. Especially since Xavier was getting them from practice and taking them home so I could work later.

I cleaned my hands on a dry towel and tapped the screen to wake my phone up. It was from Goldie.

> We're going shopping tomorrow night. I need something to wear for a work dinner, and you need something that isn't yoga pants and tees.

I looked down at my yoga pants and tee and scowled.

> I like my clothes.

> They're perfectly fine for work when you're up to your eyeballs in flour, but they will not work for a date. Have you gotten any matches yet? You never mentioned.

I'd forgotten all about the app.

> I don't know. Need to check when I'm not at work.

> And after you have date appropriate attire. When time are you off work tomorrow? Xavier said he can get the kids again.

He's getting mine today.

And he'll get them tomorrow. I told him I'd take an extra day next week since I only had one day planned.

Think of this as part of your quest. Find new clothes that make you feel good. Silky fabrics and sexy cuts and something that shows all the men of MC that you are open for business.

NO! I'm not open for business! I'm barely even divorced.

You can't pull that on me. I've been there. You need to remember that you are a strong, smart, beautiful woman who deserves a damn good orgasm once in a while. One that isn't delivered by your own hand, or something in your hand.

I can't believe you just said that.

Yes, you can. And you know it's true. You don't have to marry a guy for making you scream, but you have to get out of those yoga pants if you're going to let him try.

I'm going back to work now.

Be ready at five tomorrow. I'll pick you up.

Fine.

Love you!

Love you.

I shook my head as I locked the phone and set it back on the counter. My yoga pants were perfectly fine. And so were my orgasms.

I nibbled my lip.

They could be better with Brantley.

I groaned and shook my head. I was not going to use my best friend to have some orgasms. No matter how good he was at kissing. It wasn't fair to him. No matter how much I wanted him.

GOLDIE PICKED up a neon green slip dress. I tried not to be horrified. It was the worst possible shade of green for her complexion. I'd never seen her in anything that bright. It wasn't hideous or unflattering, just not at all right for her.

"You should try this on," she said, thrusting the garment toward me.

"What? Why?" It wasn't me at all. Too bright. It would draw too much attention to me. I preferred to be invisible, not the brightest thing around.

"Because it's a great color for you, and you need something in your wardrobe that screams, *look at me.*"

"That definitely screams it," I muttered.

She chuckled. "Just try it on. If you hate it, you don't have to get it. Ooh, or try the blue one. Same style, but less neon."

I reached for the blue without thinking about it. The color was still bright, but being blue instead of green, it wasn't neon. It was stunning, and I loved it on sight. "Fine." I wasn't going to admit to Goldie that I hoped it fit. I was there to help her find clothes, and all we'd done so far was find stuff for me.

A few more racks and a few more options, and we headed to the dressing rooms. Goldie had three dresses to try for her dinner, and I had three times that to try for my date nights.

I saved the blue dress for last, opting for a red one, a pink one, and a black one to start. I hated them all.

"Your face says it," Goldie said as we met in front of the mirrors. "It's not bad, but it doesn't flatter your body."

"Not much does."

"Except Brantley," Goldie teased.

I rolled my eyes to keep her from seeing the way her words affected me. I hadn't admitted how I felt about him. Just confessing we'd kissed was bad enough.

"What do you think of this?" she asked, changing the subject without requiring a response.

I turned to face her in the black dress she chose. It was a good cut, fitted with enough stretch to flatter her curves. The pink pin-striping gave it movement that it wouldn't otherwise have. And the length was long enough to be appropriate for a work event.

"It looks amazing on you. What's the event you have?"

"Mayor Knight is hosting a dinner. He wants to get some of the other local mayors together to plan some joint events for next summer. Something the entire area can do to work together to bring in tourists."

"That's a great idea." I was a fan of Omar Knight. I didn't know him well, but he was always friendly and kind when I saw him in town. He didn't keep to himself or act like he was too good to mingle with the rest of MacKellar Cove.

"It is. He's been great to work for. He has tons of ideas, and he's very open to suggestions from everyone. He stops and talks to all the staff. I was at Town Hall one day and he was in a meeting with one of the custodial staff. The woman's father was sick, and Omar was checking in with her and offered to cover her salary for a month so she could be with her father during his recovery."

"Really?"

Goldie nodded. "He paid her out of his own pocket since the town doesn't have the funds for something like that. Said MacKellar Cove doesn't work without everyone being part-ners. He's working to change the town's bylaws to offer better coverage for employees in those situations. She was going to apply for FMLA, but it would only cover sixty percent of her pay, and she couldn't afford that."

"Yeah, that's a big hit."

"Yep. But he had her go out on FMLA so her job was protected, and he paid her the balance to make sure she was whole. He's really just amazing to work for."

"Wow. That sounds like exactly who we need in charge of this town."

"I agree. So, I need to make a good impression at this dinner so the other mayors are willing to work with us."

"Well, I think that one's a good option. Let's see what else you have."

"You, too."

We went into the dressing rooms and changed. I tried on a pair of jeans and a gray sweater, surprised at how comfort-able both were.

"Wow," Goldie said when I walked out. "That's simple, but stunning."

"Thanks. I agree. I can't even tell you the last time I bought a new pair of jeans. Or a sweater."

"You have to get those."

I spun to check out my butt in the mirror. It looked like it was perkier than usual. I didn't know jeans could be magical.

"I don't love this dress as much," Goldie said.

I shook my head. "Nope. The other one was better. That one isn't bad, but it doesn't suit you as well."

We changed again. I tried on one top I hated, then switched to a pair of black dress pants and a moss-green top. Goldie was in her last dress, a blue one with a cowl neck that made her eyes pop.

"That's gorgeous," I told her.

"Thanks. I think it's my favorite."

"I can see why. But I think you should get both."

"I probably will. I'm sure I'll need them. I like your outfit."

"Thanks. These pants are so comfortable. And this top is the softest thing I've ever worn."

"Good. Have you tried on that blue dress yet?"

I shook my head.

"Go put that on while I change. Do you have anything else?"

"No. I wanted to save that for last."

"I don't blame you. I hope you love it."

"Me, too."

I went back into the changing room once more and set the black pants and green top to the side. I slid the blue dress off the hanger and felt like I was holding water. It was soft and slippery. I pulled it over my head and nearly groaned at the feel of the fabric against my skin. It felt so good.

I didn't look in the mirror in the dressing room because I wanted to get the full effect of it. I wanted to buy it based on how it felt on my body, but if it looked bad, I knew I'd have to put it back.

Goldie sucked in a breath when I stepped out. Her eyes went wide. "Wow."

"Yeah? I haven't looked."

"You have to wear that next time you see Brantley. He won't be able to keep his hands off of you."

"That hasn't been a concern so far," I mumbled.

"Whoa, what? You owe me that story, but first, look at yourself."

I finally looked in the mirror and did a double take. Damn. The dress looked like it had been made just for me. It fell perfectly over all my curves, accenting the ones I wanted to show off and minimizing the ones I wanted to hide. My boobs looked full and lush, my belly disappeared beneath the ruched middle, and my hips looked pin-up model worthy. "Holy..."

"Exactly. That's beautiful. You have to get it."

I nodded, unable to take my eyes off the way the dress wrapped around me. It was... I couldn't even come up with words. I loved it.

"Okay, go change, then we need dinner, and you need to tell me what's going on with you and Brantley."

I nodded, barely aware of what she was asking. I needed to talk to someone, though. Someone who might have some perspective.

We paid for our purchases, and Goldie took us to a Thai restaurant. Since our kids didn't love it, we'd gotten into the habit of going out for Thai when it was just us.

"Okay, spill," she said after we'd ordered and were waiting for our food.

"There's nothing to spill. We've kissed a few times, but it's no big deal."

"Kissing him is a huge deal. I know you're scared about getting into a new relationship, and I know you're worried about ruining your friendship, but he's also Brantley. You adore him."

"I do, and that's why it's ridiculous. I shouldn't want him.

I shouldn't be thinking about him when... you know."

"Why not?" Goldie asked. "He's a very attractive man. You're both single. There's nothing wrong with you wanting him, or with you thinking about him. I don't know why you're fighting this."

"Because I can't lose another person in my life. I can't watch him walk away."

"But what if he doesn't? What if he wants the same thing and the two of you are perfect for each other?"

I slowly shook my head, dismissing her idea as my brain tried to wrap around it. "It's not possible. He's not... I'm not his type. I've seen the women he dates and takes home from bars."

"Blake told me she said the same thing about Ian. She never considered him as a possibility because he was always with women she saw as prettier than her, skinnier, whatever. But she was wrong. He was with them to try to forget about her."

"Brantley told me he's interested in someone."

"Yeah, but he won't tell you who, and he kissed you. Maybe he's interested in you."

"No. I can't go there. I just can't."

"Okay, then let's see if you have any matches. If you won't go out with Brantley, then you can wear that dress for someone else."

The idea made my chest ache even as I handed Goldie my phone to check for any matches. I didn't want to wear that dress for another man. I wanted to see the look in Brantley's eyes when I wore it. And the look in his eyes when I took it off.

But I couldn't. I had to focus on myself. On my own pleasure. And not on tying my friend down when it wasn't what I thought he wanted.

13

T HE GIRLS APPROVED OF MY PURCHASES WHEN I GOT HOME. Bianca asked if she could borrow the blue dress sometime.

"Where are you wearing a dress like this?" I asked her.

"Where are you wearing it?" she countered.

I rolled my eyes. "I have no plans to wear it, but it was too nice to pass up. Did you two finish your homework?"

"Yes," they both grumbled. Usually, they were in better moods when I went out for the evening.

"What's going on?"

"Nothing," Bianca said quickly.

"What happened?" I asked, setting my stuff down and crossing my arms. I looked between my daughters and waited for someone to tell me what was going on.

"Bianca has a date," Samantha teased her sister.

"What?" I whirled on my oldest and caught her glaring at her sister. "Who asked you out?"

"It doesn't matter."

"Yes, it does."

"I told him no."

"Aw, Bianca, you need to get out there and live your life. You can't hide forever."

"Is that what you're doing? Is that why you bought the dress?" Bianca was far too observant for my sanity. But she wasn't wrong.

"I'm considering my options."

"You're going on a date?" Samantha asked.

I shook my head. "No. Not yet. But I don't want to be single forever. Right now, you two are my focus. Nothing is going to come between you two and me. One day, I hope to find someone, though. Someone who makes me feel like I'm special."

"You will, Mom," Samantha said.

I smiled at her. "I hope so. But the point is, I'm not putting my life on hold. Not any more. I'm figuring out what makes me happy. And part of that is eventually going to be recognizing a man who makes me happy."

"You always laugh when you're with Uncle Brantley. Maybe you should pick someone who makes you smile," Sam said. "Paul makes me smile. He says he likes the way my eyes light up when I'm really happy about something."

"Dad never made you smile," Bianca said.

"He used to," I admitted. "When we met, that was one of the things I loved most about him."

"What was he like back then?" Samantha asked.

I let the memories from long ago fill me. Dawson was charming. He was kind and smart and like no one I'd ever known before. He made me feel special, and I fell in love with him because of it.

When I thought about the people we used to be, I was sad our marriage ended. I wished things could have been different. But by the time it all fell apart, I knew those people weren't meant to be together.

I leaned back, and I told my girls about the day I met their father. About the first time we hung out together, without Brantley. About the first time I realized I cared about him, and when I believed that was love. I talked, and they listened to stories for hours, until Samantha fell asleep on my shoulder and Bianca yawned loudly.

"It's time for bed," I told them.

"Can you tell us more tomorrow?" Samantha asked as she stood up.

I nodded. "Sure."

"Good night, Mom," Samantha said. She hugged me, then headed toward her room.

Bianca hung back. "Dad sounds like he wasn't bad."

I nodded again. "He wasn't. He was a great boyfriend, and he was a good husband for a while. I think he can still be a good father, but that's up to him. I spent a lot of years doing my best to make sure you two knew he loved you."

"That wasn't up to you."

"I know. But I never wanted you two to feel like you weren't loved. He was happy when he found out I was pregnant. Anxious, like all parents, but happy. He loves you both, even though he isn't always good at showing that."

"Thanks, Mom." Bianca hugged me a little longer than usual before she went toward her room.

I double checked the doors and turned off all the lights. I went to my room and set my new clothes on my bed. The blue dress still called to me. I pulled it out of the bag and looked at it again.

Goldie said to look at my matches. I didn't have the courage to, but in the dress, I could do anything.

I changed into it quickly, feeling silly for needing a dress no one was going to see me in to feel better about myself. But it worked. I felt like I could do anything. I opened Book Boyfriends Wanted and tapped the part with my messages.

I had six matches. Six men who were interested in me enough to send me a message.

I read through their profiles and laughed when I saw one for a guy called NerdyByNature. I liked that he had a sense of humor, and that he wasn't afraid to admit that he was smart.

His message was funny and caught my attention and got me to reply.

NERDYBYNATURE

Which is worse… Getting weird messages from random guys or not getting them? I guess on a dating app you want to get them, right?

I tapped to reply and realized what Goldie had entered for my screen name. Oh my God.

BAKERBABE

Is there a third option where the messages are not weird? Because I want that one.

I started to put my phone away, but it buzzed almost immediately.

NBN

There you go changing the game. Hi, by the way.

BB

Hi. How are you?

NBN

I'm good. How are you? What are you doing tonight?

BB

I'm about to go to sleep, but earlier I went shopping and spent time with my kids.

NBN

Whoa, I'm not that kind of guy. You need to buy me dinner before you take me to bed.

I snorted a laugh and shook my head. Definitely a plus for making me laugh.

BB

Maybe you should buy me dinner first.

NBN

Ooh, I like you. We'll do it. Sometime. But I need to admit to you that I'm not sure I'm going to be on here much longer.

BB

That's okay. I need to go to sleep soon, too.

NBN

That, yes, but in general. I've been thinking about closing my account.

BB

Oh, okay. Can I ask why? Is there something wrong with the app?

NBN

Not at all. It's great. I've met a lot of great people. But there's this one woman I really like, and I'm hoping it might work out. It's nuts because it never has, but things have changed recently, and I don't want to mess up any potential relationship.

BB

I get that. I'm not looking to get serious right now. Truth be told, my friend filled this out. She asked me the questions, so they're my answers, but I did not choose my name.

NBN

Maybe she knows you better than you know yourself.

BB

She means well.

NBN

Our friends usually do.

BB

That's very true.

NBN

Should I let you go, or do you want to chat for a few minutes?

BB

Why don't you tell me about the woman you like? I could use some positive inspiration these days.

NBN

Sorry to hear that. Hopefully, you find some. As for the woman… She's the strongest person I've ever met. She doesn't know it, but she is. She's smart and brave and so gorgeous. She's been through some crap lately, but she's picking herself up and moving on. Figuring life out all over again.

BB

I'm not surprised you like her. She sounds pretty great.

NBN

She is. But like all of us, she doesn't know
it. She doubts herself. I wish she could see
herself the way I see her.

BB

Maybe one day she will.

NBN

I hope so. She deserves the world.

BB

I really hope she sees that you want to give
it to her one day. We all deserve that.

NBN

I keep telling her that, too.

BB

Smart and enamored with her? Color me
jealous.

NBN

She doesn't see me that way. At least, I
don't think so.

BB

You don't sound sure about that.

NBN

We've gotten close a few times, but she
pulls back.

BB

That sucks. It's not good to toy with
people's emotions.

NBN

I don't think she's doing it on purpose. I
think she doesn't realize. She's a friend and
crossing that line makes me nervous.

BB

Ah. I get that.

NBN

I do, too. Trust me. But it's hard to stay on the other side of that line sometimes.

BB

She'll come around.

NBN

I hope so.

BB

I should go. It was good talking to you. Keep me posted on how things go.

NBN

I will. Have a good night, BakerBabe.

BB

Ugh! That name. Enjoy your night, NerdyByNature.

I closed the app and smiled. It was nice to flirt with someone, even if I didn't know who he was. I put my phone on the nightstand and reached for the bottom of my dress when my phone rang.

Brantley was calling me.

I let the dress fall and answered the phone. "Hey, Bee. How are you?"

"Good. I was just thinking about you. I saw Xavier picked up the girls. Everything okay?"

"Yeah. Goldie wanted me to go shopping with her. She has a work dinner coming up and needed something new to wear."

"Oh, good. I was a little worried."

"All good. How was practice?"

"Good. Although I think Andrew is a bit crushed that Bianca turned him down."

"That's who asked her out! I should have known. She

wouldn't tell me. Just said it didn't matter because she said no." I paced my room, hating that she was messing with the kid.

"She's always talking to him. Why is she rejecting him?"

"Dawson."

"What?"

"She's worried all men are like Dawson and is afraid to get involved with someone."

"Ah, shit. I didn't see that one coming."

"Neither did I."

"Is there anything I can do to help?"

I shook my head. "I think she just has to work through it. But she might come around. What do you think of Andrew?"

"He's great. Wonderful kid. Kind. Always encouraging the other runners. If she were my daughter, I'd want her to date someone like him."

"Well, she's basically your niece, so I'll take that as the same. You're more of a father than Dawson has pretty much ever been. Except for the whole conception thing."

Brantley choked, coughing loudly for a second before he sounded far away.

"Are you okay?" I hissed into the phone. I waited while he kept coughing until he came back.

"Sorry. Water went down the wrong way."

"Are you good?"

"Yeah. All good. Hey, want to try something else this weekend for your Quest for Pleasure?"

"Does it require me being up before the sun again?"

"Nope, just after the sun has gone down."

"I can work with that. What did you have in mind?"

"Leave that to me. Wear a dress if you have one and bring a bathing suit."

I looked down at my blue dress and smiled. "I can make that work."

"Sounds good. See you tomorrow after practice?"

"I'll be there."

"Have a good night."

"You, too, Vee. Love you."

"Love you."

My smile wouldn't fade as I hung up the phone and got ready for bed. When I slid between the covers, I felt good. Really good. Flirting with one guy, then talking to Brantley, I was flying high.

I reached into my nightstand and found the toy I kept in my drawer. The soft buzz had my body tingling before I even touched it to my skin.

What would Brantley do with something like that?

I debated for a second, then lowered it to my nipple. I gasped at the sensation. It was new, but it was good. I moved to my other nipple and closed my eyes.

Pleasure. Sure, I knew orgasms could bring me pleasure, but I'd never given myself the freedom to experiment with what other parts of my body would heighten that.

I moved the vibrator around on my body, testing out different spots that would feel good. By the time I lowered it between my legs, I was dripping wet and hanging over the edge. It didn't take long for the vibrations to send me into bliss, a silent scream pulling me under.

My body ached as I withdrew, something that rarely happened. I was usually a one and done kind of woman, but need rippled through me. I pressed the vibrator against my clit, the jolt buckling my body in half. My throat burned with the need to cry out. Dawson was never one for noisy sex, but I wondered what Brantley would like.

"Talk to me," his imaginary voice whispered.

"Yes," I whispered in the darkness. Brantley would want to hear me. He would whisper dirty things in my ear and make me come even harder.

I tried to think of something sexy, but my mind was blank. All I wanted was another orgasm.

I focused on the vibration again and dipped the toy inside me. It hit the right spot, and I groaned. I bit my lip to keep more noises from escaping me as I thrust against the vibration.

It had been far too long since I had sex that blew my mind. A lifetime of mediocrity left me wondering if I was doing something wrong. But conjuring up Brantley's face and imagining him pounding into me brought a full awareness to my body.

It wasn't me. It was my partner.

Sex wasn't part of my Quest for Pleasure, but lying there in my bed, alone, struggling to breathe and picturing Brantley's smirking face above me, told me I was selling myself short. I was selling sex short. I needed to know what it felt like to have someone so deep inside me I couldn't feel the difference between us. To know what it felt like to have my toes curl and my lungs freeze and my entire body sing with an orgasm that shattered my world and reformed it into something new.

I wanted all of that with Brantley. As that realization crashed over me, so did my orgasm, one that had me shaking and bucking and aching to scream. One that made me desperate for more. Not from my own hand, but from his. His hands and lips and tongue and cock.

The vibrator fell to the bed and buzzed as I came down from my high. After a minute, I reached for it and turned it off, leaving it on the sheets while I struggled to find my consciousness.

I finally stood and went to the bathroom. I used the toilet, then washed my hands and washed the vibrator. I left it on the counter to dry overnight and carried myself back to bed.

My thighs tingled, and my core burned. I wanted more, but I wouldn't be able to hold back if I gave in. And I didn't want to give them to myself. I wanted to know what it felt like to be with Brantley.

But it would mean crossing a line we couldn't uncross. We'd already kissed, and the ridge in his shorts said he was willing to do more, but was I?

Orgasms were counted and numbered with Dawson. Equal and measured and in exchange for something. If he got one, I did, too, but if he didn't get what he wanted, I was out of luck.

I never wanted to think of sex that way with Brantley. Or anyone else I had in my life in the future. Orgasms were meant to be mutually beneficial. If I gave in and added that part of it to my Quest for Pleasure, the only one I wanted to share it with was Brantley.

Was that fair?

I didn't want to end up like the woman NerdyByNature was interested in. Someone who toyed with his emotions and pulled back every time we got close.

I guess I sort of did that with Brantley, but it wasn't on purpose. It was because of the situation. It was...

Not fair to Brantley. He told me he was interested in another woman, and instead of respecting that and keeping my distance, I pounced on him like a cat in heat. I definitely owed him better than that. He was my best friend, and I needed him to know what I was thinking.

I was thinking I wanted to know what really good sex was like. And I was thinking I wanted him to show me. I was also thinking we could keep it casual. Friendly. Like everything else we did together.

If the woman he liked finally figured out he was a catch, then I'd back off. I'd let him find the kind of love he deserved. I'd never stand in the way of Brantley's happiness. I was his friend. And I wanted him to be happy.

But until he was, maybe we could share a few dozen orgasms or so.

14

BRANTLEY

I WENT THROUGH EVERY SINGLE LINE OF KEVIN'S TEST, looking for any possible points I could give him. We'd been working together all week, and he was smarter than he gave himself credit for, but he was still struggling.

I didn't think about what the grade would do to his average because I couldn't. I had to be a teacher first and a coach second. That was the promise I made to myself when I took the coaching job. School always had to come first. And if that meant benching one of my stars, I would deal with it.

It was also why I came up with my system of putting grades in every Sunday. It eliminated any manipulation of grades. If I was consistent, then I was fair.

But it wasn't easy.

I wanted to give all my students A's, but when they didn't earn the grade, I couldn't do it. The only one that hurt was the kid who believed they knew what they were doing when they didn't.

I finished Kevin's test and moved on to the next one, repeating the process of searching for every single point I could give each student. They all deserved the chance to earn as much credit as possible.

It took longer to go through the tests multiple times like I did, but it gave me a clearer picture of what each student was capable of. When I finally finished my notes, I added up the scores for each test and entered the grades into my record book. Yes, I was still old-school and kept a book. It meant I never had to worry about the computer being down or maintenance on the system. I always knew what the kids were facing.

I drew a breath and double checked I'd put each grade down correctly, then worked on calculating their averages for the quarter.

Kevin was passing again.

I exhaled a sigh of relief and smiled. It was just barely, but it was passing. I knew how hard he'd been working, and I was really proud of the effort he put in. I hoped he would be, too.

I was eager to enter the grades, but I wouldn't let myself until Sunday evening. I had to stay consistent. But I needed a distraction before Valentina came over for our next adventure.

Telling her to wear a dress was impulsive and stupid. I planned to take her dancing, but she didn't need a dress for it. Still, it would be fun to see her a little fancier than her usual.

She used to love going out dancing in college. Every weekend, she would try to talk Dawson and I into trying out a new club. Sometimes all of us would go, and other times I would beg off and let the two of them go. Dawson bitched about it every weekend, sometimes telling me about other girls and other times telling me he wasn't a fan of dancing. Either way, I should have seen some of the signs. But I was too busy lusting after Valentina to notice Dawson half the time.

I knew it had been years since she'd gone dancing. I wasn't sure if it was something she would enjoy doing, but I'd signed us up for a tango class. In the first hour, an instructor would show us the steps and encourage everyone to dance. After that, the club opened up to a public venue where people would come in and dance. The club was about an hour south of us, but if she enjoyed it, we could go back again.

Since I went for a run that morning to watch the sunrise, I decided to tackle a few more projects in my kitchen. The flooring was down, the new slider was in, and the cabinets were on order, but I'd been wanting to paint the room. With no obstructions, it should have been an easy job.

If you had skills. Clearly, I did not.

By the time I was done, I had almost as much paint on myself as I had on the walls. Thankfully, I kept the floors paint free because of a heavy-duty drop cloth Knox insisted I get. I wasn't sure if I could admit to him that it saved my ass when I dropped the paintbrush.

I stepped back and admired the new color. My floors were a light gray vinyl plank that looked like wood. The cabinets were a dark gray stain with plain doors. Knox called them shaker style. I just liked the simplicity. The countertops were white quartz with gray and blue lines running through it. I was a little unsure about that one, but Knox insisted I would love it. He said the light color would brighten up the space, and the veining would tie everything together. I just swiped my credit card and hoped for the best.

The more I looked at the countertop sample in the corner of the room, the more I liked it, and when it came time to pick a paint color, I chose the blue that was in the quartz. It was a blue-gray color, but the lightest one on the swatch. Just enough of a color to not be white, but the blue came through once it was on the walls.

I had to admit, Knox was dead-on with everything so far.

I also had to admit I was enjoying remodeling the kitchen. Even though I did it with Valentina in mind, I liked the little I'd finished in the first month and was happy with it. The leak I found behind the sink was cleaned up and would not happen again. The floors were solid and softer than I expected. The tile I had in there before would have my feet aching after I finished cooking dinner, but the vinyl wasn't as bad. I still had a lot of work to do, but it was starting to feel like it might come together.

Before I allowed myself to get sucked into another project, I checked the time. I was supposed to pick Valentina up in forty-five minutes, which meant I needed to get moving.

I cleaned up the paint and made sure the can was sealed. The drop cloth was stained, but I didn't want it to soak through to the flooring, so I carried it outside and hung it over the old laundry line I'd never bothered to take down. The brush and roller would have to be cleaned later, but I set them in the utility sink out in the garage and ran water into a bucket to cover the paint.

My shower was quick, and unfortunately, I didn't have time to jerk-off before I hurried myself out. I didn't want to pick up Valentina sporting a hard-on. I'd been hard pretty much full-time since she told me about her Quest for Pleasure. Helping her and talking about pleasure was keeping me right on the edge constantly.

I made it to her house with under a minute to spare. I

debated opening the door like she kept telling me to, but I knocked at the last minute.

She opened the door with a laugh, and all conscious thought fled my body.

She wore a blue dress that hugged her curves like it was painted on her. It wasn't tight or inappropriate, just sexy and stunning and impossible for me to not harden instantly.

Her hair was natural, with her tight spiral curls all around her head like a halo. She wore a touch of makeup, just enough that I noticed her eyes were brighter and her lips were glossy and tempting and so fucking kissable I almost did.

"You look nice," Valentina said as she stepped out of the house. "I'm guessing you're ready to go, right?"

I nodded, unable to form words. She smiled, her eyes squinting, then turned back to lock the door.

"The girls are home, and I'm anxious about leaving them. Even though they've stayed home alone a million times."

"Did something happen?"

She shook her head. "No. I'm just having one of those days where I'm worrying about everyone around me and not focusing on myself. There's no reason I should worry, other than I always worry."

"Then let me distract you for the evening."

A slow, sexy, sinful smile tipped her lips up and lit her eyes. She turned her head, and I saw the teardrop earrings she wore, silver and sparkly and teasing me as they rested along the pulse point in her neck that I wanted to lick and suck.

"I'm definitely open to that," she whispered. Her voice was husky, sexy.

Was I insane, or was she acting like this was a date?

And did I mind?

I definitely knew the answer to the second question. I offered her my arm and smiled when she took it. I escorted her to the passenger door and opened it for her, waiting until she tucked her long, curvy legs inside before I gently closed the door.

On my walk around the SUV, I gave my dick a pep-talk. "Do not push. Do not beg. And for fuck's sake, do not demand."

I wanted to do all of it, and the stubborn bastard was leading the charge to get into Valentina's pants. Or panties, I guess. Assuming she had some on beneath that dress.

I groaned as I opened the door. I could not imagine Valentina without panties. It would just end in a mess in my pants.

I sank into the driver's seat and headed south. We talked about the week and the girls, and not once did she ask me where I was taking her.

That was significant. Valentina trusted me enough to not question my plan for the evening.

When I parked in front of the club, she looked up at it with confusion. "What is this place?"

"They have tango classes and open dancing."

"What?" she gasped, her eyes and grin widening together. "Are we here for that?"

I shook my head. "I thought we could watch. No need to actually dance."

She shoved my shoulder and laughed, scrambling to get inside.

I met her in front of the SUV on the sidewalk. She practically vibrated with joy. I couldn't wait to get her inside to the class and to dance with her.

WHAT THE FUCK was I thinking?

Dancing with Valentina was the worst kind of torture. Not because she was bad. Oh, no, my woman had some serious moves. But that was the problem. When she swayed in my arms and spun and shifted those hips, I was gone. I lost count of the number of times I almost came in my pants. She was a temptress, a tease, the most tantalizing of torturers.

And all I wanted was more.

The class ended, and we took a break for a few minutes. She hadn't stopped smiling the entire time, and I knew it was a great idea to bring her there.

"Are you having fun?" I asked as we sipped water and nibbled on pretzels.

"So much. I'd forgotten how much I loved dancing."

"Forgotten or just stopped reminding yourself?"

She shrugged, a bit of the light in her eyes dimming. "A little of both, I guess. I told myself it was selfish to do things for me. Especially when Dawson didn't want to join me. He hated dancing, and after we got married, he refused to go with me. I asked for a while, but eventually, I guess I convinced myself I didn't miss it that much."

"Well, I'll come dancing with you any time you want me to."

"You will?"

I nodded. "Of course."

"Why would you do that?"

I huffed a laugh because she still didn't get it. She had no clue. "Because I love you, Vee."

I knew the words wouldn't sink in because I'd said them a million times. Telling her I loved her was significant for me. I'd never told another woman I loved her, except family. I'd never loved another woman.

And for all my attempts and wishes and hopes that I would one day get over Valentina, I knew it would never happen.

She was the woman I wanted to spend my life with. If that was only as a friend, I would stick by her side and watch her love someone else, like I'd done for decades. But if there was the slightest chance she might one day feel the same about me, I was going to be there and be available for her to love right back.

"I love you, too. Thank you for this. It's the best night I've had in a while."

"Good. It's not over, though."

She smiled as the band announced they would resume playing in three minutes.

Song after song, I held her in my arms and spun her around the dance floor. We weren't very good at following the steps we were supposed to take, but we enjoyed the hell out of trying. No one else cared. We were all there to have a good time.

By the time we took another break, I'd lost my fight to keep my distance from her. Having my hands on her body all night, that silky fabric of her dress slipping through my fingers, was painful. I needed her in a way I'd never needed another person.

But I wasn't going to be the one to start something.

We returned to our booth, but instead of sitting on opposite sides, I slid in next to her. She looked up at me with a grin and winked.

"I was wondering why you were sitting all the way over there."

I shrugged. "Because you said your Quest for Pleasure was all about trying things and having fun."

"What if I told you I've been thinking about expanding that quest?"

My dick twitched. I shifted on the bench seat and tried to stop the throbbing pain of my erection behind my zipper. I was failing. "What do you mean?"

She shrugged and avoided my gaze. "I've just been thinking I haven't enjoyed sex before, and it would be really nice to be able to."

I choked. Damn. Just the thought of Vee...

"I think you should definitely do that."

"Well, you inspired the idea. Kissing you was a tease."

"Um, thanks?"

She breathed a husky laugh. "I don't mean that as a negative. Just that you opened my eyes to the way it could be. I signed up for an account on Book Boyfriends Wanted. Goldie and Anna said I should think about dating and be open to it. Even if I'm not ready now, I want to be one day."

"So, you're going to fuck some random guy?" I barked.

She looked up at me and shook her head. "Actually, I was hoping I could fuck you."

The fire in her eyes swirled deep inside me. She was pissed, but so was I. I thought she was going to meet some guy on the app and ask him to make her crazy in bed. No. Fuck no. If she wanted a few good orgasms, I was going to be the one to deliver them.

I leaned in before she could push me away and claimed her mouth. She fisted her hand in the front of my shirt and pulled me closer. Lips parted and teeth clashed. Tongues mingled and fought for control. I put my hand on her thigh, needing the touch of her to ground me.

She moaned into my mouth and reached up to pull me

closer. I leaned over her, pressing her back to the wall. I shifted, my body getting closer to hers. Her thighs parted, begging me to bunch up her skirt and test how wet she was.

But I stopped.

The first time I felt Valentina's body wet and ready for me was not going to be in a booth at the end of a dance floor. It was going to be in private. Where she would know she was respected and cared for and not violated and insulted.

Her lips were swollen. Her eyes stayed closed. Her cheeks were flushed. She looked like she'd just had an orgasm, even though all we did was kiss. I felt the same, like I'd been run over by the pleasure bus and hit every single axle along the way.

"Bee," she whispered, part question, part fear.

"I'm not going anywhere." I pressed my forehead to hers and breathed her in. The scent of her arousal wafted toward me, begging me not to stop.

But I had to. I had to make sure she was asking me for the right reasons.

The part of me who'd wanted her forever said *who cared*, but the man I was had to know. If I fucked her because she was vulnerable and turned on, and she regretted it, I'd never forgive myself. But if I knew she was going into it with a clear mind, I'd have no reservations about filling Valentina and making her come until the only name she knew was mine.

"Why did you stop kissing me?"

"Because I need to know you want this to happen."

"I thought I was pretty clear."

I shook my head. "You want to add sex to your Quest for Pleasure. You said you joined that dating app. I'm more than willing to be your quest partner, but I need to know it's because you want to be with me. If we cross that line—"

"Haven't we already? That kiss was not the kind of kiss friends share. That was the kind of kiss that leads to sweaty bodies and bliss and more orgasms than I've had in the last year."

"I need to know you won't regret this. Nothing matters to me more than you do. I can't risk hurting you. Ever."

"I will not regret it."

"Why did you ask me tonight?"

"Because we're here. And dancing is sexy. And being in your arms has had me wet and ready for you all night."

"I feel the same, Vee, but I can't do it tonight. Not that I can't, but I won't. If you still want to next weekend, you can come to my place. I'll cook something, or order in, and we will make sure we aren't interrupted. But I need you to think about it. To know this is what you truly want."

She drew a shaky breath and finally nodded. Her eyes were clear and focused. "Don't make any other plans for next weekend."

I grinned. "I definitely won't."

15

———————

We headed back onto the dance floor and spent the rest of the evening torturing each other with touches and teases. I made mental notes about the places I touched her that made her gasp, and I made sure to kiss her every chance I got.

By the time we left, it was after midnight, and I decided not to push my luck by inviting her back to my place for time in the hot tub. We could do that next weekend, either before or after sex.

Or during. I'd never fucked anyone in the hot tub, but I'd always wanted to.

I reminded myself a hundred times before I dropped her off that she might say no. That it wasn't a guarantee. And that even if she agreed, it didn't mean we were together. We were best friends who had amazing physical chemistry and were exploring it.

Me being in love with her wasn't relevant.

"Thank you for tonight," Valentina whispered on her porch.

It was like all the nights I dreamed of having a date with

her in high school. Dropping her off on the porch and being quiet so we didn't get caught. Except we were trying not to get caught by her daughters instead of her father.

"I had a lot of fun."

She looked up at me through those endless dark lashes. Her brown eyes glittered in the porch lighting. I never thought of something like that as sexy before, but the way Valentina's eyes sparkled and the way her body moved toward mine, I'd never stand on a porch again and not think of her.

"Me, too. I can't wait for next weekend," she whispered.

The meaning was thick behind her words, just like my dick behind my zipper. I groaned and closed the distance between us, letting her feel how hungry I was for her. I said I wanted her to think about it, but that didn't mean I was going to play fair and keep my hands to myself between now and then.

She opened her lips for me as we connected, her tongue diving into my mouth first. I angled my head and sucked hard on her tongue. My hands went to her hips, then lower to cup her plush backside.

She rubbed herself against my erection, moaning at the hardness against her belly. Her hands fisted in my shirt again, holding me close.

I had no intention of going anywhere. Not for a while.

I tugged her closer, grinding my cock against her. She hitched her leg up, settling me between her thighs, and her breath caught.

"Vee?" I gasped, pulling back just enough to let the question hang between us.

"Please," she whispered. Begged.

My control was firmly in her grasp, which meant I no longer had it, and that one word was enough for me to stop thinking about not having her and start thinking about what she'd been telling me.

Sex had never been good. She'd never ached for it. She'd never wanted sex.

I had a chance. In that moment, I could be honorable and walk away, and wonder forever if that choice fucked up a future with her. Or I could give in and make her quiver and come and cry out my name. Right there on her porch.

"Away from the light," I hissed, moving her from in front of the door to the side, where a pair of chairs sat in the darkness.

Her body relaxed, like she'd been tight with anxiety, waiting for my response. She took the few steps out of the light and turned back to me, pulling me down to kiss her again.

I'd never felt so out of control with a woman before. Never been so lost in lust that I couldn't say no when she wanted something. But I'd never had the woman I loved begging me to make her come.

Her leg went wide again, her ankle hooking around my shin. She steadied herself on one foot while she rubbed against me. A whimper escaped her before a frustrated groan tore from her throat.

I was not going to lose her. Not in this. Not like this. She was going to know exactly how good we could be together.

I thrust against her, rubbing my erection against her center. Her dress resisted me, but the way she tensed told me it didn't matter. She was just as gone as I was.

"Vee," I whispered. I needed to hear her voice. To know she wasn't thinking about someone else. To know she knew I was the one making her crazy on the porch in the dark September night.

"Please, Bee. Oh, God." Her voice was strangled, needy, like nothing I'd ever heard before.

"Do you want me to make you come?"

"Yes."

"Have you been thinking about this all night?"

"Yes. Touching you. I need you."

"I want to hear you, Vee. Tell me what you want."

"You feel so good," she whispered.

Every thrust had her moaning, her breath catching, her body shivering. But it wasn't enough. It wasn't going to get her where she needed to be. I could feel the tension rising in her, the moment not coming quickly enough.

"Hold me," I told her.

Her arms went to my shoulders. I slammed against her, pressing her weight to the side of the house. She shook.

"Yes," she cried, her voice soft, but the intention of the word clear.

I lifted her leg higher, spreading her thighs farther apart. I pounded against her. Our clothes dulled the sensation, but I knew I wouldn't be able to stop the lust racing through me. I was going to come with her. I didn't care. I needed her.

"Oh, God," she hissed. "Yes. Brantley. Oh... my... YES!"

Her release was quick and sharp, like the bite on my shoulder. She trembled in my arms, aftershocks wracking her body and sending need pulsing through my blood.

The bite pulled me just far enough out of the moment for my orgasm to pause, and when Valentina looked up at me, I knew I'd missed my chance.

But I also knew it couldn't have possibly been better than seeing the blissed out look of pleasure on her face.

"So adding sex to the Quest for Pleasure is good?" I teased.

"So damn good," she whispered. "It's never been that good."

"Just imagine what it'll be like when we aren't dressed and on your porch."

She groaned and dropped her head to my shoulder. I barely contained the wince when she hit the already bruising bite.

"I really used to think people were lying about how good sex was. I used to think it was this big conspiracy theory to get people to reproduce. I didn't get why people would lose their minds for sex."

"And now?"

She looked up at me and grinned. "I'm starting to get it."

I smiled and gently pressed my lips to hers. She smiled against my mouth, kissing me back in a way that only lovers did. Without a second thought to what was coming after.

"I feel like I'm leaving you hanging. Or not hanging." She chewed her lip and looked up at me with those bedroom eyes that had me hanging on by a thread.

I could ask her to return the favor, and she would. But I didn't want it like that. I wanted to feel her skin against mine, to have her touch me before I let go. And it wasn't the right time for that.

"Maybe we can change that next weekend. If you want."

"Not now?"

I shook my head and kissed the tip of her nose. "I had a really good time tonight."

"Me, too."

I kissed her again, gently teasing her lips apart to get a taste of her. If it was going to be my last chance, I was going to enjoy every second of it.

"I should go inside," she said a minute later. "Get cleaned up and go to sleep."

I nodded and stepped back, releasing her so she could walk away. It shouldn't have been so hard, but it was. I wanted to go inside with her. Go to bed with her. Wake up with her.

Dammit. We hadn't even had sex, and I was picturing myself in her life. I wanted to be in her life.

As more than her best friend.

No. That's not what we were doing. She never said anything about a relationship. Sex. It was just sex. I was going to get her out of my system, and we would go back to being friends. It was fine. No futures. No forevers. Just friends.

"Thanks for tonight," I told her.

She cupped my cheek and held my gaze for a long moment. She nodded and whispered, "I couldn't do all this without you, Bee. You're amazing. Thank you."

"Happy to help."

She breathed a laugh, then unlocked her front door and stepped inside. She was gone.

ALL WEEK, Valentina and I sent each other flirty texts. It was new for us, but definitely not unwelcome. I tried to keep my texts on the border so they were still friendly, even if they toed the line toward sexy.

After practice Thursday, I stopped by Al's Hardware to pick up the cabinet hardware. Knox sent me a text saying they were in, and I could grab them so they weres at my house before the cabinets were delivered.

It was also a good excuse to get advice about things with Valentina.

Knox was behind the counter when I walked in, closing

the drawer. Before he looked up, he said, "We're closed."

"What is this, banker's hours?" I teased him. It was almost six, and he'd likely been behind the counter for twelve hours already.

Knox replied with his middle finger. "Are you coming to O'Kelley's tonight?"

I shook my head. "Hadn't planned on it. What's going on?"

"A bunch of guys get together every Thursday. Pretty much whoever's available."

"They still do that? I think I went once or twice. I didn't know it was a regular thing. And I'm not super close with those guys."

"So? That's why you go. Talk, drink a beer, get to know them. It's good for business."

"I'm a teacher. I don't own a business."

Knox rolled his eyes. "Fine. It's good for my business. Come talk about how great I am."

"Yes, your customer service is impeccable," I droned.

Knox snorted. "Only for you." He came around the end of the counter and turned up his nose. "Dear God, did you get caught by a skunk?"

"Nope. This is what a man smells like when he works his muscles."

"A dead animal? You need a shower."

"No shit. I was going to do that once I grabbed the hardware from you."

"Good. Because you need it."

"In the plans."

"Then come to O'Kelley's. We can talk about whatever has you all twisted up."

"Who said I'm all twisted up?"

"Your face."

I flipped him off, then followed him to the storage lockers as he chuckled. He handed over the box of hardware and told me he'd see me soon. We walked out together, and I drove home, debating on bailing even as I knew it would be good to talk to someone else about Valentina. They didn't need to know it was her.

It wasn't long before I was walking into O'Kelley's, smelling clean so Knox didn't give me more shit. I took a seat at the bar next to Xavier and smiled when he greeted me.

"Coach P! Nice to see you off the field." Xavier slapped me on the back.

"Thanks, Xavier. Knox said I should come. I hope it's okay."

"Always," Hudson said, nodding from the other side of the bar. "What can I get you?"

"Beer. Whatever's on tap. Pale ale or IPA?"

Hudson nodded and held a glass under a spout, filling it with expert hands. He set it in front of me and said, "First one's on me. Glad you joined us."

"Thanks."

"Ian was just telling us Blake's talking about having another baby, but he still hasn't been able to get the first one out of their room. Any advice?" Xavier asked.

I looked down the line at the other men. I knew Xavier since McJenna was on the cross-country team. Everyone in town knew Hudson Grant and Trent MacKellar. Trent was married to Ian Jameson's sister, and Ian built custom wooden boats and was beyond talented. Gavin Holbrook owned the MacKellar Cove Inn with his wife, and Sebastian Parks was married to Gavin's sister. Knox was between Sebastian and Colin Jones, who owned the Jones Family Maple Farm.

All of them were smart, talented men who helped to make MacKellar Cove what it was. I'd grown up with a lot of them, met more, and knew the wives and girlfriends of most of them. Small town living was one of my favorite things about MacKellar Cove.

"Well, since I've neither had kids nor a wife, I'm probably the last one to ask for any advice on either," I told them.

Xavier grinned at me while the others continued the conversation. "How are things going?"

"Good. Team is great. How's McJenna liking it?"

"She's pleasantly surprised that she's having fun. She fought hard against Bianca, but she's doing better than she thought. It helps that you and Coach M have created such a welcoming environment."

"That's the goal. We have kids who are die-hard runners and will end up running marathons for fun and going to college on scholarships, and we have kids who will develop a lifetime habit of running to stay healthy or reduce stress or some other reason. There are always a few who decide it's not right for them, and that's okay, too. We want to make it a good experience for the kids while they're with us."

"You've definitely done that. I don't think J would have joined if Bianca hadn't spoken so highly of you. She said you're like family," Xavier said.

I nodded and sipped my beer to give myself a minute. "Valentina and I grew up together. Graduated from MCHS together. I've known Bianca and Samantha their entire lives."

"Nice. It's good for them to have someone around who supports them. Especially after Dawson turned out to be such a dick."

"Dawson was always a dick," I spat. "I just didn't realize

he was a big enough one that he would throw away a relationship with Valentina."

Xavier smirked, a gleam in his eye that said he was goading me.

"What?"

"Nothing. You're pretty invested in them."

"They deserve better."

"It sounds like they have better."

The back of my neck tingled. "What does that mean?"

"It means how long have you been in love with Valentina?" Trent asked.

I swept my hair back from my face and shook my head. "I'm not."

"Bullshit," Hudson said.

I glared up at him. He smirked back.

"Is that what you wanted to talk about earlier?" Knox asked.

He got a glare, too.

"We're all friends here," Ian said, leaning forward to catch my eye. "And don't let any of these assholes fool you. We've all been right where you're sitting. Including me."

"Which is where exactly?" I asked him, not willing to admit defeat just yet.

"Crazy in love with a woman who can't see how amazing she is or understand why you'd tie yourself to her forever. Basically beating your head against the wall and wishing you could stop, but stopping loving her would be like stopping breathing. You'd die if you succeeded."

I looked at the others down the line. Aside from Knox, the rest of them didn't look like they were smirking as much as I thought. They looked a lot more understanding. "Yeah, well, all of you convinced the woman you love to give you a chance. Valentina just wants to be friends."

"Are you sure about that?" Hudson asked.

I looked at him and narrowed my eyes. "That's what she's told me. Why?"

Hudson shrugged. "Just not the way Anna tells it. She's pretty convinced Valentina's just as gone as you are."

I shook my head. "Not a chance. Things are crazy hot between us, but—"

"Whoa, seriously?" Xavier asked. He smiled like he was proud.

"I'm not going to share the details," I growled.

"Don't want them. Just happy to hear it. Karissa thinks very highly of you. So does Goldie and everyone else who's mentioned you. Valentina is a good person. Great person. She should have someone good in her life, and if that's you, then good for both of you."

I glared at Xavier for a long moment, but he didn't smile or crack a joke or do anything that made me think he was being a jerk. "Thanks."

"So, back to the *crazy hot* thing," Knox said. "He might not want details, but I do."

I flipped him off, and the others laughed.

"We let Knox come because he has all the good building supplies in town, but being single means his perspective is a bit skewed," Ian said. He jerked his chin toward Knox, who rolled his eyes at Ian.

"You're all living vicariously through me," Knox said, puffing out his chest.

I watched as the others shook their heads and sipped their beers. That was what I was after. No vicarious or live one-night stands. No anonymous hook-ups. No morning after in the dark trying to sneak out. I wanted a future. A life. A commitment to Valentina.

"Does she know you're in love with her?" Sebastian asked.

I shook my head. "She'd cut line and run if she did."

"I thought the same with Zoey. She was just divorced when we got back together. It was supposed to be fun for a few weeks while she was in town, but I couldn't let her go when it was time."

"Finley and I met because we had a one-night stand. I was a first class asshole to her, and she finally let me in so I could prove I was worthy of her." Trent MacKellar was the richest guy in MacKellar Cove. His net worth was likely three times that of everyone else in the bar combined.

"Still working on that," Hudson told Trent.

Trent grinned and nodded. "Every damn day. She's worth it."

"So, what are you going to do with Valentina?" Gavin asked.

I shook my head. "I wish I knew."

"Be there for her," Sebastian said.

"Show up for her," Trent said.

"Don't give up on her," Gavin said.

"Be vulnerable," Hudson said.

"Above it all, be her friend first. If you want her in your life, you have to be willing to walk away from a relationship if that's not what she wants. I don't think that's going to be the case, but you need to be prepared for it," Ian said.

I nodded at all their advice, knowing they were all right. "Thank you. I guess having Knox as a friend comes in handy once in a while."

The guys laughed, and the conversation changed from my love life to sports. I pulled out my phone and sent Valentina a quick text, knowing it was the right thing to do.

16

VALENTINA

> Thinking about you tonight. I hope you're
> doing something that brings you pleasure. I
> hope you always are, Vee. I love you.

THE TEXT FROM BRANTLEY SAT ON MY PHONE. I READ IT WHEN he sent it, but I was helping Bianca with homework, and then I didn't know how to reply. Flirty almost seemed appropriate after the way we'd been talking all week, but it didn't feel like that kind of moment. It felt different. Like what I said would determine what happened between us.

I still wasn't sure what I wanted to happen between us. Not beyond the weekend. The weekend I knew. I wanted to sleep with Brantley. I wanted to know what claw the sheets sex was like, and I knew he would deliver. The man gave me an orgasm without even touching my skin, on my front porch! I was looking forward to learning what he was capable of without clothes on.

I also trusted him. I knew Brantley would not just fuck me and kick me out. We would be able to talk. To be honest. To stay friends after.

Did I want that?

I shook my head. That was never in question. I wanted Brantley in my life. Toeing the line was dangerous, but if I was forced to make a choice, I'd always want him as my friend.

When the girls went to bed, I turned off all the lights and went to my room. I stared at the text and finally typed out a response.

> Always thinking about you. Spent the evening with the girls. Tried another new recipe. Not a success, but not the worst thing we've had this month. I hope you did something that brought you pleasure tonight. I love you, Bee.

I set my phone down and went to the bathroom to get ready for bed. When I crawled into bed, I picked my phone up to see if he'd replied. He had.

> Sorry it wasn't a winner. Next time. I went to O'Kelley's with Knox. It was a good night.

My body flushed with a combination of jealousy and possessiveness. Knox was single. So was Brantley. If they were at O'Kelley's, did that mean they were looking for women?

> Sounds fun. Out on the prowl?

> Ha! Not even a little. Met a bunch of guys. Hudson said they get together every Thursday. Invited me back.

It wasn't fair that I was relieved. I shouldn't wish for him to be single and lonely like I was. I wanted him to be happy. I just wanted him to, maybe, be happy with me.

Anna mentioned it. I forgot. Nice to have
friends to hang out with.

Yep. Friends are always good. But I missed
my best friend. How was your day?

It was good. Uneventful. The new blondies I
made were a big hit today.

Ah, so you did do something that brought
you pleasure.

I did. And I spent time with my girls, which
is always nice. Bianca even put the dishes
away without me asking, and Samantha did
a load of laundry. I asked if they were feeling
okay.

LOL! That was my first thought, too.

Great minds.

Definitely.

I'm also enjoying talking to you right now.

Me, too, Vee. I always enjoy talking to you.

Thanks. Are we still on for the weekend?

You know I'm leaving that completely up to
you. No pressure from me.

Bianca is spending the night with McJenna,
and Samantha is spending the night
with Amy.

So you'll have the house to yourself.

I'm hoping the house will be empty. I
thought I was coming to your place.

Bring your suit. We can use the hot tub.
Might be the last time this fall.

Sounds perfect.

I yawned and looked at the clock. It was late, far later than Brantley usually stayed up.

I just saw the time. Don't you need to go to sleep?

I was talking to you.

You should have said something. I don't want to be the reason you don't get enough sleep.

No worries. I'm always going to be here for you, Vee.

I know. Thank you for that. But for now, get some sleep.

You, too. Talk tomorrow.

Yep.

I set the phone down and turned off the lamp, my lips curling up at the thought of a full night alone with Brantley.

It was going to be a good weekend.

"THIS IS THE WORST WEEKEND!" Bianca shouted as she stomped into the house after their meet Saturday.

It was Homecoming weekend, and Bianca was going to the dance with McJenna. Both girls were going without dates. At least, that was the plan.

"Why are you upset that McJenna has a date?" I asked her.

"Because we agreed! We said we would go together. Screw the patriarchy and all that. We don't need men in our lives to make us feel whole. And now she has a date. What am I supposed to do with that, Mom?"

I drew a breath because teenage drama was so big and overwhelming and stupid. God, it was so stupid. Not because it didn't matter, but because none of the things they were so focused on would be on their radar in five or ten years.

But at the moment, it was the biggest issue on the planet.

"Are you two still going together?"

Bianca shrugged. "Yeah, I think so."

"And are you still staying the night at her house?" I crossed my fingers and prayed.

Bianca nodded. "Yes."

"So, why is this a problem?"

Bianca huffed. "Because she's going to be dancing with Kevin. She isn't just going to hang out with me."

"What about Andrew? Are you going to dance with him?"

"I don't know." Her lips tried to curl up at the edges, and she went from angry rhino to coy mouse.

"Tonight is supposed to be fun. It's supposed to be a chance to dress up in beautiful dresses and dance and be silly and enjoy a night with your friends. Did you say no to Andrew because of McJenna?"

"No. Not totally. No one asked her, and I didn't want it to be weird, but I also just... don't know about dating."

"I thought you were willing to consider it."

"Consider it, yeah. But jump in the deep end? Nope."

"Why is going to a dance with Andrew jumping in the deep end?"

"Because she loves him," Samantha answered. She'd been hanging out behind me, silent through the conversation, but she clearly was paying attention and had the missing pieces.

"Shut up!" Bianca screamed. "You don't know what the hell you're talking about!"

Samantha made kissing noises toward Bianca, and Bianca lunged at Sam. I got between them and told Sam to go to her room to start getting ready while I talked Bianca down from killing her sister.

Once Sam was out of the living room, Bianca stopped fighting me and went to the couch.

"What if I pick the wrong guy, Mom? What if Andrew is like Dad?"

"What if he is? What's the worst thing that can happen?"

She shrugged. "He cheats on me."

"And then what?"

She shrugged again. "I dunno."

"Well, I do. You pick yourself up, brush yourself off, and get the hell back out there. Because no man has the right to destroy you."

"But Dad destroyed you."

I shook my head. "No. He didn't. He broke me a little. More than a little. It hurt. My pride was wounded and my heart was bruised, but I am not willing to hide from love in the hope that I never get hurt again."

"You're not?"

"No. I'm not. I'm not out there dating half the men in town, but once I've figured out who I want in my life, the kind of man I'm going to choose this time, I'll be open to finding him."

"I want a man like Uncle Brantley."

I nodded as my heart fluttered in agreement. "Uncle Brantley thinks very highly of Andrew. He said if you were his daughter, he'd want you to date Andrew."

"He said that?"

"He did. I don't think denying yourself happiness is really a slam against the patriarchy. It's letting them get away with it. It's denying yourself something that brings you happiness. How is that a move in the right direction?"

Bianca shrugged, looking years younger than sixteen. "Did I screw up, Mom?"

"I don't know, sweetie. You can ask. And you can try to fix things."

She thought for a second, then nodded and hurried toward her room.

TWO HOURS LATER, they were both dressed, their hair was perfect, and the night was about to start. Everyone was coming to our house for pictures since we all knew each other, so it wasn't long before things got busy inside. I had out treats and snacks for the parents and kids to munch on while we waited for all of them to arrive.

"Are we ready for pictures?" Goldie asked me.

I looked around the room and nodded. "I think everyone's here."

Goldie stepped forward. "Let's take some pictures, everyone. Ladies first. In front of the fireplace."

Goldie directed the pictures, lining the kids up how she wanted them. We took pictures of all the girls, all the boys, siblings, dates, and each kid on their own. It was a zoo, but it went quickly thanks to Goldie's instructions.

Bianca walked over to me as the last of the kids were getting pictures taken and hugged me.

"What was that for?"

"For encouraging me to be true to myself."

"You should always be true to yourself," I told her. I cupped her jaw and made sure she was paying attention. "The only person you should never let down is you."

"Thanks, Mom." She was quiet for a minute, then said, "I called Andrew."

"Oh yeah? And what did he say?"

"He said he was hoping I changed my mind and wanted to be my date tonight."

"Is that so? Well, I like him even more now."

She beamed. "Me, too."

"So, does that mean things with McJenna are okay again?"

Bianca nodded. "They were okay before, but I was jealous. I wanted to say yes to Andrew, but then I got scared. I thought J understood that and was going to be my partner for the dance, but when she accepted her date, I..."

"I get it. It's not always easy to say what you want. But it all worked out."

One of the parents had a large van and offered to drive all the kids. They called out that they all needed to get outside.

"You should go," I told Bianca.

"Thanks, Mom. Have a fun night at home alone."

My body heated. "I will. Have fun at McJenna's. Be good for Xavier and Karissa."

"I will. Love you."

"Love you."

Samantha came over as Bianca was walking out and hugged me and said good night.

I waited for everyone to pull out of my driveway, sleepover bags securely in the vehicles of the other parents. I went to my room and took out the tiniest bikini I owned. The one I had since college that would be indecent on its best day, but that I hadn't been able to bring myself to part with hoping that maybe one day I could wear it again. I threw that into a bag, smiling that today was the day, then added a change of clothes, a scarf, and my toothbrush.

And all the nerves I could find. Those little fuckers were dancing all around me.

I took a breath and reminded myself of what I just told Bianca. I needed to be true to myself. And the most true thing at the moment was that I wanted Brantley Pierce.

His porch light was on when I pulled into his driveway. My heart raced as I walked up the path. Everything inside me was ready for the night, and for whatever was going to happen between us.

I rang the bell and waited a minute for Brantley to open the door. He wore well-worn jeans that cupped and hugged him in all the right places and a white tee that stretched tight across his chest and left very little to the imagination. His feet were bare, but his hands were not empty.

"Hey," he said, like it was any other night. "I was just finishing with the grill. Come on."

He turned and left me to follow him. Unable to resist, I trailed him outside, leaving my bag at the front door and walking through the house to where he was on the back deck.

Tiny lights were strung from the gutters to the posts at the edge of the deck, creating a magical glow over the whole space. The hot tub was open and bubbling, the water glowing blue with an underwater light.

A charcuterie board was on the table, under a food tent

to keep the last remaining bugs of the season off the meats and cheeses artfully displayed on a slate board I'd never seen before.

"You went all out," I said.

He turned to meet my gaze. "Anything for you."

His words both warmed me and teased me.

I picked up a few pieces of cheese and some sliced meat and popped them into my mouth. The spicy bite of the meat melted into the softness of the cheese. Neither overwhelmed the other, but worked together to tease my mouth and make me want more.

"This right here is an exercise in pleasure," I told Brantley.

He turned off the grill and set two plates on the dining table I was standing next to. Two steaks were on one plate and foil-wrapped vegetables were on the other. "I hoped you'd like it."

"Did you put this together?" I gestured to the slate board.

He nodded. "It looked good, so I started grabbing things I hoped would pair well together. With the steaks and asparagus, I thought something like that would be a good compliment."

"Look at you being a foodie."

He grinned. "I've learned a few things from you over the years."

"You've paid attention."

"All the time, Vee."

My breath caught in my chest. We were really doing this. We were really going to have sex. It was real.

"Nothing has to happen," he whispered. He'd stepped back a bit, putting distance between us that wasn't there a minute ago. "We're just two friends having dinner."

"We both know that's not what this is."

"That's all it has to be. I don't expect anything from any woman, but especially not from you. I love you, and I'd never forgive myself if I pushed something or stepped over a line or changed everything between us and we couldn't get back to who we are."

"I feel the same."

He nodded. "Okay. Then let's sit down and eat, and we'll go from there."

I nodded back and took my seat. With the truth out in the open, we talked like we always had. He asked if the girls were excited about Homecoming, and I told him about Bianca and Andrew. When we finished eating, Brantley carried our plates into the kitchen and set them in a bin on top of a folding table.

"That's how you do dishes?" I asked.

He chuckled. "It works for now. I use the utility sink to wash and carry them back to the bedroom at the end for storage."

"How long are you going to live like this?"

He shrugged. "The cabinets should be here in a few weeks. They're on order. After they're set, someone will measure for the countertops. Those won't take as long. It's moving a lot faster than I expected."

"I love the blue. It's gorgeous. Your painter did an excellent job."

"Well, thank you."

"You painted this?" I asked.

He nodded.

"Who knew you had so many skills?"

"You have no idea," he said.

His words and his tone sent a shiver down my spine, and I was right back to a quivering mess of hormones and need.

"Sorry," he muttered. "I didn't mean to mess this all up."

"You're not," I told him, putting my hand on his arm before he could walk outside again. "I came here with every intention of ending up in your bed, Bee. But just like you won't force me, I won't force you."

"Trust me, I'm more than willing, Vee."

"Good." I looked up at him with what I hoped was a sexy look and said, "How about that hot tub?"

He swallowed audibly and nodded. "All warmed up and ready for us."

"Should I change here or go to the bathroom?"

"You can use my bedroom if you want."

I nodded. I grabbed my bag from by the front door and followed Brantley down the hallway to his room. I knew which one was his, but I'd never spent much time in there. It was clean and smelled good. The walls were a soft gray color. A green comforter laid across the well-made bed. The door to his bathroom was open, but it was too dark to get a good look inside.

"Let me grab a suit and change in another room. I'll meet you out there."

I watched him move around his room, pulling a pair of gray swim trunks from a drawer and heading right back to the door. He pulled it closed behind him, leaving me alone in his space.

I exhaled slowly, knowing my nerves were useless. It was Brantley. I trusted him, and I adored him, and it was just sex. Just another experiment in my Quest for Pleasure.

I set my bag on his bed and unzipped it. I found my bathing suit, regretting the choice I made when I pulled it out. It was tiny. Miniscule. It was barely going to cover anything.

But it was all I had.

I took off the jeans and top I wore to his house and

folded them into my bag. I glanced at the door and made sure it was closed, even though I knew it was, then put my bra and panties with the rest of my clothes.

The bikini bottom was the kind that tied at the hips. That was the only reason it still sort of fit me. Not that the tiny triangle masquerading as a bikini bottom actually fit, but it covered my pubic hair and my entrance, so I guess it worked. The top wasn't any better, barely covering my nipples and leaving most of my breasts exposed.

I turned on the light in his bathroom and gasped. It was bigger than I expected, and high quality. The rainfall shower-head was straight out of my dreams, and the double vanity with a full mirror was smart and essential when two people shared a bathroom.

My throat tightened at the thought of Brantley one day sharing the bathroom with someone.

Friends. Just friends.

I shook my head and forced my gaze to the mirror. The red bikini popped against my brown skin. The strings almost disappeared into the folds of my body, but I refused to be embarrassed by the way I looked. If Brantley was turned off by my rolls, he could go fuck himself instead of me.

I left my bag on the floor of his bedroom, in the corner where it wouldn't be in the way, and left his room. It was quiet in the house, but I heard the water bubbling outside. I followed it to the deck, hoping I'd find Brantley out there.

I saw him before he noticed me. He looked like he was talking to himself. When I stepped onto the deck, he stopped and looked up at me.

"Jesus. Fuck. I was wrong, Valentina. I don't think I can say no to you. If you aren't completely sure about this, you need to leave right now."

17

———

The pained growl in his voice had me pausing. But once his words sank in, I knew I made the right choice. I continued forward, my gaze locked on his as I walked toward him.

He stood when I reached the edge of the hot tub. Water rippled down his body, catching on his chest hair and creating new pathways to his shorts. My gaze followed the water, stopping when I reached his full erection, tenting his wet shorts and telling me I wasn't the only one ready for this.

Brantley took my hand in his and held it tight while I climbed the steps to the raised hot tub. He didn't let go as I joined him in the hot water. My body flashed hot, and not because of the water. This was happening.

"You're so fucking gorgeous," he said.

The words skittered up my spine and slid south again, landing between my wet thighs. I trembled.

His gaze skipped around my body, landing on my saggy breasts barely contained in the triangles, then lower to where my belly hung over the edge of the even tinier bottom. His grip tightened the longer he looked at me.

"I meant what I said, Vee. I'm not sure I'm going to be able to stop myself. I've never seen you in so little and—"

I reached behind myself and untied the bow that held up my top. I held his gaze and the strings, knowing he knew what I was doing.

The world paused. We didn't breathe or speak or think. I waited, needing him to say yes. To agree. To do something before I bared my breasts to him.

"Fucking hell, let me see them," he growled.

I let go of the ties, and my top fell.

My breath was stuck in my throat while Brantley stared at my exposed boobs. I watched him as he just stared, wondering if I should cover myself up again. Just as I moved to do so, he lunged at me.

He lifted my body effortlessly in the water. He spun us and sat on one of the benches beneath the surface, bringing my breasts to his eye-level. He buried his face between them and cupped them around his cheeks.

Then he turned his head and sucked one nipple into his mouth. He groaned as he licked my nipple, his hips pumping against me under the water.

I clutched his head, running my fingers through his long hair and using it to hold him where I needed him. Where I wanted him. Where I ached for him.

He growled at me and moved to the other nipple. He bit down, making me cry out before he flicked the tip with his tongue.

"Oh, God," I whispered.

"I know I'm not being fair right now, but I don't know how long I can hold out. I promise you, I'll make tonight good. But first I need to fuck you hard."

"Please," I whimpered. The raw edge in his voice was unlike anything I'd ever heard before. His need came through in his tone, demanding and sure, contrary to my lust-filled begging. I didn't care how he fucked me as long as he did.

He lifted our bodies in the water and eased me off his lap. He reached for a condom and put the edge between his teeth, but I stopped him.

"I want... I shouldn't even ask you this, but I'm on the pill. I want to feel just you inside me. I was tested after Dawson, and it's been more than a year. You can say no, but—"

I didn't get a chance to finish my sentence before he hauled me against him and thrust his tongue between my lips. I hung on, knowing I couldn't do anything more than that.

His kiss erased every other kiss I'd ever experienced in my life. It shredded all hope I had of coming out of this on the other end without wanting more from him. It ruined me. And it was just a damn kiss.

One hand skimmed my back before pausing at the other tie for my top. He tugged it, then pulled to remove the scrap of fabric from between us. His hands circled my ribs and cupped my breasts, pinching my sensitive nipples and caressing my boobs.

He shook as he inhaled, drawing back enough to look at my eyes. "I need you to know one thing before we do this. It's not a favor. It's not a duty. I didn't agree to this because you're my friend. I'm here because I love you. Because you're the most beautiful woman I've ever known. Because you're strong and I've wanted you since we were in high school. Because I'd never forgive myself if I didn't learn what it felt like to be inside you. So don't act like I'm not a selfish bastard, because that's exactly what I am right now. I'm going to enjoy the hell out of tonight. I promise you that, Vee."

I nodded once, my throat as tight as my core. I ached to have him inside me. To feel him stretching me. To come with him over and over again.

He kissed me again, a soft kiss that flipped the script on everything that had happened so far. I expected hard and demanding and animalistic. But this was gentle. Sweet. Loving.

Until his hand pressed my thighs apart. "Let me feel that pussy."

My legs moved apart for him, my bathing suit falling into the water. I didn't even feel him untie it, but he must have while he was distracting me with his kisses.

One finger pressed inside me, and he groaned. "You're tight, Vee. I'm not going to fit right now, but I promise you I'll make sure you're ready for me before I fuck you."

I nodded.

"Do you like me talking to you? Or would you rather I stop?"

"I like it," I whispered.

"But you're not used to it."

I shook my head, even though he didn't need an answer.

"When I get you in my bed, I'm not going to be able to talk because I'm going to lick you until you come on my tongue, but right now, I'm enjoying the way you squeeze my finger when I tell you what I'm going to do to you."

"Please."

He moved to the side and sat down, drawing me over him. I straddled his hips, his hand still between my thighs. His erection brushed against my butt, his trunks still separating us.

"How do you like to come, Valentina? Do you like it inside or on your clit?"

"Both," I confessed.

"Nice. That's going to be fun. How about inside first? Do you want to ride my hand a little bit, sweetheart? Want to fuck it for me?"

I leveraged myself up in the water and lowered back down. His finger slammed deeper into me, and I moaned.

"So, good. Again, Valentina. Fuck my hand."

I did it again, my breasts bouncing in his face as I slammed my body down on his hand. It wasn't long before I tightened around his finger, then he changed the game by adding a second one and I came hard.

"Oh, God. Yes!"

"There you go, beautiful. There's a little more space. Let's see if I can get a third finger into you when your clit comes for me." His thumb pressed onto my clit, and my legs shook. "Ooh, you like that. Come for me, Vee. Come again."

He rubbed my clit and pumped his fingers into me, sending me flying again in record time. My body tingled. I wasn't done, but neither was he.

"I can't wait to taste you," he whispered. "To feel your pussy tighten around my tongue and have you flood my lips the way you're flooding my hand right now." He groaned and pulled his hand from me. He brought it to the surface and slid his fingers into his mouth. "Oh, fuck. It's not enough, but you taste good. Come for me some more."

His hand went below the water, and he fingered his way between my legs again. Three fingers slammed inside me this time, with his thumb pressed tight to my clit.

"Brantley," I moaned, sinking down as my body pulsed around him and began to throb.

"Just one more, then I'm going to fuck you, Vee. Give me one more."

His gritted words and punishing rhythm sent lust pouring through my veins. I'd never felt so wanted, so desired in my entire life. I'd never had a man begging me to come for him, let alone begging me to come a third time before he fucked me.

The dirty words were new, and the man I straddled was a surprise a minute. I'd never imagined Brantley Pierce to be the man I begged for an orgasm, but the words fell from my lips, anyway. "Make me come, Brantley. I can't wait to feel you inside me."

He grunted and shifted. He caught one bouncing breast with a free hand and brought it to his lips. He bit down on my nipple and I screamed. I knew we were outside and all his neighbors could hear me, but I couldn't care. I was so beyond blissed out, I couldn't care.

"Fuck me, Vee."

His hissed words were accompanied by the withdrawal of his hand. I thought he was done, upset or angry that I made so much noise, then he replaced his hand with his erection and slammed me down on top of him.

His strangled cry mixed with mine. He stretched me to the edge of my body's limits, then stretched me farther. The tinge of pain mixed with the unfamiliar throb of pleasure and nearly sent me over the edge.

"Brantley," I whispered.

He looked up at me, lust fogging his gaze before he realized emotion clouded mine. "What's wrong?"

He moved like he was going to pull out, but I clamped my thighs around his and lowered my body. "Don't. Please. You haven't even moved and you feel so good. I didn't mean to cry, but this is just..." My body rippled around him, and he closed his eyes. "Thank you for giving me this. I know it was a huge ask, but I've never felt this good in my entire life."

He sucked in a shaky breath and met my gaze. "Trust me, Vee. I'm right there with you. Not all sex is like this. I've never been with anyone that makes me feel the things you do."

"Thanks," I said, knowing he was just saying what he thought I wanted to hear.

He cupped my jaw and lifted my gaze to his. "I mean that. You can't imagine how much I mean that."

I swallowed roughly and nodded. Brantley didn't lie to me. He never had. There was no reason he would now.

"Do you want...?" he trailed off, letting me make the decision. For all his doubts that he couldn't stop, he was buried inside me and still asking if I was sure I wanted him.

I leaned in until my breasts flattened against his chest. I slid my hands around his neck. I pressed my lips to his ear and whispered, "Fuck me hard, Bee."

His hands locked on my hips. He slammed up into me, hitting me so deep I thought I was going to choke on him. I unleashed something in him with my words, something I didn't know I wanted until he did it.

Water splashed around us, waves pushing it over the edge of the hot tub, over our bodies. He pounded into me, using the water to aid in moving me how he wanted me. I flopped around, unable to control myself as everything became Brantley's.

I was his. In every way, I was his. I'd never understood what it felt like to belong to another person, but I finally got it. I'd been telling him forever that I loved him, but feeling him inside me, his cock throbbing and rubbing along all my walls, I knew those words were so much bigger than I ever believed them to be.

Brantley Pierce was my best friend. He was my lover. And he was my forever.

Everything tightened inside me with that realization. My body pulled him in deeper, wanting to hold him inside me forever.

"Vee, I'm having a hard time holding back. Are you going to come for me again? Are you going to let me feel that pussy come all over my cock?"

I snapped when he whispered his dirty words into my ear. I moaned and dragged my nails down his back. My teeth landed on his shoulder, and I bit down hard. My body released, flooding around him as he slammed into me and roared.

His cock twitched inside me, pumping everything he had into me. The water slowly settled as we stopped moving, holding each other in the darkness of the night.

Brantley nuzzled against my neck and kissed my throat. He trembled, but his lips never left my skin, like he was keeping himself from saying something.

"I had no idea," I whispered.

"Had no idea what?" he asked, not lifting his head.

"I had no idea it could be so good. That if sex was with someone amazing, it was that much better."

"You are amazing," he whispered.

"So are you, Bee. Thank you."

He chuckled. "Like I told you before, I'm just a selfish bastard who's always wanted you. There's no medal waiting for me."

"I think you deserve one. Best orgasm producer in town. Or best orgasm giver in the state. Ooh, maybe best Pleasure Quest partner in the world."

He hugged me tight and pressed his lips to my collarbone. "I'm happy to help. Should we head inside? It's getting a little cold."

He got out without waiting for me to say anything, which felt less than amazing. He grabbed a towel and dried his hair and rubbed it over his body, then wrapped it around his waist. Only then did he look up at me.

"What did I say?" I asked.

He shook his head and avoided my gaze again. "Nothing. Let's go inside. I don't want you to get cold out here."

"I'm not going inside until you tell me what I said. What changed. We were fine a second ago, and now you're all pissed off."

He clenched his jaw and looked away from me. When he looked back, his eyes were blazing. "We just had this amazing sex, the best of my entire fucking life, and you trivialized it to your pleasure quest. It was transactional. That's not what this was for me, Vee. I told you before that it wasn't about that for me. But it was for you. You took something that meant something to me and made me feel like you're going to leave some cash on my nightstand when you leave."

"Are you serious?" I asked.

He glared at me, then shook his head. "Don't worry about it, Vee. It was fun while it lasted." He turned to walk back inside.

"Don't you dare walk away from me," I growled. I stomped out of the hot tub and stalked over to him bare-ass naked, not bothering with a towel.

His gaze drifted down my dripping wet body, but he clamped his eyes closed and drew a deep breath.

"We don't do this. We don't throw caustic words around and walk away. I spent twenty-two years married to a man who did that kind of thing to me. Who turned around every-thing I said, then made me feel like shit for it."

"I—"

I held up a hand for him to stop. "I'm talking right now. You're right. What I said was... not okay. Because this wasn't transactional for me either. This was special. It was sexy and beautiful and I've never felt that good in my life. What I said was careless and wrong, because being with you is so much more than finding out what brings me pleasure. This was selfish for me, too. When we were in high school, I liked you, but I was too young to understand what that could mean. With Dawson, I never questioned things. But when you kissed me, and when we went dancing last week and you made me come on my porch, I used my Quest for Plea-sure as an excuse. I didn't want you to reject me. Asking you scared the hell out of me because you mean everything to me, Brantley. I knew this was crossing a line we couldn't uncross. I knew it would change things between us. But I was willing to risk that because I wanted to feel the kind of pleasure you gave me just once. I wanted to know how good my body could feel in the hands of a man who knew what he was doing. A man who cared about me. And if I ruined our friendship for good, I will regret that forever, but I will always carry tonight with me. I will always carry you with me. Because I will never forget the way you made me feel."

He exhaled slowly, taking a step toward me. I retreated out of reflex, but he reached for me. "I need you to be honest with me. Always. Even if you think I'm going to reject you. But I will promise you right now, I'm never going to reject you, Vee. Never."

"But—"

"Never. Now, if I made you mad and you want to go,

that's fine. If not, we can go inside and dry off and I can make you wet all over again."

"Option two, please," I said without hesitation.

"Thank fuck for that," he whispered against my lips. He pulled me in close, my naked chest against his. He lifted me until my feet hung off the ground, then he carried me inside.

He stalked through the living room and kept going to his bedroom. He didn't set me down until we were in his bathroom.

"Did you want to take a shower?"

He nodded. "The saltwater from the hot tub will leave a film on our skin. I was going to clean you up, then make you dirty again."

Wetness flooded from me, and I moaned. "Yes, please."

He grinned and dropped his towel, and I got my first good look at him. His cock stood straight out, long and thick. So damn thick. A nest of dark blond hair circled his cock. It thinned as it moved north, away from his dick to his belly and chest. His shadow of a beard led to upturned lips and laughing eyes. "Are you checking me out?"

I nodded. "You're a work of art."

He grabbed my ass and hauled me against him. "Same, Vee. So fucking beautiful."

His mouth covered mine, and he led us into the shower. Hot water ran over us as we kissed and touched and teased.

How had I gone so long without this in my life? And how was I going to survive without it?

18

BRANTLEY

MY TONGUE WAS GOING NUMB. NOT THAT IT WAS GOING TO stop me. I'd been licking Valentina for the better part of an hour. Long, lazy, slow licks that had her body weeping come and readying for me. Every so often I'd flick my tongue over her clit, and she'd jump, then I'd go right back to the licks that were torturing her.

I came so close to telling her how much I loved her when we were outside, but I stopped myself just in time. She said she wanted to feel good, so I was making her feel good.

I'd lost count of the number of orgasms she had. Between the hot tub and the shower, I stopped caring. All I knew was she would feel me for days, and if I was lucky, she'd want more.

"I want you inside me again," she whispered.

"Is that your way of asking me to hurry up?" I peered up at her over her rounded belly. The lighter brown stretch marks on her belly made me jealous. It was irrational, but I wanted to be the man who got her pregnant and shared a family with her. Knowing those weren't from my baby made me want to mark her in another way.

She smirked at me and raised one eyebrow. "Not exactly. Then I'd say make me come and fuck me hard."

"But you're not saying that?"

She shrugged. "Maybe I'm saying this feels good, and you inside me feels good."

I grinned. "So you're indecisive."

She shook her head. "Oh, no. I've definitely decided you are the master and I'm going to simply enjoy all the pleasure you give me tonight."

"I'm getting just as much out of this," I admitted.

"You're getting pleasure from licking me?"

I nodded and blew on her damp flesh, watching as it clenched. "Seeing your pussy like this. Watching it drip for me. Licking all your come. Holding your thighs back so I can taste you. And then being able to kiss you and hold you and slam my dick deep inside you and hear you scream my name? Trust me, I'm enjoying this."

"Brantley," she whispered.

"Yes, beautiful?"

"Make me come and fuck me hard."

I grinned as I lowered my lips to her body again. She dripped, and I lapped it up, bringing the moisture to her clit. She bowed her back when I licked the hardened nub.

I never expected sex with her to be so good. I knew it would blow my mind, but I not that it would be like an out-of-body experience. There were moments when I felt like I was watching myself pleasure her, and moments when I felt like I was so gone I couldn't even function.

Through all of them, the only thing was Valentina. Seeing her lose her mind, watching her fall apart, and hearing her whisper dirty things to me when she didn't realize she was doing it was enough to make me wish the night would never end.

I curled my fingers deep inside her and sucked hard on her clit. She was already plump and ready for me, but I couldn't resist flooding her pussy a few more times before I entered her. She screamed, her knees closing around my ears, as I flicked the tip of her clit and pounded four fingers deep into her.

"Brantley! Oh, God, Brantley!" My name shouted from the top of her lungs as she fell apart on my bed would go down as the best moment of my life. Hands down, forever, nothing could possibly top that.

Before she came all the way down, I hovered over her. I waited, wanting to watch her beautiful face as I entered her. The look of pure bliss on her face was better than seeing one of my kids beat their own personal record on the cross-country course. Which was saying something.

"Look at me, beautiful," I whispered.

Her eyes cracked open. She smiled when she saw me above her. She reached up for me and pulled me down to her. She moaned when she tasted herself on my lips, wrapping her thick thighs around my hips.

Her wetness guided me in. I eased inside her while we kissed, the move feeling intimate and private and so very right. I didn't get to watch her, but I got to feel her as she accepted me. Her chest bowed up, and she flicked her tongue over mine. She wrapped her arms tighter around me.

I pumped my hips slowly. The way she held me didn't give me much space for leverage, but it was more like making love to her instead of fucking her. I'd never done that before, even with ex-girlfriends. I'd had sex or I'd fucked them. Love was never part of the equation.

None of them were Valentina.

She lifted her feet and set them on the bed next to my

thighs. Her channel opened wider, giving me more room to stroke into her, more room to go deeper. She moaned at the change, lifting her hips to meet my strokes.

I leaned on my forearms and kept my thrusts short but deep, not retreating far from her body before I plunged in again. We kissed and we made love and I forgot what was happening between us wasn't real.

My orgasm raced down my spine and settled in my balls. She hadn't come yet, but I was barely able to hold back. Her nails ran across my back, like she was encouraging me to go ahead. My body burst, split open at the seams. I broke our kiss to shout her name, burying my face in her neck as I shook with the power of my orgasm.

She held me, her hands running up and down my back, letting me have my moment.

"You didn't come," I said.

She smiled. "We agreed this isn't transactional. I wanted to watch you. To see the look on your face and to memorize the feel of you coming inside me. When I'm barely conscious from my own orgasm, I feel like I miss yours. I wanted to experience it with you."

Her words stitched me back together, but left a piece of me with her. A piece of me had always been with her, but this time it was more. It wasn't part of my heart. It wasn't something I could live without. She had my entire heart. My whole being. She was it for me. If I couldn't have her, I didn't want anyone else. I was done thinking about moving on or wishing I could find someone who compared to her. Valentina was everything to me, whether I ever told her or not.

"Thank you," I whispered, knowing I couldn't explain exactly how much that meant to me.

"Are you tired? Should we sleep a little while?"

I nodded. "We probably should. Do you need to use the bathroom?"

"I should. I have to brush my teeth."

"I have two sinks. Unless that's weird."

"Nothing is weird with you, Bee."

We got ready for bed, then climbed under the covers. She curled up against me, letting me hold her as she fell asleep.

I wanted to stay up and enjoy holding her, but it wasn't long before sleep pulled me under and I followed her into it.

I WAS UP EARLY the next morning. Far earlier than I wanted to be. I didn't know what time Valentina was planning to go home, but I wasn't ready to say goodbye just yet.

I eased out of bed and let myself out of my room. I walked naked through the house, stopping in the kitchen to start the coffee before I grabbed a towel and wrapped it around my waist.

The deck was still wet from the night before, and the hot tub had a good six inches less water than before we got in. I picked up the food we'd left out and the condoms we never bothered to use and carried everything inside. Our bathing suits were tossed into puddles and still soaked, so I laid them on the chairs so they would dry during the day.

With the outside taken care of, I went back in and poured two mugs of coffee. I added cream and sugar to them and carried them back to the bedroom.

Valentina was still passed out when I walked in. She looked peaceful in sleep, her long lashes fanned out over her cheeks. She had beard burn on both breasts and probably on her thighs, too.

My dick twitched. Best mark ever.

Valentina groaned and rolled over. Her eyes fluttered open just enough to see where she was, and she smiled. "Good morning."

"Is it? I seem to remember you not being a morning person."

"I seem to have an easier time in the morning when I spent all night being ravished by a sexy physics teacher."

I chuckled. "I'm happy to make all your mornings better."

She grinned. "Why aren't you still in bed?"

"I figured you'd want coffee."

She sat up quickly. "You have coffee?" She reached for it with grabby hands and wrapped both of them around the mug when I handed it to her.

"Good?" I asked as she took her first sip.

She nodded. "Delicious. Although I had thoughts of starting my day with my lips wrapped around something other than a coffee mug."

My step faltered, and I nearly fell on my damn face. "That can be arranged."

She smirked at me over the edge of her mug.

"But you weren't in bed when I woke up."

I set my coffee on the nightstand and stretched out next to her. "I am now. You weren't really awake yet, anyway."

She shook her head. "No, I really wasn't." She put her coffee down and climbed over me, kissing her way down my body until she wrapped her lips around my cock.

"Fuck," I hissed.

She moaned deep in her throat, the vibration going straight to my balls. She pumped her hand and her mouth together, bringing me straight to the edge in under a minute.

I was seconds away from blowing in her mouth when I yanked her up.

She didn't fight me or argue. She crawled onto my lap and eased onto me while I held my cock in place. As soon as she was fully seated, she rose up on her knees and went fucking crazy.

My hands went to her hips to guide her. She moaned and whined and fucked me. Her hands held my shoulders, every slide into her body partnered with a tightening of her channel.

"Touch me," she begged. "Please."

I dipped my hand between us and dragged the wetness from her up to her clit. She moaned again, her stroke faltering. "Come on, Vee. Don't stop now. Ride me. Take my cock in."

She kept going, my fingers plucking her clit and making her move faster. She huffed her breath and slammed her body onto mine. Her clit plumped as I played with it.

"Brantley," she moaned.

I felt it as she said my name. She lost control, her body going limp as the orgasm claimed her. She slumped against me, her core milking me and demanding my orgasm follow hers.

"Fuck," I groaned. My vision went black. My ears rung. My entire body tightened.

Then she sank onto me, her weight crashing to my chest as all the exertion drained her.

I held her, kissing her neck and shoulders. She heaved for breath, shaking as she drew in one after another deep breath.

"How does it keep getting better between us?" she whispered.

I kissed her jaw. "Because I love you, and you love me."

She wrapped her arms around my neck and held me tight. "Yes."

We laid there like that until I softened and slid from her body and she fell asleep on my chest. She snored softly for a while. I just held her. There was nowhere in the world I wanted to be more than right there in that moment.

Or any moment.

WEDNESDAY AFTERNOON, Kevin walked into my classroom for our daily tutoring session. I could tell instantly it was going to be a tough session. He'd been quiet all week in class, but he'd seemed responsive to the work we were doing.

"How's your day going?" I asked. First and foremost, he was a person, and I wanted him to know I was aware of that.

"Great," he said sarcastically.

"Want to tell me what's going on?"

"Not really. Let's just do this. I'm sick of being the stupid kid."

"Who said you're stupid?"

"Don't worry about it. Let's just get this over with."

"Kevin—"

He glared at me hard enough to make me stop. For a second. I was the adult.

"What's going on?"

He shook her head and avoided my gaze.

I'd worked with enough students to know it was a tactic. Like when kids hid under a table and thought if they couldn't see you, then you couldn't see them. Teenagers did it with avoidance.

"Is something going on at home?"

He snorted. "Home. No."

"Then on the team? Are you having an issue with someone on the team?"

He shook his head.

That left school. "Another teacher? A student?"

"Just drop it, Coach P. It doesn't matter. I don't matter."

"Don't say that, Kevin. You matter a lot. To me and others. I know for a fact your teammates enjoy hanging around you. They've all seemed to have welcomed you."

He shrugged. "Not all."

"What happened?"

"Why do you care? No one ever cares. I'm not important. I'm a paycheck. That's all until I turn eighteen and then I'll be a burden."

"Whoa, what are you talking about?"

He looked me dead in the eye and sneered. "Are you really going to pretend you don't know I'm a foster kid? That you aren't being nice to me because it helps you out some-how? I know how the system works. I've been in it long enough. The ones who are nice to you are only biding their time until the paycheck comes. And the ones who aren't... Let's just say they have other benefits in mind for a kid who no one else gives a shit about."

Kevin stood and moved toward the door, but I caught him before he left. "You can't say something like that and walk out. Are you in danger? Is someone hurting you?"

He shrugged me off. "Wouldn't matter. No one does anything about it."

"I will do something. But you have to tell me what's going on. Is the family you're living with hurting you?"

He huffed a breath and shook his head. "No. They're... nice, I guess. She works a ton. He does, too. They said they have adult kids."

My heart rate finally slowed as he spoke about his foster parents. I didn't know he was in foster care, but a lot about Kevin made sense with that bit of knowledge. Kids who were bounced around tended to be behind in classes because there wasn't a lot of consistency in their education.

"Talk to me. What's going on that has you so upset right now?"

He sighed. "Why do you want to know?"

"Because I care, Kevin. I didn't ask you to come here for tutoring because you're on the cross-country team. I asked you because I'm your teacher and I want to see you succeed. You're not the only student I work with on a regular basis. I don't know if anyone's told you, but teachers don't usually do this for the money."

That got a little smile out of him.

"I didn't know you were a foster student. The district doesn't share that information because it's not relevant. The teachers are here to help you do well, whether you're here as a foster student or you've lived here your whole life. As for me, I do this job because I love science, and I love helping others love science."

"You're such a dork," he teased.

I laughed. "I am. Very much so. And I'm proud of that. Not all of us can be good at everything. Most of us are lucky to find one thing we excel at. My one thing is teaching. Which is kind of cheating because teaching means I'm pretty good at listening and figuring out what someone is struggling with and explaining things in new ways."

"I don't think I have one thing."

"Maybe you have a dozen."

He snorted. "More like I have zero."

"I doubt that. I heard you took McJenna to Homecoming. She's a nice girl. If she said yes, you must have done something right."

"Yeah, well, don't tell Danny that."

"Danny Bieler?"

Kevin nodded. "He told me to stay away from her from now on."

"What did McJenna say?"

Kevin shrugged. "I haven't talked to her."

"Then I think the first thing you need to do is ask McJenna because the women I know are not going to be interested in a guy who bullies others or in a guy who gives in to bullies."

Kevin stood a little straighter at that news. "Yeah?"

I nodded. "I'm not saying go after him, but let McJenna make up her own mind about who she wants to spend her time with. Women aren't property. They deserve to be respected. If you ignore her because Danny said to stay away from her, you're no better than he is."

Kevin nodded thoughtfully. "Thanks, Coach."

"You're welcome. Is anything else going on?"

Kevin shook his head.

"Good. Think we can work on some physics now?"

Kevin grinned. "Yeah, we can do that."

19

———

AN EMOTIONAL AFFAIR WAS STILL WRONG. I KNEW THAT. I refused to be the guy who hurt Valentina again, which meant I had to close my Book Boyfriends Wanted account.

The only person I'd talked to recently was BakerBabe. I enjoyed talking to her, but after spending the night with Valentina, I knew I would never pursue something with BakerBabe. But I felt like I owed her an explanation.

NERDYBYNATURE

How was your week?

BAKERBABE

Hi. It was good. Busy. Sorry I haven't been in touch.

NBN

Nothing to be sorry about. I actually wanted to tell you I'm closing my account.

BB

You mentioned you might. Does that mean things are going well with the woman you told me about?

NBN

Let's say I'm enjoying the time we're
spending together, but trying not to get
ahead of myself. I hope it means we're
moving in the right direction, but either way,
I'm in love with her. I don't feel like I'm being
fair to anyone I meet here, or to her. I have
no interest in dating someone else.

BB

Funny. I feel the same way about someone
in my life.

NBN

Yeah?

BB

Yeah. It's kind of sudden, but I hope it might
turn into more.

NBN

Maybe it will. You never know. Maybe we'll
both get lucky and everything will work out
for both of us.

BB

Fingers crossed. It was nice talking to you.
Maybe one day we'll meet in person.

NBN

Maybe we already have. Wouldn't that be
crazy?

BB

Ooh, I never thought of that. Now I'm going
to wonder. But I don't want to know. I like to
think of you as some mysterious stranger
who's out there bringing happiness to a
woman who has no idea how much she's
loved.

I smiled and closed the app. I hoped she found happiness. I hoped everyone did. It was hard to live a life without joy. But Valentina brought me joy, and I wanted to give it my best shot.

I held the icon until they all wiggled, then tapped the X to delete the app. Just like that, my online dating life was done.

I took my morning run to the high school the next day, watching the sun rise and thinking about my next experiment with Valentina. As much as I enjoyed sex, I wanted more with her. I wanted to make sure she knew I wasn't just there for the amazing sex.

The sky brightened as I thought about Valentina. I knew the teenager version of her and I knew the parent version, but the woman was one I never let myself get too close to. But I wanted to know what made her feel good.

As I started my run home, I decided I'd do some digging. If she was up for it, I'd invite myself over for dinner and cook with her. I knew she liked to cook, but I also knew doing it alone was not as much fun as sharing the task with someone else. Maybe we could do dinner and a movie together. With the girls, of course. She loved her daughters, and I didn't want her to think I only wanted to spend time with her alone.

I showered and changed and was back at the high school before anyone else. Our meet for the day was about an hour away, so we had an early pickup. As the kids arrived, we gathered in the school entryway to make sure everyone was there.

Jana and I counted kids and double checked our lists, then had them all load onto the bus. We both stared at our phones while the kids talked behind us.

Once we arrived, it was busy getting our spot picked out and setting up the tent. When we were ready, we started the kids on a slow run to see the course. It wound through the wooded area behind the school, and even though the course stayed on the path, it wasn't marked.

The kids worked through their stretches and spread out into smaller groups while Jana and I made sure the officials had the complete rosters for each run. The modified teams were there, too, so the day was going to be longer than usual.

We got everyone checked in, and made sure they all had numbers and chips for their shoes, then we went to cheer for the seventh and eighth graders running first.

As the girls finished their race, I noticed Kevin and McJenna walking together and talking. He smiled at her, and she laughed at something he said.

I was happy for the kid. And happy to see he took my advice and talked to her instead of bailing and letting Danny intimidate him.

As the modified boys race started, I went back to our tent to get our first group of girls to the start line to check in. When I walked by Danny, I heard him mouthing off to his friends.

"He's such an ass. He thinks he's all great, but he's nothing. He's such a loser. She's not going to stay with him for long."

I stopped and faced Danny. "Who are you talking about?"

"No one, Coach. Nothing to worry about." Danny's cocky stance told me I didn't intimidate him. Nothing did.

"Well, I hope you aren't talking about one of your teammates, because something like that can be grounds for dismissal from the team."

"What? Why? I didn't do anything." Danny dropped his hands to his sides and tightened them into fists.

"It's sportsmanship, Danny. If you're trash-talking about a teammate, that's not okay. And if you're talking about a competitor, you're getting too personal. If this is what I think it is, you're arguing over a girl."

"You don't know anything."

"I know a woman should be allowed to make her own choice about who she spends time with. And if you are going to threaten someone to get them to stay away from another person, you're the problem. If McJenna doesn't want to date you, that's not Kevin's fault."

Danny snorted. "Whatever."

"Not whatever, Danny. Do you want to be that guy people are friends with because they're worried about what he'll do if they stand up to you?"

Danny glanced at his friends, who were all mysteriously busy looking somewhere else. "No."

"Then don't be that guy. Don't be the guy who threatens someone because you like the same girl. Do you have any idea how many times that's going to happen in your life?"

"I..."

"If I remember, last year you asked out Christy after Marco said he liked her. But Marco's still your friend."

Danny glanced over at Marco. "Sorry."

Marco shrugged.

"If you threaten Kevin again, or McJenna, I will have no choice but to kick you off the team. I don't want to do that. I don't think your teammates want me to do that. But I will if you're disrupting things."

Danny nodded. "Got it, Coach P."

"Good. Now warm up. Stay loose. Be ready."

Danny and his buddies jogged off. Danny kept his head down. Hopefully, something I said sank in and there wouldn't be any more issues.

I sent the junior varsity girls to the starting line to get ready for their run. I warned the JV boys they were next, then followed the girls to the start line to watch them take off.

Samantha was talking to one of her friends and beaming. I didn't know what she was so happy about, but it was good to see her smile after so many months of sadness.

It was a huge race with over a hundred girls lined up. When the last of the modified boys had crossed the finish line, the official stood in the middle and counted down the girls. He fired, and they all took off.

Jana and I watched them take the first turn. When they disappeared into the woods, we checked the time and waited for the first of the girls to reappear.

The race went quickly, everyone finishing three miles in under forty-five minutes. We congratulated our runners as they finished and marked all their times for our records.

The boys JV teams were next. Followed by the girls varsity, then boys varsity. As each group ran, we made notes and realized three of our JV kids had set new personal records, including Samantha.

Jana went to tell Sam, leaving me to record the incoming times for the varsity boys. When Andrew ran across the finish line, beating his best time, I saw on his face he knew.

"Nice race," I told him.

Andrew couldn't stop smiling. "Thanks, Coach. I just PR'd."

"I know. We've had a few of those today. Hell of a race."

Andrew nodded and moved to the side as the other kids came to the finish line.

At the end, we had three JV and four varsity kids who'd PR'd. "We need to celebrate," Jana said. "This is amazing."

"I agree. They deserve something for working so hard. I think all of them beat their average times, so it was a good race for everyone."

"Pizza party?"

"That's not a bad idea. Let's talk on the bus back."

"Yeah, definitely. I told the JV kids. You want to tell the varsity kids? I think Andrew knows, but Kevin, Danny, and McJenna might not."

I swallowed a groan and nodded. "Yeah, sure. I'll tell them."

Some of the students were leaving with parents, but our tent was still busy. Kevin and McJenna were talking on one side, and Danny was on the other with his back to them.

I approached Danny first. "Can I speak to you? And Kevin and McJenna?"

Danny tensed. "Coach, I listened. I didn't do anything."

I jerked my head to the side for him to follow me, then went to get the other two. When Kevin saw where I was leading him, he hung back, taking a few steps away from McJenna.

"Hey, Danny," McJenna said. "I heard you ran a heck of a race."

"Who said that?"

"Kevin did," McJenna told him, hooking her thumb at Kevin. "He said you were awesome and encouraged him to keep going into that hill at the end."

I looked between the three of them. Danny nodded, and McJenna beamed at him.

"What did you need, Coach?" McJenna asked, turning her focus to me.

"I wanted to let all of you know you beat your personal records today."

"Really?" McJenna asked.

Kevin and Danny both jerked their heads up, eyebrows high, thinking they were in trouble for some reason. They glanced at each other and grinned.

"It sounds like when you guys work as teammates, amazing things can happen."

"No kidding," McJenna said. "This is awesome. I need to tell my dad and Karissa." She took off running, leaving me with the two boys.

"You two have the potential to be friends. You clearly have a few things in common. But you have to stop fighting and accept that you're better as teammates than enemies."

Kevin swallowed and faced Danny. "Thanks for encouraging me today. I was fighting some soreness before the race and that hill about took me out. I wouldn't have PR'd if it weren't for you. Not even close."

Danny nodded. "Just trying to do what coach said. I'm sorry I've been such a dick about J. I was jealous."

"I get it. She's a pretty great girl," Kevin said.

Danny nodded, and the two of them walked away together, talking about how amazing McJenna was.

That went better than I expected.

I went back to the tent and grabbed a few of the kids to help me take it down. We packed up all our gear, and I went over the list of kids who'd been signed out. We only had twelve riding the bus back to the school.

Jana jogged over with the bag of chips from the kids' shoes and put them in our team bag. She went through to make sure we had everything, then called the bus driver to come back and pick us up.

"I'm going to go flag him down," Jana said. "He said it's busy."

I nodded. "I'll meet you up there with the kids. Just want to make sure there isn't anyone else who's planning to get picked up. We'll bring the tent if you can take the gear bag."

"Got it," Jana said, grabbing the bag and taking off toward the parking lot.

I called out to the kids hanging around to make sure a parent signed them out if they weren't going on the bus. I held up the clipboard, knowing the parents didn't always know where it was.

One parent came over and took the clipboard from me to sign out her daughter, then handed it back. I held it up again as I waited for word from Jana that the bus was ready for us.

My phone buzzed, so I pulled it out to check if it was Jana, then told the kids it was time to go. We gathered the last of our things, making sure we didn't leave anything behind, and headed toward the parking lot.

"Hey, Coach Pierce," a man said from behind me.

I paused, not wanting to be rude to my team parents, even though I was trying to get out of there. I turned to say hello and stopped dead. "Dawson."

Dawson smirked at me. "Good to see you, *friend.*"

I nodded and crossed my arms over my chest. The students continued ahead of me, but I could see the bus and Jana, so I let them go. "Glad you could make it to see the girls run. Samantha was pretty upset last time you said you'd be here and didn't show."

"Yeah, well, she's like her mother. She gets emotional. But I heard you were there to make her feel better."

I straightened up. "I did what I could. Your girls have needed you. You weren't around."

Dawson snorted. He rolled his eyes and tossed his hair. It had grown longer over the months since he walked out of their lives and disappeared. He looked harder, more of a jerk than he once was. "My supposed friend threw me out on my ass. Where was I supposed to go?"

I shrugged. "Get an apartment. Or stay at the inn. Somewhere so you could be here for your family."

"I had a home. One I shared with my wife. You know, the woman you've always wished was warming your bed."

I sucked in a breath. I never told Dawson I liked Valentina. Not once.

"You thought I didn't know?" He threw his head back and laughed. "How rich. You always were too dumb for your own good."

"You're the one who messed things up with her."

Dawson snorted. "Yeah, well, it was fun while it lasted. Stealing her out from under your nose was easy. You were never man enough to claim her. But man, once I had her, I knew I had to keep her. For a little while, at least. She was a damn good fuck. For someone who didn't know what she was doing. Not very inventive, but she made up for it with that tight pussy. Until she had kids." He shuddered. "Then everything stretched out, and it was all I could do to force myself to fuck her. I would have left her years ago if she hadn't been so willing to do whatever I wanted to try to keep me happy. That and if I wasn't able to get some on the side when I traveled."

"How could you do that to her? How could you treat her like she didn't matter?"

Dawson chuckled. "Because she didn't. She was just a challenge."

"What?"

"A challenge. A bet. The guy who lived across the hall told me about her when I moved in. Said she was following you around like a puppy, but you were so clueless you thought she was just a friend. I told him I'd have her in my bed before you even knew what was going on. And I did."

"You son of a bitch," I growled. I lunged at him.

He put his hands up. "Be careful, Coach Pierce. You wouldn't want to lose your job for assaulting a parent."

"You're not a parent. You were a sperm donor. You don't deserve to call those girls your own."

Dawson shrugged. "Maybe, but they are mine. You're not going to slide into my life. No matter what you do, you'll never replace me as their father."

"I never tried to."

"Bullshit, Brantley." Dawson stepped closer. He hissed at me. "You always wanted my life. My kids. My wife. I'll be generous and let you have my ex-wife. She hasn't been worth the energy to fuck in years, so you might not want to bother, but maybe you can live out some old childhood fantasy. Just know it's really not worth it."

"You fucking—"

Dawson stepped away, and I stopped. Valentina was less than two feet away. Tears ran down her cheeks. She clearly heard everything Dawson said.

20

VALENTINA

"Valentina," Brantley said. He took a step toward me, but I held up my hand to stop him.

"Not right now," I whispered. It was the only thing I could force past my lips.

Dawson walked away, whistling like he hadn't just blown up my fucking world. I was a bet? Someone he only slept with to be a dick to Brantley. And then he married me and had kids with me and cheated on me until I caught him.

God, I was such a fool.

I stumbled away, knowing I needed to get to my car before I fell apart. I couldn't let him see that. Let him enjoy that.

The son-of-a-bitch knew I was there. He knew I could hear him. He knew what his words would do to me. He did it on purpose.

Fucking asshole.

"Hey, Valentina!" another voice called out.

I drew a breath and pasted on a smile before I saw Goldie waving. She was standing next to my car.

"Are you— Whoa. What the hell happened?" she asked.

Her eyes went wide and scanned me. Like she could see something just by looking.

I resisted the urge to squirm. To hide. To protect myself. It was Goldie, but I was raw. Vulnerable. Exposed.

"Are you okay?"

I scoffed. "Not even a little bit."

"What happened? Talk to me."

I glanced around to make sure the girls weren't close. The last thing I wanted was for them to overhear what Dawson said. "I ran into Dawson."

"Oh, shit. What did he say? Is that the first time since you threw him out?"

"Yes. And he told Brantley he only slept with me in college because the guy across the hall in their dorm made a bet he couldn't. Dawson said he only did it because he knew Brantley liked me. I was a game to him."

"Oh, my God. Where is he? I'm going to kick his ass." Goldie shouldered past me and stood at the edge of the parking lot, scanning the thinning crowd.

"You know what? He's not worth it. He's out of my life forever."

Goldie turned back to me. Her blonde brows pinched in the center, her gaze doubtful. "You can't possibly be okay with what he said."

"Oh, no. I'm not okay with it. But I can't change it. He's an even bigger asshole than I ever thought he was. Haley was one thing, but knowing we spent more than twenty years together and he never cared is another."

"I have a hard time believing that," Goldie said. "You don't marry someone if you don't love them. You don't spend half your life with someone for a bet."

I shrugged. "I don't know. Maybe he did. Maybe there was a time when he loved me. Maybe he was playing the long game and making sure Brantley was not a part of my life. It doesn't matter, though. I'm done with Dawson. I have been for a very long time. It hurts... the things he said. He knew it would hurt, though. He wanted to hurt me."

Goldie shook her head. "I wish I'd been there. I definitely would have made it harder for him to find someone to fuck for a few days."

I snorted. "That would have been great. But he really isn't worth it. I just... I spent a long time wanting to make him happy. Putting aside everything to do what I thought he wanted me to do. Now, even a chance that what he said is true, it just makes me feel like an idiot. I really did love him. I wanted a life with him. The last few years were hard, but I was willing to honor my vows. It sounds like he never did, and I can't change him."

"Wow. You sound very... okay right now."

I drew a breath and let it out slowly. Bianca and Samantha were heading our way with Paul. "I have to be. For them. I don't want them to know what he said."

Goldie looked back at the kids and nodded. "I would never."

"Thanks."

"Hey, do me a favor and hold on to that bravado you've got going on. Do something you enjoy tonight."

"We're making pizza and watching movies tonight. Something low-key after the meet."

"Good. Then take a nice hot shower or bath after they go to bed and make sure your day ends on a good note."

I snorted a laugh and rolled my eyes. Only Goldie would whisper something like that with our kids a few feet away.

"You guys ready to head home?" Goldie asked the kids.

"Yeah," Paul said.

"Mom! Did you see Dad?" Samantha asked.

I nodded and forced a smile to my face. Just because I hated him didn't mean I wanted my daughters to hate him. "I did. I'm glad he made it."

"Me, too. He said he wants to take us out to dinner tonight." Samantha squealed and clapped. She was practically vibrating with excitement.

Bianca was a different story. She looked like she'd rather do just about anything else.

"Oh, yeah? He didn't mention that to me."

"Because he knows you'll say yes if she asks," Bianca snarled.

I gave her a look that said she didn't need to bring so much sass. "I will say yes either way. I am not going to keep you two from spending time with your father."

"What if I don't want to spend time with him?" Bianca snapped.

"Don't ruin this," Samantha whined. "I want to see Dad. We haven't seen him in months."

"And whose fault is that? He's the one who walked out! He's the one who was cheating on Mom! He's the one who's ignored us and hasn't come to visit us in months, Sam! Months. Why should we drop everything just because he bothered to show up?"

"Because he's still your father," I told her. "Listen, I'm not going to force you to go out to dinner with him, but I'm not going to stop you either. And I think you owe it to yourself to not only hear what he has to say but to ask him these things. I don't have answers for you. I don't know what he's been doing or why he hasn't been around. He does, though. The only way you're going to find out is if you ask him."

Bianca kicked the dirt with her toe. She scowled and hissed, "Fine."

"Yay!" Samantha jumped up and down. "I can't wait. This is so exciting."

"You're delusional," Bianca muttered.

"Bianca. Don't." I glared at my oldest. She was outwardly angry, but I saw the pain in her eyes. She was hurt. She came across as mad, but it was a mask for the wound caused by her father's dismissal.

Samantha looked between us, her excitement banked with the tension. "I don't care if you don't want to go. I'm excited to see Dad."

Paul grabbed Samantha's hand and tugged her a few feet away. He said something to her that I couldn't hear but that made her smile.

"Hey, Bianca?" Goldie said. "I think your mom's right. You should talk to your dad. But be willing to listen to him, too. It's not easy. None of this is easy. But you guys are all getting older. You'll be adults soon. You need to make your own choices about things. About whether you want your dad in your life or not."

Bianca sucked in a shaky breath and nodded. "Thanks, Ms. Goldie. You're right. I think it's good for me to go."

I nodded and pulled her close, kissing the top of her head.

We turned up the radio and sang along on the drive home. I wanted to lighten the mood and celebrate the excellent meet. My phone buzzed a few times, but I never checked it when I was driving. The two most important people were with me, and everyone else could wait.

When we got inside, I pulled up the text messages I'd gotten on the drive. The first one was from Brantley, asking if he could come over tonight for dinner and a movie. And to talk. I knew we needed to, but I wasn't sure I really wanted to.

The other texts were from Dawson. Four of them. Each a few minutes apart. Ugh.

> I told the girls I want to take them to dinner tonight. Sam said it would be fine.

> Is this your way of giving me the cold shoulder? Are you really going to stand in the way of me seeing my daughters?

> I expected better from you, Valentina. I thought you cared about our daughters.

> You're so selfish! You're really going to stop me from seeing them. I came all the way here, and you're being a petty bitch. I'm not letting you stop me from seeing my daughters.

What. A. Dick.

He didn't think I'd be driving? That I might not be able to reply to a text message when I had our daughters in the car?

My blood boiled. I wanted to fire off a nasty reply and keep the girls home just out of spite, but I wouldn't give him the satisfaction of knowing he got to me.

> Just got home from the meet. I was driving and don't check my phone. Sam told me about dinner. They're getting ready now. Are you going to pick them up or do I need to drop them off somewhere?

I'll be there in fifteen minutes.

> I'll let them know.

I rolled my eyes as I closed the chat. I should have let Goldie go after him. He deserved it. And more.

I relayed the message to the girls. Sam was almost ready and grinned. Bianca looked like she was heading toward her execution.

When Dawson pulled into the driveway, he honked the horn. It took everything in me to let the girls walk out the door and go with him. He didn't even have the decency to come to the door?

Fucking asshole.

I locked the door behind them and remembered the text from Brantley. I pulled out my phone again and headed toward my room. I needed a shower.

> Dinner and a movie sound perfect. That was our plan for tonight, anyway.

Was?

> Dawson took the girls out for dinner.

You let him?

> He's their father. I was not going to stop him. What time did you want to come over?

Bus is not back to the school yet. By the time parents all get there and I go home and shower, it'll probably be an hour. Maybe longer. Is that too late?

> Nope. Sounds good. Let yourself in when you get here. I'm going to open a bottle of wine as soon as I get out of the shower. I might be half-drunk or sleeping by the time you arrive.

You deserve it after today. See you soon.

I locked the phone and set it on the counter. The water

was hot, and as I reached in to test it, I thought about what Goldie said.

Don't let Dawson ruin my night.

That fucker took everything from me. From my virginity to my happiness to my chance at something with Brantley. Dawson stole too much. He made me doubt who I was for too long. I started my Quest for Pleasure because I spent too many years without pleasure in my life.

But I was done. He didn't get to take anymore pleasure from me.

I opened my top cabinet drawer and grabbed my waterproof vibrator. I set it on the shelf in my shower and stepped under the spray. The heat felt good after the coolness of the mid-October day. Even though the sun was bright, there was a breeze all day, and I hadn't been able to shake the chill. I turned and let the hot water beat down on my neck, easing the tension brought on by Dawson. I closed my eyes. No more. He wasn't causing me tension anymore.

I washed my body, cupping the soap bubbles around my breasts to tease myself. The slipperiness of them had my core growing wetter, getting me ready.

My body was tense as I reached for the vibrator, but it was a good kind of tense. The kind that was anticipating and excited. I turned on the vibration and took my time playing with it over my body. By the time I slid it between my thighs, I was soaked.

The vibrator slid into me easily, just like Brantley did the weekend before. The thought of Brantley sent a fresh wave of need through me. He wanted to talk, but at the moment, talking was the last thing I wanted.

I spread my thighs wide and pressed the vibrator deep into my body. I gasped when the external stimulation hit my clit. "Yes."

My knees softened, but I grabbed on to the handrail for support. I leaned back against the cool tile. The hot water ran down my front, the cold tile pressed against my back, and the rapid vibration centered inside me all confused and excited my body.

"Brantley," I groaned, imagining him there with me.

I pumped the toy in and out, every stroke in hitting my clit and making me cry out. I moaned his name with every move. I was so close. My body tensed, I pushed the vibrator deep inside, holding the buzz on my clit and shouted his name.

"Brantley! Oh, God, Brantley. Yes. Brantley!"

"Holy fuck," a male voice said.

I screamed. The toy dropped to the tile floor and rattled around as I came, my body finishing what it started even as fear gripped me.

"Don't stop," he growled.

"Brantley?"

"You said to let myself in with my key. I'm early. I heard you shout, and I thought something was wrong. I... Fucking hell. I need you. Can I have you, Vee? Right now? I will walk out if you say no, but I—"

"Yes," I whispered.

Our gazes locked as he yanked off his clothes in jerky, hurried moves. His jeans got caught on his sneakers when he tried to take everything off at once, but his gaze never left mine.

He stroked himself as he walked toward me. Stalked me, really. He tugged the shower door open and scanned my body with his eyes, his cock still in his hand.

"Pick it up," he growled.

I bent down and picked up the vibrating toy.

"Show me."

My breath hitched in my throat, but I wasn't ashamed. Of all the people in my life to share something so personal with, he was the only one I could imagine.

I spread my thighs again, using my fingers to ease my folds open. The first touch of the vibrator against my sensitive walls had me gasping.

Brantley dropped to his knees and pressed my thighs wider. "God, you're beautiful. This perfect pussy. You were thinking about me?"

"Yes," I confessed. He already knew, but admitting it made it real.

"I can't even count the number of times I've thought of the way you taste or the way you feel while I jerked off. At least a hundred in just the last week, but in my lifetime it's probably in the millions."

"Show me," I parroted to him.

His gaze snapped to mine. He stood, wrapping his hand around his dick. "Nothing feels as good as your pussy around me when I come, but watching you fuck yourself might be a close second as far as pleasure goes."

"Brantley."

"I'm right here, Vee. Always."

He wrapped an arm around me, one supporting my weight while the other stroked his dick. He pressed himself against my side, both of us working to bring ourselves to orgasm while we also watched the other.

"Brantley," I whimpered.

"I got you, beautiful. Come for me. Then I'm going to lick you and fuck you some more."

As always, his dirty words sent me over the edge. I moaned and shouted, and my knees buckled. But Brantley held me, keeping me from getting hurt while the vibrator sent me over the edge.

"Let's get out," he whispered when I was finally back in my body. The vibrator was off and on the shelf. Brantley turned off the water and stepped out, wrapping me in a towel before grabbing one from under the sink for himself.

He was still hard.

"Did you come?"

He shook his head. "I wanted to watch you. I would have preferred to see from up close, but someone had other plans."

"I wanted to see you."

"Any time you want. But first, I need you, Vee. If you're willing."

"Always."

He closed his eyes and nodded, a faint smile on his face. When he looked at me again, there was something there that wasn't a minute ago, but he pressed his body to mine and kissed me until I forgot all about whatever he was hiding from me.

21

BRANTLEY

Always. She said always. So simple. So easy. So... not true.

I knew always didn't mean the same thing to her that it did to me. Not yet. Maybe not ever. Valentina told me more than once she wasn't looking for a relationship. She was focusing on herself and the girls. She was doing this stupid quest to figure out what she enjoyed.

I was the idiot who got sucked in and let myself believe there was more to it than just pleasure. Sure, it was a lot of damn pleasure, but it was physical. She didn't love me. This was a childhood curiosity fulfilled.

We sat on the couch, the open bottle of wine on the coffee table near our feet, and watched a movie. A sappy rom-com that she loved and only reminded me that I was alone. I was the chick in the movie who thought she'd never get the love of her life to pay attention to her.

Except for me, Valentina paid attention to me. All the damn time. But it wasn't enough.

"Are you okay?" she asked, startling me out of my thoughts.

I shifted and nodded. "Yeah. Of course. Why?"

"You just seem tense. Like something's bothering you. Were you... Did it upset you to see me... Was it bad?"

I lunged over her, pinning her to the couch, and shook my head. "God, no. It was amazing. You're supposed to be finding things that bring you pleasure. I'm more than happy to share that pleasure with you, but if you can't stop yourself from thinking about me, I'm not going to tell you to wait."

She looked away from me, like she was ashamed. "I've never... It's only been recently that I've tried things."

I eased back to look at her. "Tried what kind of things?"

She shrugged. "The vibrator. I told you sex wasn't something I got a lot out of. It's only been since Dawson and I stopped sleeping with each other that I tried anything like that. Before..."

"You never have to explain yourself to me. It wouldn't matter to me if you'd been building a collection since high school or if that was the first and only time you've touched yourself. You need to be comfortable with your own body."

She smiled shyly. "I'm getting there. It's still more fun when I'm not alone."

I leaned down and kissed her hard. I thrust my hips against her. "Yeah, it is," I growled in her ear, licking the shell and making her shiver.

"I don't know how you do that."

"Do what?"

"Take me from hiding myself to ready to come in just a few seconds."

"I like making you come. A lot."

She met my gaze and circled her arms around my neck. "I like it, too. A lot."

She pulled me down, and we kissed on the couch like teenagers. It was different for us, chaste and sexy and simple. It was perfect. I wanted her to feel how much I loved her because even if always wasn't real, I never wanted her to doubt that she was loved.

After a few minutes of making out, and my cock trying desperately to get out again, I sat up and pulled her up with me. I kissed the top of her head and tucked her under my arm. She rested her hand on my chest and exhaled a contented sigh.

We were still sitting like that when the girls came home from a long dinner with Dawson. As soon as the door opened, Valentina jumped up to see how they were, and asked if Dawson was coming in.

"He said he had to go," Samantha said. "But he promised to come back and visit soon."

"Good," Valentina said, but her tone was flat. "Are you guys tired, or do you want to finish the movie with us?"

"I need to text Paul," Samantha said, already heading toward her room.

"I told McJenna I'd let her know how dinner was," Bianca said. Her faint smile said dinner was better than expected for her, too.

"Okay. Well, good night then."

"Night," both girls said before giving Valentina a hug, then me, then disappearing into their rooms.

Valentina took a minute getting back to the couch. When she sat down, she stayed on the other end, away from me.

"You okay?"

She nodded. "Yeah."

"You sure? Because you're really far away now." I tried to keep my tone light, but it stung. Dawson pulled into the driveway, and Valentina shut down on me. He didn't even come inside. Maybe that was worse because it meant she had to wonder what he was thinking instead of being able to ask him.

But what the hell did I know?

"He's infuriating," she whispered.

"Dawson?"

She nodded. "How do I look at him ever again after the things he said today?"

I drew a breath. I knew we needed to talk about it, but after the way I arrived, we pretended nothing happened. "I don't know."

She glanced at me. "Do you think it's true?"

"That he did it to piss me off and prove he could?"

"That I was a bet."

The air that filled my lungs felt like it was full of barbs instead of oxygen and nitrogen and other elements. It felt like I'd sucked in a mouthful of smoke. I wanted to choke it out, but there was nowhere for it to go.

We heard what Dawson said so differently. I internalized the part about him knowing I liked Valentina and fucking with me by stealing her. She heard the part about him making a bet with the guy across the hall. Both truths hurt. And both were likely true.

"He fooled us. For years. I don't know if we ever really knew who he was."

"So, you think it's true."

I shook my head and forced myself to defend the man who didn't deserve it. "I don't know what to think. If it's true, and he married you and had two kids with you in order to win a bet, that's the worst bet ever. Even Dawson isn't that low. Even Dawson wouldn't marry you if he didn't fall in love with you. Maybe it started out that way, but I believe he loved you. I believe he loves your girls."

Her lower lip wobbled. She nodded after a minute,

then looked up at me. "Thank you. Goldie said the same thing. I'm kind of bouncing between angry, hurt, and indifferent right now. I really want to not care. I don't love him anymore. I don't want him back. But it was hard to hear him say those things. And then his texts."

"What texts?" I growled.

She dismissed me with a roll of her eyes. "He was just being a dick. He texted me about taking the girls to dinner while I was driving home from the meet and got nasty when I didn't reply immediately. He thought I was trying to keep him from the girls."

"He never should have come back."

"You can't say that. Samantha misses him. Bianca is angry and hurt, but she came home smiling. I can't wish him out of their lives."

"As long as he's out of your life."

"He is," she said vehemently. "For good. I don't want him in my life."

I nodded. "Good."

The movie finished, but I didn't think either of us really watched it. I stayed lost in my thoughts, and she stayed in hers.

"I should go," I said as the credits rolled.

She nodded, but didn't make a move to get up. "Are we okay?"

I reached for her hand and squeezed it. "We will always be okay, Vee. You're the most important person in my life. I love you."

She looked up at me and nodded. "I love you, Bee."

I forced myself to smile. I'd made my bed, and now I had to sleep in it alone.

She walked me to the door and gave me a quick kiss that

proved to me things had changed. She could say Dawson didn't bother her, but he did. All of it did.

My house was quiet and lonely and depressing as fuck. I wanted to leave as soon as I stepped inside, but I knew being around others was an even worse idea. I carried myself into my kitchen and wished I had more demo to do. I could really go for smashing the shit out of something.

I grabbed a bottle of water and chugged it. The cold of it slid down my throat and reminded me I had nothing to complain about. My life hadn't gotten worse. I had a job I loved. I had a home I loved. I had friends and a great family and I was healthy. I'd been in love with Valentina most of my life. Getting the chance to taste her and touch her and love her, and having to walk away when she was done, was going to be painful, but the truth was, it was no different from where I was at since high school.

People always said it was better to have loved and lost than never loved at all. I loved her. I hadn't lost her yet. I was not going to feel sorry for myself and act like she was gone. She was still there. And she was still my best friend. That was what mattered.

I STAYED busy through the week so I didn't notice that Valentina wasn't reaching out to me. I worked on my kitchen, I tutored Kevin, and I went to guys' night at O'Kelley's. I had a full life without Valentina in it.

"I heard Dawson showed up at the cross-country meet last weekend," Ian said. "How's Valentina?"

I shook my head. "Not great. He was a jackass and said some things he shouldn't have."

"Like what?" Hudson snarled.

"He said he only went after her in college because he knew I liked her. Said she was a bet with the guy across the hall. She heard him say it, too."

"Fucking asshole," James hissed.

"Agreed."

"Did you kick his ass?" Knox asked.

"She wouldn't let me."

"You could have after he left the meet," Knox suggested. "Followed him to his hotel or whatever."

I shook my head.

"He deserved it," Nico said.

"He still does, but it was more important to me to be there for Valentina than to kick Dawson's ass."

"You should have done both," Knox said.

"He's saying he was with Valentina," Sebastian interpreted. "He didn't want to leave her."

The other men looked between Sebastian and me as understanding dawned on them.

"So, you two are doing well?" James asked. "Trinity really likes Valentina."

"Everyone likes Valentina," Ian said. "What's not to like about her? She's beautiful, she can bake, and she's smart."

"Smart enough to keep this one at arm's length. How come you two are still keeping things quiet?" Knox asked.

I shook my head. "She's not interested in a relationship."

"You're just sleeping together?" Sebastian asked.

I shrugged.

"You want more." It wasn't a question. It was a declaration from a man who understood.

"Yeah, I do. I always have. Dawson might have been an asshole, but he wasn't wrong about me wanting Valentina when we were in college."

"Wait a minute. You've never gotten serious with another woman because you're in love with Valentina?" Knox asked.

I nodded. No use hiding from the truth.

"Damn," Nico said. "I thought I had it bad. I dated some after Laura came to work for me, but I always felt like I was being unfair to the other women."

"That's how I feel. I was talking to this one woman on Book Boyfriends Wanted. She was great. But it felt like I was cheating. The last thing I wanted was to risk Valentina thinking I was screwing around behind her back. Especially when it was just a woman I was talking to."

"What did you do?" Ian asked.

"I told the woman I was closing my account."

"Did you?" Knox asked.

I nodded. "I had to. Like Nico said, it felt unfair to the other women. And to Valentina, if I'm being honest. I want to spend the rest of my life with her. If that's not what she wants, I'll deal with it, but it's what I want. I want her to be happy, and I think I can make her happy, but it's her choice."

"And what if she chooses not you?" Knox asked.

"Then I'm still her friend."

"You'd stay friends with her? If she said she doesn't want to be with you, you'd be fine with it?" Knox pushed.

"Fine? Hell, no. But it's not like I can force her into a relationship. If she doesn't want me, I can't change that."

"How's her quest going?" Hudson asked. A smirk lifted one side of his mouth.

I chewed the inside of my mouth to keep from grinning back at him. "Well."

Hudson snorted. "In other words, you two are incredibly compatible between the sheets, and you're best friends, but you honestly think she doesn't want you?"

I huffed. I was right there with him until the end. "Our

chemistry is better than I ever imagined it could be. Like a rocket ship, or a flamethrower. It's fun and hot and so fucking good. I've never been with a woman who was so perfect for me. I've always enjoyed sex, but it's on a different level with her. It's just different."

"That's what happens when you fall in love with your best friend. All the women I was with before Blake were nothing compared to finally being with her. I'd been waiting for her my entire life, and the sex was just on a different level. But it's so much more than that. I had to be her friend, too. That isn't always easy. I give you a lot of credit for making that choice, but when things ended with Blake, I wasn't sure I could handle being her friend still. It hurt just to look at her." Ian rubbed his chest, a move I wasn't sure he was even conscious of.

"You're all nuts," Knox declared. "Sex is good when it's good sex. When it's a woman who's eager and willing. No matter who I'm with, I'm always going to make sure she has a damn good time, and I'm going to enjoy getting her there. That's how you make sure sex is good."

The married guys smiled and sipped their beers. The guys who were in serious relationships followed suit. I sat there, stuck between the two, because I agreed with Knox, but it was different with Valentina. It was better. Because there was more to it than just mutual pleasure. Even though that's why we started sleeping together.

"You'll understand one day," Sebastian told Knox.

Knox rolled his eyes. "Oh, whatever. You guys suck."

The rest of them laughed at Knox, but he took it in stride. He told me he wanted to settle down. To have something solid and steady. To have what the rest of them had. But he wasn't going to sit on the sidelines and wait for love to bash him over the head. He was out there looking for it, and testing out opportunities every chance he had.

A part of me was jealous of Knox. He hadn't found love yet, but he was open to it. He had a chance to find someone and fall for her and build a life with her.

I'd found the person I wanted to share my life with. And if she didn't feel the same, I was shit-outta-luck.

"We all felt that way," Ian said. "That's how it should be. But when you meet that one, it's going to rattle you so hard you're going to think you're losing your damn mind."

"Mostly because you will be," James added.

"But in a way that'll make you never want to find it again because it's that good with the one person who makes you feel like nothing can ever go wrong again," Sebastian said.

"Or who makes you feel like when shit does go wrong, you can get through it with her by your side," Nico said.

"Because that's exactly what love is," Hudson said. "Love is splitting yourself wide open and letting her inside to stitch all your pieces back together with little bits of herself in there so she's always with you. It's knowing every experience is better because you're sharing it with her. It's waking up every morning with a smile—"

"And a hard-on," James said with a smirk.

"Because she's yours," Hudson finished as though James hadn't interrupted. "And what he said." He hooked a thumb toward James, and everyone laughed.

"I think Valentina wants you just as much as you want her," Nico said after a minute. "I think you two are good together. And we all know I'm the smartest one here."

I chuckled with him as the others protested his assertion.

"Regardless of Nico's misguided inflation of his intelligence, I do think he's right about you and Valentina," James said. "Give her a chance to realize how great you are together. More than one of us messed things up before we realized what we would be walking away from if we didn't pull our heads out of our asses and make it right. And the women are not exempt from the same idiocy."

"You're talking about yourself, right?" Hudson asked.

James flipped him off, but nodded.

"See? He admitted he's an idiot," Nico said. "Anyone else willing to confess?"

"Didn't you fuck things up with Laura and sequester yourself on Doc Rock so she couldn't find you?" Ian asked. "I'm pretty sure I loaned her a boat to get out there."

"You ran away?" I sputtered.

"Not my finest moment. Okay, fine. Maybe we're all idiots when it comes to the women we love. But that's part of it. Being an idiot and knowing she's still going to love you when you figure it out yourself."

"Smartest one here, my ass," James snarled.

"Smarter than you," Nico argued.

"Just because you have some fancy degree..."

I chuckled and let them argue around me because they were right. They were all right. If I was going to let Valentina make the choice, then I had to let it go. But that didn't mean I had to let her decide if she could love me without playing a little dirty.

And I knew she enjoyed dirty.

22

———

I took the test out of my bag. I didn't typically share the results with students before I gave them to the entire class, but I knew Kevin needed to see his test.

"We need to talk about the test you took on Tuesday. I graded most of them and will be reviewing them in class on Monday, but I wanted to go over a few things with you today."

Kevin nodded. He slumped down in his seat. He avoided my gaze and crossed his arms.

I dropped the test on the desk in front of him, the eighty-nine big and bold and circled.

"No way," Kevin breathed. He sat up and picked up the stapled packet. "Is this a joke?"

I shook my head. "Nope. It's your test."

"I got an eighty-nine?"

I nodded. "You should be really proud. You've been working hard."

He huffed a laugh and smiled up at me. "I've never done this well on a science test."

"You earned that grade. You've been working really hard this semester."

"Because of you."

I shook my head. "Because of you. You could have blown me off and not put in the effort, but you didn't. You show up here every day, you work hard, you study. You're the one who made this happen. Needing a little extra help is normal. Putting in the work to bring your grades up this much in just a few weeks is exceptional."

His lips lifted as he stared at his test. It was obvious he didn't believe in himself, not the way he should. He was a smart kid with huge potential, but he hadn't been given enough encouragement. He'd been dismissed too many times by teachers and foster parents and maybe even his own parents. But he deserved a chance.

"Thank you, Mr. Pierce. No one has ever believed in me like you do. You and my foster parents right now. I... it means a lot."

"I hope you take this and believe in yourself more, too. You have a ton of potential, Kevin. You can do anything you want to do. You have classmates who make things seem easy, but our struggles are what define us. Our struggles are what make us who we are. You've struggled more than some people ever will, and I hope this shows you that pushing through is better than giving up."

He nodded. "Yeah, it does. Thanks." He flipped to the second page of his test and saw the questions that were incorrect. "Can you explain this to me?"

I looked at the question. We'd been studying kinematic equations. It wasn't easy, but he only missed one step. I sat down at the desk next to his. "Do you understand the question?"

"I think so. If a car starts up an on-ramp at one speed, accelerates at a constant rate, and has a given distance to travel, will it reach the speed of the rest of traffic when it merges?"

"Yes, perfect. That's exactly what we're trying to figure out. So, what did you do?" I knew where he went wrong, but I wanted him to see it himself.

Kevin studied his work, looked at the question, and went back to what he did. "I did... wait a minute. I didn't count the starting speed. I went from zero instead of the speed the car was going when it got onto the on-ramp."

"So, what would the answer be?"

Kevin dug out his calculator and reworked the numbers. It took him a minute, but when he finished his calculation, he wrote down the correct answer and wrote *YES* next to it. "The car would exceed the speed of traffic when it merges, if it maintains a constant acceleration."

"Exactly."

He grinned and tapped the page. He shook his head. "Wow. It's... this is just..." He looked over at me. "I knew what to do. I almost got an A on this test."

"And you will on the next one. Because you do know what to do. You're figuring this out."

He smiled, a look of pride filling his gaze. "Thank you, Mr. Pierce."

"You're welcome, Kevin."

The bell rang, and he gathered his stuff, leaving the test on the desk. "My foster mom is coming to the meet tomorrow. She wants to meet you, if that's okay."

I nodded. "Of course. I look forward to meeting her."

"See you at practice."

"Yep. Have a good last class."

"Thanks."

Kevin walked out with his head held a little higher, his shoulders a little straighter. The lightbulb went on for him. It was why I kept teaching. After years of students, fights with administration, problems with parents, I kept coming back because of the students. Because of the ones who didn't give up and who worked hard to succeed. The ones who pushed through their mental roadblocks and saw the possibilities.

I loved what I did, but working with Kevin kept sparking something else in me. I saw my students as my kids, but kids like Kevin needed more than that. They needed a family. A parent. A support system.

I'd never considered being a foster parent before, but the need existed. The kids were out there. Waiting for someone to believe in them.

My next class filtered into the room, and I pushed the idea to the back of my mind. It would take some research, but the more I thought about it, the more I wanted to be there for kids who were forgotten and left behind. No one deserved that.

THE DIFFERENCE in Kevin was so clear at practice that Jana asked me if I noticed it when the kids left.

"He had a lightbulb moment today."

She beamed. "No shit. That's awesome."

I nodded. "It really is. He's a good kid. Just hasn't had anyone to believe in him."

"He's lucky to have you."

"He has both of us. And his foster parents, from what

he's said. It just sucks he's sixteen and only now finding people who are willing to support him."

"Better than never finding that support. A lot of kids go through the system and just age out with no one. Once they turn eighteen, they're just done. Abandoned and alone."

"I don't know how people walk away from a kid like that."

Jana shrugged. "Most don't have the extra money to support a kid without getting the assistance. It just sucks for the kids."

"Yeah, it does." And it was another thing that made me want to take in foster kids.

"See you tomorrow, Coach."

"Have a good night." I waved as Jana got in her vehicle and left. I was sweaty and tired and needed food, but I was vibrating with excitement.

Before I could think twice about what I was doing, I parked in front of Valentina's house. I was on the porch before I realized I hadn't given her a head's up.

Are you home?

Yeah, why?

I wanted to see you. Just for a minute.

The girls are showering from practice. You
can come in.

I don't want to interrupt your night.

The door opened a second later. "Why would you be interrupting?"

"I had a good day. When I left practice, my SUV came here."

She grinned and stepped outside, closing the door

behind her. "Well, I'm glad it did." Her gaze slid over my body. "How was practice?"

Was it my imagination, or was she a little more breathy than a second ago?

"Practice was good."

"Is that what your good day was about?"

She stepped closer.

I shook my head. "One of my students had something click today. He struggled all quarter, to the point where he was failing a few weeks ago. He got a B on his last test, and he could have gotten an A. He will next time."

"That's good."

I leaned closer to her. "It was. It's the reminder I always look for that I should keep teaching."

"Are you thinking of quitting?"

"No. I love my job. But there are times when it's harder than others. The students, the ones who work like he has, they make it worthwhile."

She nibbled her lip. "You care so much. It's really good to see you like this. To know you're so excited because you got through to one of your students. You helped him to get there."

"How do you know that?" I didn't remember telling Valentina about Kevin or any of the kids I tutored.

She looked up at me. Her lashes fluttered down. She smiled. "Because that's who you are, Brantley. You're the best man I know. You give so much, and you never take for yourself."

I stepped closer to her, close enough that I could feel the heat of her body against mine. "I'm here to take something for myself."

She cocked one brow and smirked. "Oh, yeah? What's that?"

I inhaled her deep and snaked my arm around her waist. The game we were playing was turning me on and making me want her more. The slow back and forth had me desperate for her, in the afternoon setting sun on her front porch.

I yanked her body to me and leaned my head down, finally eliminating the distance between us.

Her hands immediately slid around my neck, a groan ripped from her throat. She parted her lips and met my tongue with her own eager one. Her leg hooked around mine, opening herself up for me to grind against her like I did after our first date.

I cupped her ass and rubbed my cock against her willing body. She whimpered and moaned and panted for more.

I fucked her mouth with mine. I didn't go to her for sex. I went to her to celebrate. To share my joy. I debated telling her I was thinking about fostering, but I wasn't sure what she would say. Most likely that I was crazy. The idea was too fragile for me to risk sharing it with someone and getting a negative response.

She pulled back, her glassy gaze struggling to focus on me. "Why don't you stay for dinner?"

I shook my head and kissed her softly. "I didn't want to mess up your night. I just wanted to share my excitement."

"You can share some more excitement with me later."

I grinned. "I know. And I would love to. You have no idea how much."

"I think I have an idea," she said, grinding her hips against my erection.

I groaned and nearly gave in. "You are dangerous to my health."

She chuckled. "It's okay. If you don't want to stay, I understand."

"Are you sure?"

She shrugged. "Maybe not, but that's okay, too."

"I know you haven't had a lot of time with the girls. You said earlier in the week you were looking forward to tonight. I don't want to get in the middle of that."

She smiled. "You are amazing."

"So are you, Vee. Thank you for coming out here so I could tell you about my day."

"Any time."

I leaned in and kissed her hard. "And when you're in bed later, think about me when you slide that vibrator inside you. Imagine it's me inside you instead. I'll be thinking the same thing when I get in my shower and stroke my dick until I come."

She moaned and swayed against me. "You're the one who's dangerous."

I laughed and kissed her again. The woman was an addiction. One I never wanted to be cured of. "Just making sure you don't forget how good we are."

"Trust me, I'm not going to forget."

"Good. I'll see you tomorrow at the meet?"

"Yep. And thankfully, Dawson isn't coming to this one."

"Wouldn't matter if he was. He's not a part of your life anymore."

"Damn right." She smiled. "Thank you, Bee."

"Thank you. I love you."

"I love you. Have a good night."

I kissed her once more, a quick peck before I gave in and stayed for dinner. One day, I would never have to leave her side.

HOME MEETS WERE NICE, but hosting an event was complicated and busy. It was why the only meets we hosted were with one or two other schools, not fifty or more like the invitationals we went to almost every weekend.

I shook my head as Coach Mike, the coach for the host school and a man who'd become a friend over the years, got pulled away again. He groaned as he waved to me, rushing to handle yet another crisis that he didn't have time to deal with.

Most invitationals were run by a staff, but for some reason, Mike was heading it. He was less than thrilled, and had been asking me if I knew of any openings at MacKellar Cove so he could get away from the event. I wasn't entirely sure if he was serious or not, but either way, I didn't know of any openings.

Andrew came over and distracted me from worrying about Mike, and I joined the team again. The kids were getting warmed up and ready to go. It was the biggest meet we'd had all year, and they were buzzing with excitement. Especially Andrew, who was facing the toughest competition he'd had all year.

"Are you ready?" I asked him.

He nodded, his face serious.

"You're going to do great."

"I know. All I can do is my best. If it's enough to win, then cool. If not, I'm okay with that. I refuse to run someone else's race."

Andrew was a smart kid. Wise in ways many kids weren't. When he went to college, the team was going to miss out on a true leader. But I had a feeling others would emerge.

The JV girls lined up for the first race, and the gun signaled the start. Jana and I waited, cheering them on as they ran past us before making the final loop and racing to the finish line. The JV boys followed, with two of our kids taking first and second place. The varsity girls came next, our fastest runner claiming fourth place.

The varsity boys race was tense. The energy in the air was thick. Andrew bounced on his toes as he waited for the last of the girls to finish and the official to call for them to line up.

When the gun went off, Andrew took off. Kevin and Paul weren't far behind him. A few boys from other schools were hanging in there with them until they all made the turn and went out of sight.

Jana and I exchanged worried glances, but we knew our boys would do their best. That was all we cared about.

They ran past us a few minutes later, with Andrew in second place overall. Paul and Kevin were running together in the seventh position. They all looked like they could run another five or six miles.

When they made their final turn toward the finish line, Andrew was only a bit behind the kid in first place. But Andrew ran his race, which meant he had a burst of energy saved up for when he saw the finish line.

Andrew took off, with Kevin and Paul following suit. The kid who'd been ahead of Andrew most of the race couldn't hold out as Andrew sprinted past him and claimed first. Kevin and Paul passed three other boys in the last quarter mile and took fourth and fifth place as they crossed the finish line.

The smiles on those boys' faces almost brought tears to my eyes. They did it together. They encouraged each other and motivated each other and the three of them finished top five in one of the biggest meets in the area.

Jana pulled my attention back to the finish line in time

to see another one of our runners cross. We cheered loudly for all the kids, but especially ours. They were all out there working hard and doing something few others would even attempt, let alone excel at. It was good to be a part of it.

When the last racers crossed the finish line, Jana and I grinned. Our varsity boys securely wrapped up first place. Our other groups likely didn't place, but we had another handful who PR'd in the meet. It was another great week. Another great meet.

There was a quick ceremony where Coach Mike thanked all the teams for participating and handed out ribbons to the kids who finished top ten in each race. He announced the winning teams for each group, with MCHS coming in first for boys varsity and boys JV, which was a surprise to Jana and me.

After collecting our ribbons, we all made our way back to the tent. Some of the parents were hanging around, waiting for their kids and signing them out. I saw Kevin as I approached, talking to a woman I didn't recognize. He pointed to me, and I changed my path to speak to them.

"Coach Pierce, I'm Grace. I wanted to meet you and say thank you."

I smiled at her and shook her hand. "It's nice to meet you, too, Grace. Kevin is a great kid. Smart, and a huge asset to this team."

She grinned at him. "I've been telling him that since he moved in with us this summer. He said he shared with you that I'm his foster parent."

Kevin shuffled his feet. "I'm going to talk to McJenna."

I smiled as he walked away. "He did tell me. I think what you're doing is exceptional. Kevin has spoken very highly of you."

She laughed. "I was going to say the same. We weren't

sure how the year would go. When he asked if he could run cross-country, we encouraged him to try it, but we know MacKellar Cove can feel very small, especially for someone who hasn't been here his whole life."

"I agree. I wasn't sure when I saw his transcript, but learning he was a foster kid made a lot of sense. It must be tough for him to not have stability."

"My husband and I are hoping we can change that for him. Our kids are grown, and when Kevin came to live with us, we knew he needed people who wanted him there. I'm not going to say it's always been easy, but it isn't with any teenagers."

"That's very true. But he's lucky to have you."

Grace stepped forward. "Can I hug you, Coach Pierce? Kevin is a different kid since you took the time to help him. Since you told him what he's capable of." Tears hung on her lashes. "It means so much to us."

I moved toward her and pulled her in for a hug. She sighed against me, her chest rattling with the emotion rolling off her in waves.

"My husband wanted to be here today, but he had to work. He is hoping to come to one meet. He'd like to thank you, too."

She released me and stepped back, looking up at me with a genuine smile. I smiled back at her and noticed movement from the corner of my eye.

Valentina. Looking like she was going to be sick.

My smile faltered, but I forced it back into place as I returned my focus to Grace. "I'd love to meet him. Kevin has been working hard, both here and in school. A lot of kids aren't willing to do that, but I have no doubt you've been encouraging him at home."

Grace breathed a laugh. "Absolutely. We never stop telling him how capable he is."

"Me, too."

She grinned and gripped my arm gently. "I don't want to keep you from other parents, but I'm so happy to meet you. Thank you, again."

"Thank you, Grace. It's good to meet you, too."

She walked away, approaching Kevin and asking where to sign him out. She joined the group of parents in line for the clipboard while I searched for Valentina.

She was on the other side of the tent, worrying her lip and staring at me. As I approached, she jerked her head away from the kids.

"Are you okay? Did Dawson show up?"

She shook her head. "No, he's not here. But I'm not okay."

"Why not? What happened? What's wrong?"

"That woman? The one who hugged you?"

"Yeah. Her kid is the one I told you about yesterday."

Valentina sucked in a breath. "When I saw her hug you, I thought... it just popped into my head that you were sleeping with her."

"No. Of course not."

"But that was my thought. Not because of you. Because I'm broken. Because the last man I let into my life was sleeping with someone else."

"I'm not Dawson," I snapped.

She laughed mirthlessly and shook her head. "No, you're not. And I love you for that. But that's why I can't do this anymore. I can't put you through that."

"Valentina—" I reached for her, but she pulled away.

"I can't, Bee. I love you too much to risk destroying our friendship. And that's what I would do. Because as much as I want to tell myself I'm done with Dawson, he damaged me. More than I realized. And I would never forgive myself if I did the same to you. If I ruined you. And if I don't walk away now, I know that's exactly what will happen, so I have to end it. I have to walk away from you. Now."

And with that, she turned and left.

23

VALENTINA

I walked away from the second track meet in as many weeks fighting tears. But these tears were different. They were worse. They were goodbye tears. Tears I never wanted to shed.

But I knew it was the right decision. When I saw that woman hug Brantley, my gut sank. Everything in me screamed *CHEATER!* It didn't matter that it was Brantley. And if I was going to have an inkling of doubt for him, of all people, I'd never be able to have a normal relationship again.

If I couldn't even trust the man I loved, I couldn't trust anyone.

I jumped in my car and wished I could just leave. It would have been easier to not have to look at Brantley when he was corralling the kids and getting them all ready for the bus. But I had to wait for my girls. I'd already signed them out, thankfully, but they were talking to friends.

I took the few minutes to calm my racing, shattered heart. It was my own fault, but that didn't make it hurt any less. Everything I said to him was the truth. I would eventually ruin him, ruin our friendship, and I couldn't live with that. I had to walk away now. Find a way to get over Brantley so when he moved on to someone else, I could be his friend and be happy for him. Like I was supposed to be.

Samantha and Bianca were smiling when they made it to the car. They climbed in, talking and laughing about something. I tuned them out while I drove home, letting them have their conversation and be kids. Be young. Be joyful.

When we got home, they hurried inside to shower and change. One of the kids on the team was having a get together, and they were excited to go.

After I dropped them off, I sent Goldie a text asking if she could bring them home. I claimed to not be feeling well, which wasn't entirely a lie. She said she would, and I did the selfish and horrible parent thing and turned off my phone.

I heard the girls come home, and I went out and asked them how the party was. They took in my ratty pajamas and puffy eyes and asked what happened.

"Nothing. I just don't feel well. That's why I asked Goldie to bring you home. I'm sure I'll be better in a few days."

They nodded and accepted my lies. When they went to their rooms, I returned to mine and cried myself to sleep.

FOR THE NEXT WEEK, I avoided everyone. I made sure the girls had what they needed, I went to work and stayed in the back, and I replied to texts to confirm I was still alive, but otherwise, I didn't talk to anyone or go out.

I was more upset about things ending with Brantley than I'd been when my marriage blew up. But I told myself it was because I was not only ending my relationship with Brantley, the one that was beyond a friendship, but I was also accepting that I was going to be single forever.

I deleted my Book Boyfriends Wanted account. I hadn't used it since NerdyByNature and I spoke, but I still deleted it. There was no point in keeping it when I wasn't willing to date anyone.

On Saturday, I begged off the meet, claiming to not feel well again. Goldie asked what was going on, and I told her I must have picked up something. Lies. More lies. I hated lying.

I threw myself a pity party while the girls were at their meet, knowing Brantley wouldn't show up. Not that I expected him to. He hadn't reached out all week. I didn't blame him. I made a mess of our friendship, first by asking him to help me with my Quest for Pleasure, then by asking him to have sex with me, and then by falling in love with him and not being able to be sane around him.

I heard the car in the driveway before the girls burst through the door. They were all smiles until they saw me. They shared a worried look, then joined me on the couch.

"Mom, what's going on?" Bianca asked.

"Nothing is going on," I argued.

"We know that's not true," Samantha said. "Uncle Brantley's been the same all week. He said he's sick, too, so either you two have the same thing or you're both lying."

I looked between my two girls and did the hardest thing I'd ever had to do. I lied through my teeth. "I think I caught an early flu or something. I'm just glad I haven't given it to you two."

They exchanged another look that said I was full of it. Guess my lying skills weren't as practiced as I'd hoped.

"Are you dating Uncle Brantley?" Samantha asked.

"No. I'm not." I looked between my girls and saw the disbelief in their gazes. "But I was," I confessed.

"I knew it," Bianca mumbled. "And he broke up with you."

"Did he cheat on you?" Samantha asked.

"Uncle Brantley did nothing wrong," I snapped. "This is not because of him."

"I thought he was one of the good ones. One of the guys you told us to believe in. But you've barely been out of the house for a week. How are we supposed to believe that?" Bianca asked. Her lip wobbled, and her eyes were sad.

"Uncle Brantley is a good man. The best. He did nothing wrong."

"So, you cheated on him?" Samantha barked.

"No! No one cheated. I just realized I can't trust him. Not him. Anyone." I turned to Bianca, the one who'd been more damaged by her father. "I don't want my fears to become yours. I don't want you to see me and have doubts. Every man has the potential to be a good one. Uncle Brantley is the best one I've ever known. That's how I knew I couldn't trust anyone. He would never cheat. He would never risk anything like that. He's honorable and faithful and loyal. He's perfect. But I saw him talking to a woman, and I panicked. I assumed the worst. He explained, and I know he was telling me the truth, but if I can't trust him, I can't be with him. And if I can't trust him, I can't trust anyone."

"So, you broke up with him?" Bianca asked.

I sighed and nodded. "Yes. I told him the truth. I want him to be happy, and if he's constantly having to defend himself, he won't be happy. I'll ruin his life."

"Oh, Mom," Samantha sighed. She leaned her head on my shoulder. I kissed the top of her sweaty head and remembered the meet.

"How did the meet go? Sorry I missed it. I promise to stop hiding."

"It was good," Bianca said. She looked at Samantha, and I knew they were hiding something.

"What aren't you telling me?"

"Bianca broke her personal record," Samantha said. "She did awesome, Mom."

"Oh, honey, I'm so proud of you! And I'm so sorry I missed it. No more. You two take showers, and I'll start pizza, and you can tell me all about the meet."

They nodded. Sam jumped up to get into the shower first. Bianca lingered for a minute.

"I'm sorry you got hurt again, Mom. For what it's worth, I think Uncle Brantley is just as sad as you are. Maybe that means there's a way you can be together."

"Maybe, honey, but I just don't think so."

Bianca hugged me, then said, "If you were going to date anyone after Dad, I'm glad it was Uncle Brantley. He was a good choice."

I smiled. "I thought so, too."

Sunday was strangely quiet at my house. No calls or texts or anything. It was nice, but it was weird and had me on edge all day. Maybe my friends were getting the point, or maybe they believed me about being sick.

Either way, it was good. It was how things would be, eventually. When the girls went to college and I was left alone in my empty house.

There was a knock on the door as I was cleaning up after dinner. I debated on ignoring whoever it was. They knocked again, and I looked down at my well-worn and loved sweats and decided I didn't care who saw me. It wasn't like I was trying to impress anyone.

Goldie and Anna were on the other side of the door. As soon as I opened it, they pushed their way inside and grabbed my arms.

"You're coming with us," Goldie announced.

"Whoa. What's going on?"

"We're kidnapping you," Anna explained. "Get your shoes on and a jacket if you want, but you're coming."

"I don't wanna," I whined in my best bratty tone.

"Tough shit," Goldie said. "You've had a week, and you need to be around friends who understand what you're going through."

"I'm not going through anything. I'm sick." I fake-coughed for effect, but they weren't fooled.

"Bye girls!" Goldie called out. "We'll bring her back in a few hours."

"Thank you!" they replied as one.

"What? You roped my kids into this?" I hissed.

Goldie shook her head. "They reached out to me. They're worried about you. They said you finally admitted things with Brantley ended, even though we all assumed. You can't go through this alone."

"I'm fine." I shook them off and stood my ground. There was no way they could drag me out of my house. I wasn't small.

"Yeah, I said the same thing. Now, either you go with us willingly, or we will have you removed," Goldie said. There was a ferocity in her gaze I'd never seen before. A deadly serious gleam that said she'd love the chance to force me.

I was a little afraid of her.

"Fine," I huffed. I scowled at them and stuffed my feet

into my sneakers, kicking and muttering under my breath as I followed them to her vehicle.

They talked like nothing odd was happening on the drive to Book Boyfriends Unlimited. I stewed in the back-seat like a stubborn child. My friends deserved better, but I didn't like being called on my shit. Even if it was warranted.

Goldie and Anna flanked me when I got out of the car, as though they thought I was going to make a break for it. I debated, but then I remembered there was always cake at book club and decided to stick around. Maybe I could get an extra piece since I was heartbroken.

The conversation was already in progress when we walked in, but they all stopped when we sat down. I looked around the room at the people I'd started to consider friends and hated the worried looks in their eyes.

"I'm fine," I argued before any of them could say anything.

"We know you are," Blake said. "But we're still worried about you."

"You didn't hide from the world when you got divorced. This is worse," Elise said.

"I'm fine," I repeated.

"You will be, but you're not." Melody handed me a piece of cake.

I drew a breath and shrugged. "I'm the one who ended things. I can't be upset by that."

"Sure you can," Blake said. "I ended things with Ian when we were dating, and it almost destroyed me. It sucks. Whether it's the right call or not, walking away from someone you love isn't easy."

"No, it isn't," I confessed. "But I couldn't trust him."

"Seriously?" Karissa asked. "He strikes me as a very

trustworthy person. Not that I know him well, but I'm having trouble imagining him stepping out on you."

"He would never. But that's the problem."

"It's a problem that he wouldn't cheat?" Elise asked, looking around the room for clarification.

I shook my head. "It's a problem that I still couldn't trust him, even knowing he'd never cheat. I saw him talking to another woman, and my gut reaction was that he was cheating on me."

"And after that gut reaction? What did you do?" Karissa asked.

"I told him I couldn't do it. That if I knew he'd never cheat on me, and I still thought he was, I would ruin his life and our friendship with my accusations and suspicions."

"I think you did that anyway," Anna said. Only a friend could deliver that kind of truth.

"We'll get past this. He told me before we started... whatever we were doing, that he liked someone. He'll date again and he'll be fine and I'll be happy for him."

"He told you he liked someone else?" Trinity asked.

I nodded.

"He said someone else or someone?" Karissa clarified.

"What's the difference?" I took a bite of my cake and wished they would all move on.

"Because we went on a date. More than a year ago. I was pretty convinced that he was in love with you," Karissa said.

"What? No. There's no way," I argued.

"I agreed with her. I didn't go on a date with him, but she mentioned it, and I started watching. He seems pretty into you. Has for as long as I've known him," Trinity added.

"I was married. And he said he had a thing for me when we were kids, but not now." I shook my head.

"Did he say not now, or did you?" Karissa pushed.

"Look, it wouldn't matter. I think you're wrong, but it wouldn't matter either way. I can't do it. I can't get close to him and not have those fears come up. I tried. All of this with Brantley started when I wanted to find things that brought me pleasure. And I did. I discovered I like sunsets better than sunrises, but the quiet of the morning is nice. I love dancing, which I hadn't let myself enjoy in far too long. I like spending time with my family and friends and eating good food and making my body feel good. I like orgasms that make my toes curl and movie nights on the couch. And I love Brantley Pierce. But whether it's him or NerdyByNature or someone else, Dawson stole my ability to trust men."

"Did you say NerdyByNature?" Karissa asked.

I nodded. "We were paired together on your app. I liked him. He seemed like a decent guy. He told me he was in love with his best friend, and they got together at one point. We stopped talking because he closed his account. He said things were going well with her, and he didn't want to mess it up. He's a non-starter, trust me, but he was nice to talk to."

"You never met?" Karissa asked.

"No. Why does it matter?" I wasn't sure why she was so concerned with one guy from the app.

Karissa breathed a laugh and shook her head. "I was paired with him, too. We went on one date. I thought he was sweet and funny and really good-looking. But I was pretty sure he was in love with someone else."

"I just told you he said he was in love with his best friend."

"I believe it."

I stared at her when she didn't elaborate. "What is this all about?"

"Hun, she's telling you NerdyByNature is Brantley," Trinity explained.

I drew back and shook my head. "No." I looked between them, but neither of them were laughing. "No. It's not possible."

Karissa nodded. "I promise you, NerdyByNature is Brantley Pierce. And the best friend he told you he was in love with is you."

"No. It can't be." I thought back to the times we talked.

"Brantley is in love with you. I'd guess he has been for a very long time. You're the reason he's never gotten serious with anyone else. He loves you. He wants to be with you," Karissa said.

I shook my head. "It doesn't matter. He deserves better. He'll get over me. I just... I already messed everything up with him."

"When you love someone, things find a way of working themselves out," Blake said.

I laughed mirthlessly. My throat was tight. I wanted to have their faith, their confidence, but it was gone. It vanished the day Haley knocked on my door. "I was married for twenty-two years. To a man who told me a few weeks ago I was a bet. Maybe from the time he asked me out to when we got married, things changed, but the truth is, he screwed other women as often as he could while we were married. How do I ever look at another man and not worry about the same thing happening all over again? How do I move past that?"

I looked around the room. One after another, they looked away. They had no answers for me. None of them had been through what I'd been through. None of them knew the deep stab of betrayal caused by something like I'd been through.

"When I met Dawson, I thought he was sweet," Haley said.

I swallowed. I wasn't sure I wanted her to tell the story of how she started dating my husband, but she was the only one talking.

"I was never someone who let life pass me by. I jumped in with both feet every chance I got. Sex was just an activity. We enjoyed it, so we had lots of it," Haley said.

"Do you really think this is helping?" Goldie asked, not too kindly.

Haley forced a smile toward Goldie. "I promise, there's a point."

Goldie rolled her eyes and waved her hand for Haley to continue.

Haley looked at me. "Looking back now, I feel stupid for not realizing he was married. But he did it on purpose. He distracted me with sex instead of having real conversations about who he was. We didn't go out, and he never stayed the night. There would be weeks when I didn't hear from him. But when he was there, I told myself everything was fine."

Goldie cleared her throat.

Haley smiled at her again. "Dawson was smart. He gave just enough to keep me hanging on. I'm guessing he did the same for you. He toyed with you, like some sick game. He let you do things for him and let you believe you were the bad guy. He blamed you for him not being around more often. Am I right on any of this?"

I swallowed roughly and nodded. I hated that it was one more thing we shared.

"I'm the slut who slept with your husband, and I know you have every right to hate me, but you've never treated me that way. You are the kindest woman I've ever met. You're beautiful and loving and funny and talented. You could have turned all of these women and this whole town against me in a day. Instead, you protected me. You told people not to blame me. You let me come here and have friends here. You've been an inspiration to me. That's probably not fair, but you have been. I've told myself that I have no right to complain about what Dawson did. I dated him for a year. You were married for decades. And you were willing to try again. You were willing to love again."

"But—"

"You deserve it, Valentina. You deserve better than what Dawson did. I can't imagine how scary it is for you right now, but you deserve all the happiness he stole from you. You deserve a man who's loved you his whole life. A man who waited for you. A man who never gave up hope and who loved you, even when you loved someone who never deserved you. Why would you walk away from that?"

I shrugged. My throat was closed tight, making it hard to swallow.

"Don't let Dawson take anything else from you. He stole your chance at two decades with Brantley. Don't let him steal however many decades you two have left. Don't give him the satisfaction of knowing he ruined something that could have changed both of your lives. Because he doesn't deserve that power."

Her words sank in deep and took hold.

"Damn, Haley. That was deep," Goldie said.

"I like her," Elise said.

"She's right," Karissa said. "But now you have to do the hard thing and take the power back."

"If you want it." Anna raised one eyebrow at me in challenge.

"Dammit." Hell yes, I wanted it.

24

BRANTLEY

I closed the door behind the appliance installers and sighed. My kitchen was done. Only a little over budget and weeks ahead of my three-month schedule. That's what happened when the woman you loved ended your relationship and you needed to throw yourself into something to avoid making a fool of yourself.

But it was worth it to have the kitchen finished. It was worth it to know I could move forward with my life.

I walked back into my completed kitchen and smiled. It was amazing. Better than I ever hoped it would be. Knox was right, not that I intended to tell him that. He made excellent suggestions and recommended exceptional contractors to do the work I couldn't do on my own.

The cabinets were installed the week after Valentina ended things. The countertops came in after that. And just a day ago I finished the backsplash I'd been working on all week. I didn't have time to move everything back in from the spare bedroom before the appliance guys showed up, but it meant I had something to keep me busy for the day.

I started with the coolers where I'd stashed the meager supplies from my fridge and freezer, even though neither of them were quite at the right temperature. I was fairly sure the bottles of beer, water, and ketchup would survive. Once the cooler was empty, I went down the hallway to the spare room where all my dishes were stored for the last few weeks.

My bedroom door was still closed from when I returned from the meet two weeks ago. I couldn't face my bed. After having Valentina in it, my sheets smelled like her. I wanted to wash the sheets, or burn them, but I couldn't bring myself to do it. Instead, I closed the door and slept in the guest room.

For a few weeks, the house felt just right. Like it wasn't too big since I had Valentina here to share the space. It didn't matter that she only spent the night once, she was there. She filled my home with all the things I always dreamed she'd fill it with. Love and happiness.

But she took it all away two weeks ago. It wasn't coming back.

As I put my old stuff in my new kitchen, I had the same internal debate I'd been having since Valentina said good-bye. The only thing I'd decided for sure was that I wanted to be a foster parent. I wanted to give kids who had no one else a chance at a great life, even if they only stayed with me for a short time.

Having my own kids was a dream I'd let go of, but this was a way to have kids without having to start from scratch. It was good.

The question was if I could do it in MacKellar Cove. If I could stay. And I hadn't been able to answer that question yet.

Valentina hadn't picked the girls up from practice since

she told me we couldn't keep seeing each other. Since her lies about ruining me fell from her lips. I knew she was scared, but it hurt that she would even think I could cheat on her.

It didn't matter, though. She was done. She said she couldn't do it, and she wasn't the kind of person who debated things. She made a decision, and she stuck to it. Which was why I never called her. It would have been a waste of breath to try to convince her she was wrong.

I finished putting the dishes and glasses away and was starting to move the cookware when someone rang my doorbell. Knox was supposed to come over for dinner to celebrate the kitchen being done, but I wasn't expecting him for another hour.

"You're early," I said as I opened the door with a frying pan in my hand.

I nearly dropped the damn thing on my toe when I saw Valentina on my porch.

"Oh. You're expecting someone."

If she was going to show up at my house to break my heart a second time, the least she could have done was look like shit. Instead, she wore a pair of tight jeans that hugged her curves and a bright green sweater that dipped low on her chest when she moved and offered flashes of cleavage I wanted to bury my face in and stay there until I blacked out.

Her eyes looked huge with the makeup she wore. Bright and clear and not a trace of the gut-wrenching pain I'd been feeling for two weeks.

Guess it was nice to be the one who called it quits.

"Yeah, I am. What do you want?" I asked. I was being an asshole, but I didn't have it in me to be nice.

She wasn't deterred. "I wanted to apologize."

"You're forgiven. Thanks for stopping by."

She stuck her foot in the way when I tried to close the door. I sighed and opened it again.

"I can't do this, Vee. I want to pretend I'm fine and go back to being friends, but I just fucking can't. Maybe one day. Maybe when I've stopped dreaming about the way you felt when you came apart in my arms or the way you tasted when I kissed you or how right it was to be inside you. But I'm not there yet, so please, if we were ever really friends, be my friend now and get the hell off my property."

"No," she said.

I sighed. "Fine. Great. Good to know we're not friends. That'll make it easier for me to leave town."

"You're leaving?" she gasped.

"You don't want me! You never have. I've loved you most of my life, and you've never given me a damn chance. Then I finally get it. I finally get to love you and make you feel good and show you how special you are, and you walked away. It was so easy for you to shit all over us. To blame Dawson for destroying your heart and making it so you can't trust me. It's fucking bullshit. So, yeah, I can't stay here. I can't be in this house where I made love to you and not want to take a sledgehammer to the walls. I can't stay in this town where we met, and where I fell in love with you, and where I see you everywhere. I'd rather start over and be the crazy science teacher no one knows than be here and watch you live just outside my world."

"You can go be NerdyByNature somewhere else. Maybe meet someone else."

"Yeah, sure." I huffed a laugh. "There's never been anyone else. Never will be."

"NerdyByNature dated some. Not that long ago you talked to a new woman."

"What does online dating have to do with anything? What? Did Karissa tell you my screen name?"

"She did. But only because I mentioned it."

"What are you talking about?"

"You told BakerBabe you were in love with your best friend. That you were closing your account because you wanted things to work out."

"So?"

"So, now you're leaving?"

I rolled my eyes and stalked away from her. It hurt to look at her. "I just told you I can't be here."

"Were you lying when you said you had no interest in dating someone else?"

I spun on her. "What did Karissa do? Share all my conversations? No, I wasn't lying. And that's a serious violation of my privacy."

"Karissa didn't share anything with me."

"Then how do you know what I said?"

"Because I'm BakerBabe."

"What?" I took a step back. It was not possible.

Valentina nodded. "I didn't know you were NerdyByNature until I mentioned your screen name last week. Karissa told me."

I scoffed. "I bet you had a good laugh, huh? So much for that stupid app being magical or some shit. Didn't do anything for me."

"It paired you with someone who fell in love with you."

"No, it didn't."

"Yes, Brantley, it did." She stepped in front of me and looked up at me with those big brown eyes, vulnerable and gorgeous.

"What are you doing, Valentina?"

"I'm trying to tell you I love you."

"Don't lie to me. I can't take anymore," I breathed. It hurt. Like someone punched me in the chest and snapped a few ribs.

She reached up and cupped my jaw. Her skin against mine was as much a balm as it was a flame. I leaned in, hating myself as I took comfort from her.

"I was so wrong about so many things, Bee. I convinced myself I couldn't trust you. I even convinced myself what we were doing was just for fun, about my stupid quest. But I've been lying to myself for far too long."

"What does this have to do with me?"

"I fell in love with this skinny kid when I was in high school. We were opposites in every way, but we were best friends. When you introduced me to Dawson, everything shifted. I know everything happens for a reason, so maybe we were too young back then to do it right, or maybe I didn't deserve you. I don't know why everything got all messed up for us, but I never stopped loving my best friend. I never stopped wondering what my life would have been like if he loved me, too."

"I always did," I whispered.

She nodded. "I know. But then I messed it all up again. I let Dawson win again. I let him control me. Instead of trusting you like I've been able to do my entire life, I let fear get to me. Fear of losing you. But Haley—"

"Haley?"

She laughed. "Yes, Haley. She made me see that my fear is why I lost you. It was a self-fulfilling prophecy. I was afraid to lose you, so I made it happen. But that meant Dawson still had power over me. He could influence my life. And I don't want that. He doesn't get to do that."

"I'm happy for you, Vee. Dawson is out of your life. You can start over."

She stepped closer to me. "You don't get it. I don't want to start over. I don't want to date. I don't want to meet someone new."

I threw my hands up and swore. "Then what the hell do you want?"

"You."

"You said you couldn't do this. That you had to walk away."

"I was wrong, Brantley. I was scared. God, I'd never been so scared in my life. Letting you in was the biggest leap of faith I've ever taken, and when I saw you, I felt like the safety net I've had forever was suddenly gone. I felt like the man I'd always relied on wasn't who I thought he was. But you were never like Dawson. On his best day, he's never been half the man you are on your worst day. And I forgot that. I lost sight of that. You have always been there for me. But that's not why I love you."

"It's not?"

She shook her head. "I love you because you're kind. And I love you because you're smart. I love you because you are encouraging and selfless and generous. I love you because you care more about the people around you than you do about yourself. Because I asked you to help me figure out what brings me pleasure and you dove head-first into the task. You showed me more pleasure in a few weeks than I'd known in a lifetime. And I'd be a fool to throw that away. More than that, I don't want to."

"You don't?"

"No, Bee. God, no. I want to spend the rest of my life with you. I want to know what it's like to go to sleep in your arms and wake up next to you. I want to cook dinner with you every night and share coffee with you every morning. I want to plan summer trips and college visits and beach vacations so I can look at you in just swim trunks." She broke off with a laugh and wiped a tear from her cheek. "I want to grow old with you, Brantley. I want to have a future with you. And I know I'm asking a lot of you. I know I'm not being fair. I threw what we had away, and I'm asking you to just overlook that and try again. I know I have to earn your trust. And I'm willing to do that. If you want to leave town, I know I can't stop you, but I'm hoping you'll stay and consider giving me another chance."

I shook my head slowly. "I can't consider that because I've already decided."

She let out a shaky breath, and I realized how my words sounded.

"I didn't mean it like that. I meant I've already decided I want all those things, too. It's all I've ever wanted."

"Really?"

I nodded. "Except one thing."

"What's that?"

"I want to become a foster parent. I want to give back. I always wanted to be a dad, and I don't know that I want to have babies at this point in my life, but I want to help kids who have no one else. There are a lot out there, and—"

She stepped forward and put her hand on my lips. "I think that sounds like an excellent idea."

"You do?" I asked through her fingers.

"Absolutely. And it just makes me love you more that you want to give back in that way."

I licked her hand, swirling my tongue around her palm.

She gasped, her eyes darkening.

But she didn't move her hand, so I did it again.

She moaned. "I've missed you." She finally moved her hand.

I leaned into her. "I've missed you, too."

"Yeah?"

I nodded and yanked her tight to my body. I let her feel my growing erection. "Every time I closed my eyes, I saw you coming apart. It's been impossible to sleep. I finished the kitchen so I wouldn't slow down and think about you."

"You finished the kitchen?" she asked.

I nodded again.

"Can I see?"

"Now?"

She grinned. "I can wait."

"Good. Because I'm not sure I can." I nuzzled against her jaw, hardening when she mewled for me. I nipped at her skin and took my time working my way to her lips.

I cupped her ass and turned us toward the hallway. I paused when she grabbed my hair and pulled my lips to hers in a kiss that sent my blood pressure sky-high.

She whimpered and tugged at my shirt, her hand cold when she pressed it against my back. I cupped her jaw and devoured her, more than ready to get another taste of the woman I loved. The woman I never had to walk away from again.

We made it to my room and stopped. She pulled back and looked at me, then the door, then back at me. "Why is your bedroom door closed?"

I looked her in the eye and admitted the truth. "I couldn't face going in there without you. I couldn't look at my bed and accept that you were gone."

"I'm—"

The doorbell interrupted her sentence. She looked up at me with a question in her eyes.

"You really were expecting someone."

I nodded. If she was going to trust me, it had to happen now.

"Should I wait here?"

"It's up to you."

"Do you want me to leave?"

I shook my head. "Never."

"What do you want me to do?"

"What do you want to do?"

The doorbell rang again, and Knox pounded on the door.

"Your guest is impatient."

"It'll be fine."

"You're not going to tell me who it is, are you?" She grinned and crossed her arms over her chest.

"Does it matter?"

She smiled and went up onto her tiptoes. She wrapped her arms around my neck and pulled me into a kiss.

I groaned and backed her up against the wall, grinding against her until she was panting and the doorbell was ringing again.

"I need to tell Knox to go away," I growled as I pulled away from her.

She laughed. "It's Knox?"

I nodded and stomped toward the door. "I invited him over for dinner to see my finished kitchen."

"You can let him in," she said.

I yanked the door open.

Knox started to push his way inside. "Jesus, finally. What the hell were you doing? Jerking off?" Knox stopped dead when he saw Valentina on the other side of the living room. "Um, hi, Valentina. I didn't know you were here."

"Hi, Knox. How are you?"

Knox looked between us. His face turned red as he backtracked toward the front door. "I'm a little early. I forgot to grab something."

"Come back in an hour, Knox," I growled as I slammed the door behind him.

"Make it two!" Valentina shouted.

"Fucking hell, I love you."

"I love you, too, Bee."

EPILOGUE

KNOX

I PULLED UP IN FRONT OF BRANTLEY'S HOUSE JUST AS MY phone vibrated in my pocket. I'd become addicted to the damn thing since I signed up for that stupid Book Boyfriends Wanted app.

I debated ignoring my phone, but like any obedient puppy, I fished it out of my pocket.

It wasn't the app. It was worse. It was my ex looking for a hookup.

> What are you doing tonight? Want to come over?

My dick swelled at Ivy's casual invite. We had fun. She was easy to talk to, and we had fun in bed. But there was no future. We both knew it, but we still hooked up sometimes.

I scrubbed a hand over my face and groaned. Fucking hell. I hated that the thought even went through my damn mind. A future. But shit, I wanted a future with someone. A woman who would make me want to lock up the store early and whisk her off to some fancy dinner. Or a weekend away.

Or hell, a ball game where we could scream at the refs or umps or officials and cheer for our team.

I'd never met a woman who made me want to do any of that. Ivy was a way to pass the time. The sex was great, but we weren't on the same page.

I looked up at Brantley's house. I wanted what he'd found with Valentina. It took him for-fucking-ever, but he finally got the woman of his dreams. If I wanted the same, I had to quit fucking around and quit doing the same damn thing over and over again. Ivy didn't want a family, she just wanted a fuck, and while I enjoyed that for a while, it wasn't what I wanted forever.

Or for right now.

> Sorry. I have plans.

> What about after your plans? I'll be home all night. Or I can meet you somewhere.

> It's not a good idea.

> Tonight or ever?

I sighed. I knew I was going to have to have this conversation with her at some point. Just because we agreed we wanted different things and wouldn't work long term didn't mean I'd been good about turning her down when she reached out. I hadn't been. At all.

But dammit, if I was going to find forever, I had to stop accepting for now.

> Probably ever. We both know this isn't going anywhere.

I waited for a reply from her, but one didn't come. My gut twisted. I hated being the bad guy. It didn't matter that she knew I was right. I was the asshole who told her to fuck off.

I tossed my phone on the console and went inside. If it wasn't in my pocket, I wouldn't be tempted to look at it every five seconds.

The house was busy, with all the lights on inside and music and laughter so loud I was sure no one would hear my knock. Better than a couple of weeks ago when I showed up for dinner and was sent away so Brantley and Valentina could make up.

When no one came to the door, I tried the knob. All the vehicles outside told me it was safe to enter, but I still did it with a measure of caution.

"Hey, Knox!" Brantley called out when he saw me peeking in.

I glanced around and let myself the rest of the way into the house. I waved to the people in the living room and made my way to the kitchen where Brantley was.

"Thanks for coming."

"I had to make sure you were treating my kitchen right," I joked. When Brantley started remodeling his house, I knew the kitchen would be the perfect blank canvas. The years he took to give in and do it gave me plenty of time to come up with ideas. It was like Mr. Rockaway's game room and Mrs. Florence's plant room and Ms. Mallory's master suite. I had ideas for all of them, and more, if they ever came looking for options.

"Your kitchen?" Brantley scoffed. "I don't remember you paying for all this stuff."

I slapped his arm, knowing he appreciated the help even if he wouldn't admit it. "The place looks damn good."

"It really does. You could have a job in design."

"Nope. I like the job I have."

Brantley clapped me on the back and pushed a beer into my hand. "Understood. Come on. Get a drink. Valentina baked a shit-ton of desserts for us, and Ramsey's out back grilling with a friend of his. There are kids running in the backyard. It's a celebration."

"Celebration of what, exactly?" Brantley told me to come, but never told me what it was about.

"End of the cross-country season. Things finally working out with Vee. My kitchen being done. I just wanted to get people together before the weather keeps us all indoors for the winter."

"It's coming."

Brantley nodded. "Fast, too. But for tonight, we're not thinking about Thanksgiving coming in two weeks, and we're having fun."

"Works for me."

Someone called his name, and he pointed me toward the deck before going to the living room.

I walked out and saw Ramsey talking to Derek Bailey. "If you can cook as well as you can fix cars, I'm glad I showed up here."

Derek laughed and shook my hand, pulling me in for a slap on the back. "How the hell are you? I didn't know you knew this crew."

I nodded and said hello to Ramsey. "I do. They let me crash their beer nights on Thursday at O'Kelley's. I haven't seen you there."

Derek shook his head. "I have a ten-year-old son. It's not always easy to get away in the evenings."

"Ah, makes sense. I didn't know you were married."

"Divorced."

"Makes even more sense why you can't get away," I said.

Derek nodded. "I wouldn't trade my kid, but the

divorce part sucks. How about you? One of these yours?" He gestured to the kids running around Brantley's backyard.

I shook my head. "Nope. Still single."

"I was just trying to talk Derek into joining Book Boyfriends Wanted," Ramsey said.

I snorted and shook my head. "Don't do it. You'll get addicted to the damn thing. I left my phone in the truck so I wouldn't go nuts with all the notifications."

"That sounds like a good problem," Ramsey said. "If you're getting that many matches, you should be praising it, not trashing it."

"Not trashing it. Just offering a warning."

"I take it you aren't finding anyone worth keeping," Derek said.

I shrugged. "I've met a few I went out with more than once, but no one who stuck around. I hear it's a numbers game."

Ramsey choked. "Don't let any of the women hear you say that."

"Not all of us can end up with our high school sweetheart. Or even had one. I'm not saying I'm like Brantley and have the one picked out, but I'm open to possibilities."

"So, you're looking to settle down?" Derek asked.

I shrugged. "I'm looking to not waste my time. If the right woman comes along, I'm going to enjoy getting to know her, but until then, I'm going to enjoy dating." The line rolled off my tongue easily, even though it was bitter. I'd been spewing that for years. But telling other men you wanted a family was not always well-received. Even with men who had families.

"That's how I feel, too. My marriage ended for a reason. I don't need a woman in my life, but if the right one came along, I'd be an idiot to turn her away." Derek flipped the burgers as he spoke.

"Exactly," I said, acting as though we were the same. "What's tough for me is I'm old enough to know what I want in a relationship. Narrows the pool down and means I end things fast when I know it isn't right. I think I go on two or three dates a week."

"Seriously?" Derek asked. "I don't have time for that."

I sipped my beer and avoided their gazes. My ears burned with their disapproval and judgement. I knew I dated a lot. I'd been out with multiple women in one night before. But I wanted a family, so I had to make finding the right woman a priority. When I found her, I'd already have that time in my day to spend with her.

"Maybe I'm not cut out for online dating," Derek said. "Not if I have to do all of that."

I shook my head. "I wasn't trying to talk you out of it."

Derek waved off my concern. "No, you're not."

"Not everyone goes on that many dates in a week. Not all of us are studs like this guy and get that many dates in a week." Ramsey jerked his head at me in what I took as an approving way.

I laughed off his compliment. "Just putting myself out there."

"Where do you meet so many women?" Derek asked.

"I'm on a few dating apps, friends. I'm a friendly guy. I talk to people."

Derek snickered. "Is friendly code for something?"

"It's definitely different when you have a kid to think about. Not that I dated when Mel and I were separated, but it was always in the back of my mind that it didn't matter how much I liked a woman if she and Amber didn't get along," Ramsey said.

"Yeah, I feel that," Derek agreed. "If Jude didn't like a woman, it would be over. It must be nice to be single without kids."

I nodded and pretended his words didn't bother me. He didn't understand how frustrating it was to be told my life was better without kids, or without a wife. They weren't being jerks about it, but it sucked to always feel like I was playing a game no one told me how to play. I wanted kids. I wanted a wife. I wanted more.

I just hadn't gotten lucky in that department yet.

But I was going to. I was going to make some changes. And I was going to find someone who wanted all the same things as me.

Forever, not just for now.

THANK **you** for reading Valentina and Brantley's story! Friends to lovers is my absolute favorite trope, and adding in a dirty talking hero and a heroine who needs that boost to remind herself how amazing she is, and I had so much fun with this book. I hope you did, too!

The next book in the series is Knox and Haley's story. A one-night stand was all it was supposed to be. They agreed. It was all either of them were looking for at the moment. But when she slides onto a seat opposite him the next night, he knows she wasn't telling the whole truth. Then again, neither was he. Preorder His Curvy Stranger today!

WANT MORE from Valentina and Brantley? He has that big, remodeled house all to himself, and hers holds more bad memories than good. It only makes sense that his new kitchen gets used! Bonus epilogue is only available to subscribers. Sign up now!

SINGLE MOM, Briella, is juggling her own business, her seven year old son, and her ex wants to reduce his payments. The last thing she has time for is a man who turns her inside out and makes her forget he's all wrong for her. Pick up Devil vs. Angel today!

ABOUT THE AUTHOR

USA TODAY Bestselling Author Mary E Thompson spent most of her childhood wishing she had a few less curves. She hid in the pages of books because her favorite characters never cared what size her clothes were. Now, neither does Mary, and she writes stories that celebrate women like her. Real women who have curves, chase dreams, and find love, because we should all be happy, no matter our dress size.

Mary spends her non-writing time with her husband and two kids, watching too much TV, cheering for her hometown football team (Go Bills!), and hiding chocolate from her family.

Visit https://MaryEThompson.com/ to sign up for Mary's newsletter, **Romancing the Curves**. Subscribers get free ebooks and other fun stuff, like exclusive, members only content and giveaways, plus are the first to know about new releases and sales!